UnRaveled
The Promise Keeper

Diva Dorreen

Editor: Copy Cat
Cover Designed by: Rock Steady

Because of the dynamic nature of the internet, any web addresses or links contained in this book may have changed since publication and may no longer be valid.

ISBN: 978-0-9963612-5-5 (e)

ISBN: 978-0-9963612-4-8 (sc)

Forward

Thank you for supporting me by purchasing my third book UnRaveled. This book introduces characters who are no different from people we know in our everyday life.

Lana and Fen live in a fictional version of The National Harbor. They met eighteen years ago in college and became each other's support system when they thought they had no one else.

Fen, shrewd and business savvy, builds a company with Lana, but once developed Lana becomes bored, and starts a career of her own at one of the top Hotel chains in the country. Fen's insecurities get the best of him and he starts down a road that slowly destroys them. Lana's faith keeps her in the fight for her marriage, believing if she honors the promises she made before God then things will be alright.

This story is told from Lana's perspective. Reading Lana and Fen's story show us the complexities of love and the hard decisions Lana has to make when things fall apart. These characters learn that marriage is not a game and love is complicated. Don't throw stones, because those same stones may one day come back and hit you.

You can find all my books at:

www.divadorreen.com

I am excited you are venturing into Lana and Fen's world along with a host of other new characters.
Enjoy!

Diva Dorreen

Acknowledgements

Over the years, many people have influenced my writing. I shared before that I wrote my first book in 2008 and put that story on the shelf. One day a co-worker asked me what happened to that book. Well my millennial niece had written a book and told me the ins and outs of how she brought it to print. The rest is history.

I would have to say that my mother was my greatest influencer. She read, on average, one book per day and I wasn't far behind her. I further passed my love for reading on to my daughter Tiffani who has read every movie we have seen.

You never know where inspiration is going to strike and who will influence you. People like Nikki Du, who presses me for my next contribution makes me work hard not to disappoint.

My daughter Tiffani always challenges me to be excellent. I have written and rewritten this book several times and still want to redo it again. BUT!! I learned in my studies that at some point you have to let it go.

My daughter Autumn who allowed me to read to her as she went to sleep like a four year old listening to her bedtime story.

My daughter Samantha gave me the drive to continue as I watched her develop her Religious Fashion Magazine MyBelliza.

Trey, my middle son, the motivator, told me more times than I can count how proud he was of me. Thank you.

Cameron, my eldest son, who taught me that mental disorders are real and sometimes scary.

Then there is Titus. Well Titus is Titus.

I love you all and thank you.

Chapter One

The Harbor pier was my favorite place to go to think and clear my mind. Today was no different. Sitting in the large Adirondack chair, my head swam with so many thoughts I couldn't focus on just one.

"Jesus!"

Over the past year there were profound twist and turns in my life, and I didn't know if I would survive the chaos I had created. Love had betrayed me like Judas betrayed Jesus. Unless you experienced love you might not understand how the three words 'I love you' could feel so comforting and at other times perplexing. For me, love had become my curse and my refuge.

Lost in thought, I watched a couple sitting on the ground a few feet away. Hugs and kisses exchanged, and I wondered how long they would gaze into each other's eyes before seeing the real person on the other side, that person we learned to hide as children, when we learned we weren't enough. We had to become someone else to deserve love. Her smile, bright and shiny, and his, wide and embarrassing in return, was no indication of how long they would play the game of deception?

Love is a fragile thing that needs nurturing, watering, fertilizing and sometimes weeding. Weeding was the most important of them all, because if you don't weed your relationship, their roots will choke the growth, causing the relationship to eventually die.

The girl shook out her long auburn mane and he ran his hands through it until his fingers became entangled. Pulling her close, he kissed her again.

I don't know how long I was watching, before I noticed she was looking back at me, so I redirected my gaze to the clouds pretending to mind my own business, and thought about my relationships.

We all put our best foot forward in the beginning. Didn't I when I first met my husband Fen? And didn't he do the same? Just like our relationship, in the end, they too would experience the tears that came from blindly loving another. There were always tears.

Chapter Two

No one would view my life as pitiful. My husband loved me and lavished me with trips and gifts. I had more advantages than most, a good job, successful man, and beauty inherited from my mother. But even with my many possessions, my life was dismal. It would seem the dysfunction of my childhood spilled over into my adult life.

I lived with a man who I barely spoke to and no longer trusted. So, we walked around our million dollar townhouse like roommates who were stuck with their assignment in the dorms. If the walls could talk, I'm sure they would have more to say.

Fen had to leave to take care of a service failure at work. He was gone for several hours. I tried a couple of times to call, mostly out of duty, but he didn't answer. That was always my first sign of deceit.

I was preparing for bed when he returned home. While brushing my teeth he burst into the bathroom.

"Sorry it took so long, Lana. I had to wait for my help to come."

He stripped his clothes from his lean, cut body and threw them on the bathroom floor. I stopped brushing my teeth and stared at the rude pile, knowing it was something else to add to my chores.

He was lying. It was a pattern I was used to now. There were always calls or emergencies, allowing him to leave at all hours of the day and night. I found it funny that he could never look me in my face when he lied.

And so went our life. I didn't need him, but I still wanted him. I stayed with him, allowing myself to be subjected to many disappointments and rejections. I stayed because I knew he loved me. I stayed because I still loved him. I stayed because I made a promise for better or worse.

"I understand," was my only reply.

I placed my toothbrush back in the holder and left him to take his bath. Things would be alright after a few days. My attitude would subside and the irritation would fade.

Watching the ceiling, I tried not to be annoyed as I listened to him splash around in the water, attempting to wash away the dirt that he could not. I laughed when I thought of it as the equivalency of washing away ones sins. When I heard him release the water from the tub I closed my eyes and pretended to be asleep.

The sheets were cool and comforting as I rolled over to my side of the bed. He would soon join me as though nothing were wrong. I would allow him to hold me, and in the morning go to work, leaving him to his own devices.

Lie. Role play. Repeat.

Chapter Three

I worked in an office managing one hundred and fifty people for one of the largest resort chains in the country. Most of our challenges were turn over and disciplinary actions.

I stood looking at the clamshell shaped pool just below my office's huge, scenic window. The river waters were unruly today, much like my mood. I felt restless. Today I was going to fire an employee for stealing, but as much as she deserved it, I still hated that part of my job.

The office door opened and I knew the mousy girl had arrived. "You wanted to see me, Mrs. Fenney?"

I didn't answer right away. A wave of emotion hit me, and I felt the tears come. I didn't know why, but they did. Maybe it was because I could feel the young girl's unhappiness. Unhappy knows unhappy.

My silence only scared her more. "Mrs. Fenney?"

"Give me a second Courtney."

I took the time to gain control again. Not a single tear fell. It was a technique I learned to master when I was thirteen, and my mother told me she never wanted me. She was drunk at the time, but I learned through watching my parents, when they shared drunken harsh words, those words represented their true feelings.

Tears came so easily then. My mother said I was too soft-hearted and needed to toughen up or people would run over me. Although still soft-hearted, I no longer wore my emotions on my sleeve.

My reflection in the glass showed my efforts in the gym. My waist was tight and stomach flat, accenting my hips and small round bottom. George, my new trainer, was relentless, but charming. I smiled just thinking how hard he tried to get me to go out with him. I should. Maybe all my efforts would not be in vain, because Fen hadn't noticed my hard work.

When I finally turned to face the waiting girl, I realized I had allowed her to wait much too long. Her tears were already flowing, breaking my heart. Her hair was unkempt and clothes slightly wrinkled, evidence that something more was going on.

"Courtney do you know why I asked to see you?"

"I guess." Her thumbs went around and around as she nervously twiddled them. Her head hung low and she stared down into her lap.

I looked through the paperwork and saw she made just above minimum wage. It wasn't much money to take care of three children. The story was her boyfriend recently abandoned her and their children for her girlfriend, leaving her to take care of them alone. Whatever happened to girlfriend code? I didn't expect it from the whore who was sleeping with my husband. Hell, why should I expect anything from a woman who left her husband for a married man?

In a hushed voice, I asked, "How long have you worked for us, Courtney?"

"Just over three years."

Her shoulders were shaking, and her nose running. I handed her a tissue. As I looked at the frail young girl, I could see she had recently lost weight. Her clothes were loose. Her red hair was dull and dry.

I spun in my chair to face the Woodrow Wilson Bridge to control the wave that threatened to overtake me again. Cars passed in both directions without incident as the drivers left Maryland to enter Virginia and vice versa. The beautifully architected arches gave it an artistic look, framing a stunning backdrop from my window, which seemed to calm my fragile emotions.

What would be this girl's destiny if she lost her job? I couldn't help but feel sorry for her. Although I was wondering what she would do to survive, it was not my concern? My responsibility was to the company. If I did not do what I set out to do, how could I fire the next person who stole without any pushback?

"Give me one reason why I shouldn't fire you, Courtney?"

"Because I don't know what I did."

I turned abruptly, disturbing the fragile balance of emotional calm, and looked her in her eyes. I couldn't believe she didn't know why she was there.

Her cries began to intensify, becoming frantic, bordering hysterical, letting me know she knew exactly why she was about to be fired. I stopped breathing to subdue my own hysteria.

"I'm sorry Mrs. Fenney! I will pay all the money back. I just didn't know what to do."

I handed her another tissue. "What is going on with you lately Courtney? You were one of our best employees."

"I am having a hard time right now, but it will get better. I start my second job next week."

How was she going to see her children if she started working another job? I spun in my chair and faced the bridge again. I couldn't keep her in the casino and let her continue to steal. Now that she was caught I was sure it wasn't her first time. It was the first time she was caught.

"I am not going to fire you today Courtney. You have been a good employee up until now. Can you type?"

"Ma'am?"

I spun around in my chair to face her yet again. "Can. You. Type?" The irritation in my voice annoyed even me.

The confused girl was speechless. Suddenly, she blurted out, "Yes, fifty-five words a minute."

I spun back around to face the bridge with the cars running like my emotions traveling in two directions. "Then go home now, and return Monday to my office." I turned again. "I need you to wash your face and put on some makeup and do your damn hair."

Shame filled me as I immediately felt convicted for my harshness. My last comment might have gone too far.

"There will be no next time Courtney. You will be on the street looking for another job. Do you understand?"

She nodded her head, as the realization sank in that she was not losing her job. She started crying again, but this time her tears were joyous. I felt as if God was leading me.

"Have a good weekend." I closed her file and put it back in my drawer. I would have to explain my decision to my director Wayne, but I could make it work.

She didn't move. I made a motion, waving to the door, dismissing her. The girl stood from her seat and scurried from my office, still wiping her tears.

"Thank you, Mrs. Fenney. I appreciate this, and I won't disappoint you. I'm a good worker," were her last words before disappearing on the other side of my door.

Who would rescue me? My heart became full again, but this time I allowed myself that moment of emotional weakness as my overwhelming helplessness overtook me.

"Mama I can cry if I want to."

Chapter Four

It was Friday night, and I was home alone. Something came up. Something was always coming up. It had become a cycle for us.

We moved to the Harbor so I would be closer to work. Fen worked more since we moved there. He said he had to pay for our new lifestyle, but the funny thing was, we could afford this lifestyle before moving here.

The sky was clear, and the Harbor lights felt festive. From our rooftop deck, I could see the small line at the lit Ferris wheel, and the excursion boat docking to release its passengers returning from Georgetown.

The rooftop was my favorite place in the house. It was serene and allowed me to sit and meditate. From its vantage point I could become a part of the living, watching people leave the restaurants or the carnival when it came to town and set up on the open parking lot, across the street from our town home.

The breeze became chilly coming off the water. I took the throw blanket I brought with me and pulled it tight around my shoulders. Then came the loneliness that sometimes plagued me, so I decided to head to the sports bar and exist with those I watched.

The restaurant was crowded, which was usual for a Friday. People stood in clusters or pairs laughing and exchanging stories. There were no seats at the bar so I stood leaning on its leather covered edge.

Dwight, the bartender, placed a Shirley Temple in front of me and walked away. I didn't come often, but when I did we shared thoughts, events and sometimes looks with unspoken words, like the look you give when someone's breast are about to pop out of their top, or the look that says 'that man is too drunk to know he's drunk.'

I watched those around me interact and sipped my drink slowly. The man at the end of the bar was smiling hard, pretending to be interested in the busty woman's conversation, but he was more interested in the mounds that sat in his face with their own zip code. Although my drink was non-alcoholic, I felt included.

The digital screens were lit with a different basketball game on each. I stood pretending to watch them. People cheered and talked trash to one another. Dwight was busy, so I had no one to talk to. I should have stayed home.

A seat at the bar near me became available, so I hopped up on the stool and took more interest in what was happening on the nearest screen. That was the night I met my distraction.

He was a tall drink of water, six feet two, broad-shouldered, with chestnut brown skin. I thought to myself he must have been a dentist because when he smiled, his teeth were so bright, it was like sunshine on my face. We hadn't formally met but had exchanged smiles and nods when we saw one another in the past, but tonight, I felt like I was seeing him for the first time.

He must have come from work because he was wearing a suit that sculpted his tight chiseled body perfectly. His muscles strained against material every time he flexed his arm. I definitely had a type.

He stood next to me as he ordered his drink. I caught him stealing a peek at me, here and there, but I said nothing. We had never been this close before. His voice was like silk and his cologne was subtle, taking my mind somewhere it should not have gone.

"How are you this evening?"

I coughed as I choked on my drink realizing he was talking to me.

"Oh, I'm sorry. Do you have some health issues?"

I laughed. "Why? Are you a doctor?" I felt myself blushing like a school girl. This was the most excitement I experienced all week.

"No!" He looked straight ahead, not sure of what to say next. I thought maybe he didn't talk to women very often because he seemed awkward.

I laughed. "I'm sorry."

He turned to face me again. "For what?"

He smiled. I melted.

"I've been told I have a smart mouth."

"I like smart-mouthed women."

This one was a charmer.

"I have a table right over there." He pointed to the table close to the largest screen in the room.

I smiled, making sure not to expose my teeth, so I wouldn't appear to be silly, and nodded. When he didn't say anything else I realized it was an invitation to join him.

"Oh!"

He mouthed my answer mocking my response and took his drink when the bartender returned. "If you decide to join me the invitation is still open." He headed back to his table catching the eyes of the women as he passed through the crowd.

Dwight leaned on the bar. "Don't sit here tonight, please. Allow me to make some tips and go sit with the man."

"I can't now. I didn't accept the invitation the first time he asked."

"You think he comes here to sit alone? Whenever he comes in, he looks around for you."

Shocked I turned to face Dwight. "Why do you think that?"

"Because when you're not here, he leaves after one drink. When you are here, he stays and watches you until you leave. Then he leaves."

My mouth dropped open.

"Tonight, he paid Evette twenty dollars for that table."

I discreetly glanced in his direction and thought about going to sit with him. I was nervous. How would I do it?

Dwight read my thoughts. "Just go. Tell him the bar was too noisy and you changed your mind."

I put my empty glass down, and Dwight had another waiting. I hopped down from the bar stool and headed his way. I didn't want to settle for being an observer tonight, watching everyone else laugh and talk. I wanted to be a part of the living.

He was facing the big screen when I reached the table. He didn't turn to acknowledge me, so I sat next to him. He smiled, still facing the screen.

"The bar was noisy," I said, as Dwight had advised me.

After about a minute he turned his attention to me. "I didn't want to sit alone tonight. I hope I didn't make you uncomfortable inviting you to sit with me."

"No. It was fine." Now what?

"My name is Sterling."

"I'm Lana." And just like that, we went from there.

His conversation was pleasant and not about him. To be honest, I wasn't even sure what he was saying. He had me mesmerized. I tried to keep my eyes focused on his face which shined like the sun. My smile fake, I willed myself not to reach out and touch him.

Tonight was my third time seeing him. After Dwight's revelation, I no longer wondered if it was an unspoken arrangement, rather than a coincidence that I kept seeing him.

He excited me like I had not been excited in a long time. No other man, except Fen, had done that for me, but this man, oh my Lord!

"I asked you a question." He had stopped talking, and I had not noticed. Perhaps it was because the sun was still shining on my face.

Embarrassed, I shook my head. "Oh! I'm sorry. Repeat the question, and I promise I will answer."

He laughed a hearty laugh that I knew I could grow to love. "You are too polite, and I talk too much."

He touched my hand and chills ran through my body, making me shiver. I was afraid he felt them too. His eyes told me he had, and his face became serious. Slowly he released my hand, trying to hide his awkwardness, but it was too late. His vulnerability was exposed.

"I've been talking all night about my week. How was yours?" Taking his napkin he dabbed his mouth.

Suddenly I was stumped. Fen never cared to know what went on in my world. He rambled on and on about his own until it became mine and whenever I tried to say anything about me, he cut me off to start another conversation. I no longer attempted to participate in the discussion. I was tired of pretending his conversations were fascinating.

"Oh, my week was not as exciting as yours. I was supposed to fire a young lady today, but instead hired her as my new assistant."

"Wow." He leaned back in his seat. "Did she know you were firing her?"

"Yes."

"You probably changed her life today. Why did you do it?"

I thought of what to tell him. I couldn't say because a man had just abandoned her, and she needed a break. Instead, I said, "I knew she was having a hard time and I didn't want to add to it. She needed a break."

He looked around for our server. "You hungry?"

By now, I was famished. "Yes," I answered, then blushed again at how eager I sounded.

The food arrived much too soon. A woman passed and smiled her wide grin, letting Sterling know her interest. Politely he nodded and turned his attention back to me. She scowled, rolling her eyes, switching her wide hips down the aisle; I'm sure with intent on catching his attention.

"Did you want to say hello to her?"

"I spoke."

"I mean.."

"I knew what you meant and the answer is no. If I wanted to eat with her I would have invited *her* to my table."

I smiled and bowed my head. "A little sure of yourself?"

"Very sure of myself."

He smiled his big intoxicating grin again. Normally I would have viewed him as being cocky, but I didn't get that vibe from him. He *was* sure of himself.

The young lady sat at the bar eying us. Her reaction brought back old uncomfortable memories as she rudely stared.

"It appears we have an audience."

Sterling glanced momentarily at the woman then clasped his hands under his chin grinning at me. "If we ignore her she will go away. This isn't the first time she has approached me. I'm not interested, so why don't we continue to enjoy each other." His smile eased my nerves. "So. Tell me about your job."

My insecurities were showing and I swiftly tucked them away and hid behind what I was confident in, my work.

I explained my work at the casino and my daily challenges. He listened intently as I waited for the rude interruption that usually came when I spoke of me. It never came. His eyebrows rose at the appropriate times and he reared back laughing when things were funny.

His head tilted to one side. "Wow. I didn't know all that went on in a casino."

I looked at my phone, and there were no missed calls or messages. My suspicions about my husband's evening were confirmed.

"Do you need to go?"

Realizing *I* was being rude, I placed my phone in my purse, and zipped it to safeguard its contents. "No, I'm fine."

"Won't your husband be worried about you?"

I looked down at my wedding rings then back to the stranger and wondered what I was doing. He was right. I was still married, even if Fen didn't honor his vows. I knew this interlude couldn't lead to anything, but I just didn't want to leave. I was feeling more alive than I had in a while. "No."

"Where does he think you are?"

I wanted to be honest, but honesty was sometimes ugly, and people were often uncomfortable with the truth. I didn't know this man nor did I care what he thought. "He doesn't care."

His eyes saddened and I became afraid I had ended the evening. People were looking for excitement, not baggage. I didn't want him to leave. I didn't want to be alone.

"Then let's take a walk."

Before I could answer, he raised his hand to get the server's attention. When she came, half running, he put a bill in her hand, stood and pulled my chair out then offered me his help. I hesitated. What now?

"I'm not going to kidnap you Lana, and will be glad to deliver you to your car if you change your mind."

My thoughts raced. I had read about stupid women who went with total strangers never to be heard from again. I was over reacting, and he looked harmless, but I was sure serial killers did too. I didn't want to be alone, so I reached for his hand. and then looked around to find that our stalker had given up.

That was our first of many Harbor walks to come.

Chapter Five

My weeks were long and tedious. In anticipation of new stores opening in the resort, we held job fairs to fill the future positions they would create.

Luke, my co-worker, and I stood behind the long table decorated with the company's paraphernalia and brochures for hours, greeting potential candidates. Many were college students approaching graduation and reality. There was a university nearby, so I made sure we posted a flyer on the student board.

After collecting close to one hundred fifty resumes, there were only three I kept. One boy approached the table and slammed his resume in front of me.

"Bam!" he told me. "You don't have to look any further."

I was startled by the outburst. Luke left the booth to keep from laughing hysterically in the young man's face.

The chubby boy stood proudly before me in his food stained pants and wrinkled shirt. His smile was wide and I'm sure he felt he was impressive, so I took the time to give him some words of encouragement and explained our hiring process. When I got the text to meet Sterling, I was ready for a break.

Although Sterling was a needed distraction, my mind was all over the place at dinner. No matter what he asked, I was a second behind answering, often asking him to repeat himself.

He touched my hand. "Where are you today? You seem distracted." His brilliant smile froze. "Are you okay?"

I drew my hand back slowly and looked around the room scanning each face. Was I being watched? My nerves got the best of me, and I became uneasy. The war within began.

I thought about Fen. Odd. I tried to believe in a castle made of sand, but every time the winds and waters came, it washed away. When it fell into the sea, my feet couldn't find dry land, leaving me treading water. This was my metaphor of my relationship with Fen. It started as this storybook tale most little girls dreamt of, but eventually reality hit. The castle was our fortress, our foundation. The winds represented the turmoil that constantly bombarded us and all our work was washed away by the tides that rolled in, dissolving the foundation we desperately tried to rebuild. We were beyond treading water. We were drowning. No one told us sand wasn't stable.

My beginning with Sterling had storybook written all over it as well, only there could never be a happy ending without someone getting hurt. I knew I should be running from him, but instead, I felt safe, and that made him dangerous. I had been faithful through my husband's constant infidelities because I feared God, and there was no one else who remotely peaked my interest. I realized that had changed. Sterling, I wanted.

In that instant, I felt lost. I didn't know what to do. I didn't want to disappoint anyone. I closed my eyes and talked to God. *Tell me what to do, Lord. I know this can't be good.*

Today my world felt cloudy, as though a storm had just moved in. My heart was open to this man with whom I had been spending weeks. Now What?

"I'm sorry," he laughed, exposing his nerves. "I didn't mean..."

"I know what you meant," I assured him, mimicking his favorite phase. Honestly, I had no idea what he had just said. His words were lost in my maze of thoughts. "Let's take a walk."

He helped me stand and swept his eyes over my five foot four-inch frame. The heat rose to my face and I hoped my clothes went back to the right places. I didn't want to be obvious that I dressed for him, but he began to orchestrate my every move.

I ran my hands down my sides to smooth any possible imperfections. He grabbed them, stopping me. "You look fine."

I smiled. He made me nervous.

I felt his hand on the small of my back, gently guiding me through the bar, weaving through the tables and people. Once clear of the door, he joined me, and our walk began.

Although it was spring, the night air was a little chilly. There was a light breeze and every so often I felt an icy drop of moisture.

Now I didn't have to strain to hear him speak over the other conversations that bombarded us. And the eyes I felt watching me were gone.

I listened to his voice resonate as he told me about his day. I was mesmerized by its sound, singing and calming my soul. The light breeze made me realize *I* was creating the storm. He never asked anything of me, except my time. I was exaggerating the significance of our encounters.

I rubbed my arms in an attempt to heat them.

"You cold?" He took his pin-striped suit jacket and wrapped me in its warmth before I could answer.

"You never talk about yourself."

He stopped and looked down at me.

I didn't talk about myself because I had become unimportant. My husband never listened to me, so I stopped talking about my day or what was important or even interesting a long time ago. "I'm sorry. My life is simple and not as interesting as yours."

"Everyone's life is interesting, Lana, and everyone has something to share."

He had a habit of knowing exactly what to say. *Satan, get thee behind me.* "I am the manager of a small group, mostly millennials. They keep me young, make me laugh and stress me out."

"I thought *you* were a millennial."

I wondered how old he thought I was. I looked at him trying to hide my horror.

He burst into laughter heating my cheeks as I realized he was teasing me. Playfully I pushed him.

"I am so glad we got that out of the way," he said laughing.

We were walking again. Sterling looked dignified, hands clasped behind his back as he considered my words. He reminded me of a judge listening to the accused dilemma before he made a decision. Then I realized. He was listening!

"Why do you come to MVP?" he asked.

MVP, the sports bar we frequented, was the only social place in the harbor, other than GM, that attracted people my age. GM was my work place and I would never mix business and social. I initially went to MVP to have adult conversation with Dwight, but now I came hoping to see Sterling.

"Why do you come to MVP?" I asked reversing the question. Although I now came to the bar looking for him, I wasn't about to tell him that. I could hardly admit it to myself.

"I come to see if you are there."

Bam! There was the truth for me to process. I hadn't heard honesty in so long I questioned whether it *was* the truth. "Me?"

"You had to know. Don't pretend you didn't." He abruptly stopped walking and looked at me. "I'm completely honest with you, Lana, so give me the same respect," he said authoritatively and as suddenly he began walking again.

Wow. Were there still men like him? "I didn't know." I *knew* he was dangerous.

He looked embarrassed and exposed as he turned away, attempting to hide his exposed true feelings. Looking across the slow moving river I gathered the courage to be as transparent.

"I come for you too," I admitted in a whisper. I didn't want him to feel sorry for telling me the truth while I held on to mine.

Slowly the corners of his lips curled, and I felt him grab my hand. We walked, both smiling and basking in our new revelation and friendship.

Chapter Six

I was still sleeping when Fen arrived home. The familiar voice of the security system announced he entered through the front door, which meant he would not be home long. It was ten in the morning, and he found it alarming that I was still in bed.

"Hey, sleepy head. You want to go to breakfast?"

I turned over and looked at my phone. Ten o'clock. "Sure. Let me wash and get dressed."

"Are you feeling okay?"

I felt his eyes on me. "I'm just tired," I answered as I went into the bathroom. Was I acting differently? I laughed to myself. I felt guilty for stealing a dinner and walk while he felt no remorse for screwing some whore.

In the closet my jean dress was where I left it. It fit loose these days. I had not been eating much lately due to the overwhelming need to have the new hires in place before the new stores opened. Sometimes I forgot to eat. Wayne, my director, noticed the weight loss and ordered lunch for my team, just the day before, to make sure I ate.

My peep-toe booties were sitting on my shoe rack. I sat on the small stool in the closet, reminiscing about the evening before and the honest conversation shared with Sterling.

I looked in the mirror and decided to wear a belt to hide the looseness of the dress. I didn't know why I was taking care to dress presentably when Fen obviously didn't notice, and I wanted him to notice. For us, in that moment, I needed him to care. It seemed an eternity since I received a compliment from him. They seemed to come from strangers lately.

Fen was flipping through his mail at the kitchen table when I came downstairs. "I'm ready."

"Where do you want to go?"

"It doesn't matter. The Diner is fine."

"Then let's go."

I pushed my food around my plate as he rambled on about work. The more he talked, the more it irritated me, knowing he was not where he claimed to be. I never understood why he felt the need to volunteer lies when I didn't question what he did. His conversation was as cold and stale as the food on my plate.

I never snooped through his things, although the opportunities always presented themselves. There was the time when his phone rang in the middle of the night. It was her, thinking he was working. He was asleep and didn't have the opportunity to look and see who was calling before he answered. He thought it was one of the workers.

The sound of her voice caused him to jump to his feet for fear that I would hear her. The conversation sounded unintelligible as he attempted to answer her questions. "I'm home!" Then without warning, he disconnected the call, without as much as a goodbye.

"Why is she calling you?"

Startled by the question he was slow to return to bed. He paced the floor. "I don't know," he answered. "I don't know how to make her stop."

"Put a restraining order on her," I suggested. "She should get the message."

He became quiet.

"I don't have any control over who calls me Lana. What do you want me to do? Change my number?"

"If that's what it takes."

"You know I can't. I have too many business contacts with this number."

There it was again, another excuse. He had one for everything.

We blew up so badly one time I was prepared to leave. Anything was better than always wondering where he was or if he was telling the truth. If I left, I wouldn't have to care what he did. Not caring was so much easier than waiting for him to do the right thing. I didn't know if I would continue to surrender my life to a man who appeared to have no intentions of stopping his escapades, even if he believed he could. But I never did anything easy.

The two had a history together. When I realized he was still seeing Rose after ten years, I shutdown. Ten years... that was almost our entire marriage. It wasn't like he was seeing different women, it was just her.

I withdrew. His relationship with her was like having a second marriage. How was he going to let that go? He made unsolicited promises I knew he wouldn't be able to keep.

"You have two marriages. Why should I expect you to walk away from her?" I yelled. I was so frustrated the night of the blow-up.

"But I will," he promised.

"You are making promises you cannot possibly keep. You have a whole other marriage!" I screamed.

"Lana I love you."

"You don't know what love is. Your parents have screwed you up."

"And yours haven't?"

I was hurt by the truth that spilled so effortlessly from his month, but I had just done the same to him. I knew I should apologize for the words I rudely spurted from my smart mouth, which had gotten me in trouble numerous times in my past, but I wouldn't. I wanted him to swim in those words and feel what I was feeling. Hurt.

That week was tense, but I never felt so free, knowing the truth was on the table and now the ball was in my court. It was me who held all the cards, and he waited for my answer.

The entire week I avoided thinking about our issues. I just wanted to leave, so I wouldn't have to process them at all. It was better to cut my losses and move on. It was what I did best as a youth. Run. It was what freed me to cut my mother off and move on as though she didn't exist. If she didn't exist, I didn't have to sift through the web of hurt where she had entrapped me.

On her death bed I had no last words of love to share with the woman who birthed me. It was her fault I didn't know her. She hadn't taken the time to know me, so she was a stranger, and a burden. I had finals to prepare for.

When she finally died I didn't cry. I felt she wouldn't have wanted me to wear my feelings on my sleeve and be weak. No, I was a soldier, reading the announcements, making arrangements and picking out everything while my brothers fell apart.

I felt they had betrayed me. She was the same woman who left us days at a time while we had no food in the house and wasn't there when people broke in to steal our things. She was the same woman who abandoned us with our grandmother for two years, visiting us only on Christmas and maybe our birthdays.

How would he break things off with Rose and never speak to her again, when he had no reason, other than he was married to me? Apparently that wasn't enough for him to end things. There was no reason for him to leave her, and he had everything to lose staying with me.

I went to the opera at the Kennedy Center; I went bowling, and saw a concert at the Casino that week. It was great. Although I was free, I came to the realization that freedom came with its downfalls as well. When the adventures ran out there was no one to share with, to rub my toes when they were tired, pat my behind when I felt frisky or vent to when I had a bad day. But, I didn't have most of that anyway; at least not with Fen.

Yes. That one week I felt empowered. I was going to leave my husband, and never look back. Then it happened.

He cried. He begged. He promised. Then the Holy Spirit began talking to me.

Who will stand in the gap for him?

"I don't have to be married to him to stand in the gap."

What about your promise before God?

"Why didn't He protect me from this hurt?

All things work together for the good of those who love the Lord, Beloved. He will never allow for more than you can bear.

"Then he doesn't know me."

He knows you better than you know yourself. He knew you before you were in your mother's womb. He knew you would be strong enough to withstand.

"Withstand what? Heartbreak?" He was silent.

Didn't Fen remember all the hurt from my childhood; the loneliness and feeling of abandonment? He only cared and respected himself. So, why did he need my respect and love? I could give all I had to someone else. Besides, he could get it from Rose.

I waited for an answer, but the Holy Spirit was silent for too long, and I was impatient. I needed God to tell me it was okay to leave and He would back my decision. I needed Him to turn my love for Fen away, like He did David with Michal, who ridiculed David for dancing out of his clothes in the streets. Still, He was silent, and I needed His direction.

"This isn't tough. It's impossible!"

Is there anything too hard for God? He asked, finally breaking the silence.

His words convicted me. I knew there was nothing too hard for God. "But why do I have to stand? Why can't I run? I don't want to wonder if he's with her every time he walks out the door. I don't like the feeling when he lies. Things would be better if we were apart, then he could be free to do his thing without me knowing or caring!"

There was the problem. I still cared.

He was silent again, leaving me to my thoughts and conclusions. Was He testing me? He wanted to see if I would trust Him. Right?

I was that girl who never wanted to let anyone know when they hurt me. Hurt waited for me at my happiest moments as a reminder that happiness was not a permanent part of my destiny. Instead, my happier times were there to give me a break from the heartache.

I told Fen how he hurt me, but all he said was that he never wanted me to know or find out. I bet he didn't! If I found out, he would be forced to make decisions he never wanted to make.

I reminded him how in love with me he used to be, but he only said he was still in love with me. He promised he never stopped loving me.

"Then why?"

"Do you believe you can be in love with two people at the same time?" he asked me.

I couldn't believe he was telling me he loved her! A piece of my heart broke knowing my husband had allowed another to come between our sacred union. Who was this woman and why was she there?

"I believe someone could care about themselves so much they are convinced they are and use that as an excuse to have their cake and eat it too!" There was my mouth again.

He looked at me like a child learning an important lesson from his mother. I was five months older than Fen, but I wasn't trying to be his mother. I needed a man and not a man-child.

He apologized over and over, kissing me and making promises of fidelity, using my love for him against me. He held me as if he was afraid I would walk out on him at that very moment, and he would never get to hold me again. He made love to me, offering his heart and soul for me to do with as I chose. And I believed him.

Months passed, and after many weekends at exotic hotels, dinners, walks, spas and conversations, I felt we were back on track. Fen asked me to let down my guard and let him back in. I asked him to help me, and he did. So, I stayed.

We had survived what many had not. It felt to me like Fen had pulled the trigger and shot me, but after he realized his mistake, he revived me. I had taken my vows for better or worse, and we survived. I didn't believe I could ever love another man.

Love was a fragile thing. I had fought many fights as a child for less, but now I was a woman. Wasn't my marriage worth the fight?

Four months later, I lay next to him as he slept. Suddenly, his phone lit up. I realized I had not seen it in months. I looked at him and turned back to the lit phone.

My inner feelings told me to leave it, but my flesh needed to know. I didn't just want to know, I *had* to know. I entered the code, he thought I didn't have, and the text messages from her were there for me to read.

Rose: I thought you were coming by today what happened?

Fen: Some things came up at work.

Rose: Things are always coming up lately. I accept being second. I get it, but don't make arrangements with me if you aren't going to hold to them.

Fen: I'll call you later.

Rose: I guess I'm glad I didn't hold my breath for that call. I hate you, Russell.

Quietly, I put the phone down. Staring at the wall with my back to Fen, I felt God was holding me hostage. I didn't want to be a part of this triangle. Hadn't he already said he felt bad that he brought her into his inner circle and now she was in love with him and alone?

I knew with all her pleading and whining; he would give in eventually because he would feel her hurt was his fault. He was to blame for becoming involved with her, as he told me before. Should I stay or leave? The Holy Spirit seemed to believe my place was here, but I felt disrespected and demeaned by the situation. *Subdue your flesh.*

I couldn't go back to sleep. Quietly, I slid from the bed and went to the closet to pray. God must have made a mistake. How could He want me to stay in this mess? I didn't have the resolve of Jesus.

The walk-in closet was huge, so I converted a corner into my prayer area. Fen had a separate closet. My pillow was on the floor where I left it.

I lay face down and began to worship. I thanked God for all He had done for me, and prayed as I learned to do years before. Then I prayed for our marriage, but couldn't be specific, because I didn't know what I wanted.

I mostly cried remembering my lonely childhood. I asked God why I wasn't important to anyone who was important to me. Then I prayed for my brothers who always took care of me when there was no one else to care enough to do it. I missed them.

"God you have been so good to me. I'm sorry for my murmuring. I know you love me and that should be enough. I don't deserve your love, but you're always there for me. You been kind and selfless where I have not, and still you give yourself to me."

I thanked him for protecting me from what could have been worse as my brothers and I raised ourselves. On the surface it appeared we turned out fine, but I knew I was damaged goods and the only thing holding me together was God.

I felt the relief and comfort cover me like a warm blanket as He ministered to me. It was amazing to be in God's presence. When you sense the enormity and infinity of God, it feels like your issues are so small. He reminded me that this was only temporary, although I didn't feel ten years was temporary. Obviously, God didn't measure time as I did. Soon I was calm and asleep.

Chapter Seven

My story began thirty-eight years ago and my tears began out of the womb. My parents separated and my mother, Sade, was pregnant with me on her departure. I'm sure if she could have gotten away with it, she would have named me Misery, but that would have been too obvious. Or maybe it was the sadness I felt, the time she told me she never wanted me. But here I was, entirely against her wishes.

Five pounds eight ounces, and loud as ever, I entered the universe, screaming from the indignation of being spanked for the first time. I'm sure God begged me not to leave His side, but I was stubborn even then. Had I known I would have been untouched and unloved as a child, I would have stayed with Him. I could never question His love for me.

My brothers were breastfed, the one thing Sade was selfless about. I, on the other hand, was not. Sade and I started a love-hate relationship from the beginning.

There weren't many conversations between the two of us. I remembered endless shouting matches that helped me to refine my smart mouth and quick come backs.

As a teen I feared her, but obviously not enough to stay out of trouble. Although most thought I did things to get attention from her that was the last thing I wanted. I did them, because I thought I was smart enough to get away with them. Overall I was a good girl and I stayed to myself.

My friends were my brothers. They ensured my safety and when my mother wasn't around, made sure I had food. We were our own clan, even when we lived with Grandma Ruby who took care of us, but had no time for us. After I gave up on everyone else, Fen became my friend.

But, my first earthly love affair was with my father, Simeon. Why I don't know. By court order, I spent every other weekend in the summer with him, but he was never there. When he did show up, I behaved like a love starved puppy, running behind him, willing to accept any attention he gave.

Grandmother, Virginia, didn't work, so when my father was not home, my brothers and I spent all our time with her. She was mean and ornery towards me, but cared for my brothers, who lived with my father at the time. I always believed she was mean to me because I was the darkest of my father's children and looked like my mother. Most of the time she ignored me, leaving me to feel invisible.

My brothers played outside, but I wasn't allowed. Grandmother Virginia said the neighborhood was too rough for me. The front steps became my playground and it was there that my fairytale kingdom was built. I imagined that each step represented a different element of the kingdom and the top step was my throne.

Once, I got up enough nerve to sneak off my throne and walked the concrete city sidewalk to the girl about eight houses down. She looked cool, and everyone who passed knew her by name. She took one look at the stolen pearl ring on my finger and began her scam.

"Hey I like your ring," she told me. "Can I see it?" Of course, I was going to let her see it. I was in need of a friend, but before she could leave her fingerprints on the round, hazy pearl, my grandmother appeared and pulled me, feet barely touching the ground, back to my boundaries. She ruined my only opportunity of having a playmate. Hell, she could have had the ring.

My brothers Ozi, the eldest, and Keanu, the younger of the two, had the full reign of the neighborhood. My father said they were boys and had to learn to survive in the streets, or the streets would overtake them.

Ozi was into everything from stealing, including the ring I wore that day, to drug trafficking. He could make friends with anyone and adapted to any environment. He feared no one and did things his way, gaining the respect of his peers. His natural ability to lead made him the perfect big brother and threatened his future as a gang leader.

Keanu was mild in nature. He followed Ozi wherever he went, but did more observing than participating. His adoration for Ozi could not be tainted nor soiled by anyone. Ozi was both of our heroes.

They were both my kings, which made me the princess in our kingdom. But our kingdom was dysfunctional, lacking direction, purpose and love from those we expected to love us.

I hated my Grandma Virginia's house. It stunk like dog. In fact, there were two of them, and they didn't like me either. One grabbed me by the socks and twirled me around. Grandma Virginia told me to watch where I walked and returned to what she was doing.

Grandma Virginias's floors were black linoleum, but most floors during that time were linoleum when you had no money. Black was not the color of the floor. Black was the dirt on the floor. It had never been washed.

This life was not the life I knew. My floors at home were hardwood and shiny. There were no dogs to attack me and our house was spotless. My grandmother Ruby was a maid, so everything at home shined.

I shared a bed with my grandmother Virginia on my visits. The mattress was fluffy and sheets cool at night. The worse thing was I couldn't remember my grandmother ever striping the bed to wash those sheets.

The best thing was that Grandma Virginia was a baker. Rolls were her specialty and she sold them from her East Baltimore window every weekend. They were the best rolls in the world. Just thinking of them brings back the delightful aroma, making my mouth water. My brothers, Ozi and Keanu, sopped the fluffy mounds of perfection in King's Syrup. Me, I loved to roll mine in butter... lots of butter.

I remembered being in that kitchen watching her every move. It was the only thing I could do, trapped in the house. Her long braid swung past her waist with every move, and she wore the same frown every day. I wondered if she was as unhappy as me.

Grandma Virginia's eyes were green and her skin fair. She seemed to be a black man's delight, so I never understood why she was so unhappy. If the black man's prize was unhappy, what hope was there for me with my cocoa brown skin? But of course that would be based on the assumption that to have a man made one happy. To have a man appeared to be every woman's only goal then.

My dad's eyes were bright blue, and he was fair skinned as well. I looked nothing like him, but everything like my mother. Maybe he wasn't home because I reminded him of her. She was the one that got away and he truly loved her.

Mom was high on the selection list, and my dad won the prize. Then men were known to explore outside of the home, hence the term 'rolling stone'. Today that wouldn't work, because most women wouldn't tolerate those shenanigans. Hell, now women are the ones doing the rolling.

Sade was the girl you didn't leave home alone. She had yearnings of her own. My mother was wild and unpredictable. Deep down I believed she wanted to have the same privileges as a man.

She was beautiful, with mahogany brown skin and long, jet black, curly hair that came from her Native American heritage. I know every Afro American claimed some existence of Native American heritage to explain their hair or complexion, but Sade was the real deal.

She was uncontrollable as a child. Taken from her mother at three, she was given to her barren paternal aunt, who gave her back to her father at thirteen after a physical altercation ensued between the two of them. Surely, no man was going to control her as an adult.

At the beginning of their marriage my parents lived with Grandmother, Virginia, but Grandmother's distaste for my father's choice of a brown girl often caused conflict between Grandma and my mother, who didn't know when to hold her tongue. Grandmother Virginia wouldn't tolerate Sade, the family embarrassment.

Grandmother Virginia proudly claimed her European blood, inherited from Master Harris of the great state of Virginia. The families, Greenhill, Tucker, Harris' and Hobbs traded off members many times over to preserve their privileged light skin and eyes.

Her ancestors quickly found they were treated differently from their darker complexioned Afro-Americans brothers and sisters, continuing what master had started on the plantation. My father's people were the house nigga's. Never wanting to lose their privileges, my father's people tried to maintain their color. My parent's generation was the first to disregard that tradition and the elders were in an uproar.

Due to the stressful environment my parents moved to a small apartment above a bar. A bar? I don't know what my father was thinking.

He disappeared for days at a time, and Sade was not a "leave-at-home" kind of girl. One night, he returned to find she wasn't at home, and neither were my brothers. Mom dropped them off with my Grandma Ruby, which she did often.

Dad went to the bar to wait for her return. When he got there, to his surprise, there was Sade, sitting at the bar, smiling at another man's pearly whites.

That night they fought, but didn't wait until they were in the privacy of their home. The fight started right there in the bar. I remember when I first heard this story, and I visualized my mother jumping on my father's back and fighting him as he attempted to drag her back to their apartment. She was outraged at being treated like a child, and cursed him the whole time.

Although she was small in stature, five feet, I feared her as a child because I never knew what she would use to discipline me. Shoes, belts, plastic cups, hangers, I could go on and on, describing the things she used to throw or spank me with, although I didn't get many spankings, because she was seldom home to discipline me. Most of my spankings were because of my mouth.

My parents never fought again, because two months later Sade left Simeon. That was another of many differences we shared. Sade only had allegiance to one person and that was herself. She escaped early, and I remained in my marriage that was dying a slow death. My allegiance was for everyone except me.

Chapter Eight

Over the months, Sterling and I met regularly. We met at least once a week and shared conversation about everything. Sometimes, we talked about our week, or we might talk about sports, news, and our beliefs, but never about our personal lives.

Fen spent his time so predictably; it was easy to plan our time together. Fen was spending more and more time away from home, and I began to look forward to seeing Sterling, and became irritable when we couldn't get together. Our meetings helped me through mine and Fen's times of alienation. He filled a void that I no longer expected Fen to do, thus, making my times with Fen less stressful. I thought that was a good thing.

Fen asked what was going on with me. I was short with him and we would argue. I no longer had the tolerance to hear the lies so I challenged him and my smart mouth got the best of me.

One night he left after an argument and didn't come home all weekend, reminding me of Simeon's disappearances. I felt abandoned and pushed further away from him. Our conversations became cordial, and I fulfilled my wifely duties as though doing chores. Still I remained with him. I wanted even more to leave, but I wouldn't.

The small voice reminded me. *We wrestle not against flesh and blood.* He was reminding me that our battles were not carnal, they were spiritual. I pushed it down and ignored the warning. I didn't want to feel lonely or unhappy anymore. Fen wasn't there, so why should I be?

I canceled my next meeting with Sterling. I lied, and said I wasn't feeling well and I would see him the next week. The last thing I wanted was to be moody and bring down our atmosphere. I was feeling some kind of way, because Fen had not come home.

When Fen returned home from his weekend, he was mean, but I felt relieved that he was safe. I wondered where he was, frustrating me even more, but didn't ask. I could hear Grandma Ruby say, "Don't ask a question if you're not prepared for the answer."

What was I doing?

The next week I went to church, again deciding not to meet Sterling. The more I saw Sterling, the less time I spent with God. I used church as my cover to meet him. I only had to tell Fen I'd be back, because he wouldn't believe his precious Lana would be going anywhere other than church. Fen never went to church anymore, so I didn't have to worry about him wanting to come.

I needed to reconnect with God. I needed direction. I needed reassurance that what I was doing wasn't wrong.

There was a time when I lived for Fen's love and would have died for it. But the truth was, I no longer cared what he did and wished he would decide to leave, because my promise didn't allow me that convenience.

This space I existed in was confusing and frustrating. Should I stay? Should I go? But mostly, why am I here?

I walked on eggshells for the past ten years, afraid as always, to fail. I had abandoned who I was and became Fen's wife. I hated him for who I had become. Now, no longer caring, those eggshells were broken into a million pieces, and I didn't know how to clean up the mess. Instead, I stood in them, pretending nothing affected me. The pretty bird birthed in the process was hurting and lost, and if she didn't learn from these lessons, she would die.

I was so used to pushing my feelings down and tucking them away that I had not realized something inside of me had broken. I always believed Fen and I were destined for one another and no one else. I believed we only existed for one another, but I was wrong. He chose another direction and walked a path that endangered all I once believed we were. I was always playing the game... He loves me? He loves me not? Once believing I couldn't go on without him, now I knew I could. Bound only by my promise to God, I stayed.

I don't know when Fen stopped loving me. Maybe it was something I had said or done that turned him away. He found someone to replace what I was not giving him. Why *did* he stay? I found myself mulling over those four phases of heartbreak: he's leaving; it's over, he's sorry and goodbye. I found myself waiting for them in vain. If he would say just one, things would have been easier. It would help me put my feelings in some context. That would be fair, but life was anything but fair.

Heaven had been away too long.

Chapter Nine

I was late to church but made it before praise and worship ended. Although Sterling and I had not been intimate, I felt the shame rush over me as soon as I entered and the words of the praise team penetrated my heart. Our relationship took me off course and away from what grounded me; *God's* promises.

Sure, I was destined for hell; I began to say a silent prayer. I stood swaying with the music, hiding the fact that I was feeling unconnected. I wanted to feel God's presence, but shame wouldn't let me. The tears came. I cried. I couldn't hear Him and didn't know the last time I had. I imagined Jesus felt like this when God turned away from the sin He took on at the cross.

A tissue was pressed into my hand, and I attempted to wipe away my tears, but there were too many to catch them all. The familiar voice of my Bishop quietly called to the alter all who needed prayer. I was too ashamed to go and remained at my seat with my hands up in worship.

Without warning, my knees met the floor, and I held myself. My eyes closed, I heard someone kneel with me and pray. After calming down, I stood to my feet. Prophetess Jordan hugged me and whispered in my ear. "He hasn't left you. Keep believing on Him and trust in Him with all your heart."

I nodded my head and sat in my seat. Although her words were comforting, they gave me little direction.

After church, the usual few hugged me. My Bishop's wife approached me. "We missed you daughter." She gave me a long refreshing hug and pushed me back to give me a once over.

She always reminded me of the mother I always wanted but never had. Her warmth made me want to curl up in her arms and let her stroke me and tell me things were going to be fine.

Sade wasn't that person. She ridiculed, and her words were harsh. When I left home for college, I could remember her asking me if I were still a virgin. After assuring her that I was, she turned on me and asked, "What? You think your stuff is too good?"

Stunned by her disapproval, I was at a loss for words. Most mothers would have been proud their daughter wasn't a whore, but mine saw this as a failure. Nothing was new. I could never please her, and I stopped trying once I moved from home at eighteen.

"I missed you too, Mother," I said as I hugged the woman I now addressed by the title bestowed upon her by the church. I held on to her, wishing I could share my transgressions, but I couldn't stand to have her look at me differently. If I shared with her the time I was spending in the company of Sterling, I knew it would wipe away the beautiful smile she gave me whenever I saw her and I needed her motherly smile.

"Everything okay?"

I smiled but didn't answer. How could I tell the woman I held in such high regard that my husband was cheating, and I was on the border of doing the same? I hung my head, afraid she would see through my shallow desires for a man who was not my husband.

She patted my hand. "If you need me I'm here until God calls me home."

"I know Mother. Maybe one day, but I'm not ready." I didn't want her to tell me what I was doing was wrong. I already knew that, but I wasn't ready to let Sterling go because he made me feel happy and safe.

After hugging Bishop, I hurried to my car before someone else stopped me. Once I was off the property, away from the possibility of being struck by lightning, I called Sterling but got no answer. I didn't know whether to go home or to the sports bar. Not wanting to see Fen, I decided to go to the sports bar.

Dwight wasn't working, so I had to find my voice, and order my Shirley Temple.

A nice looking man, dressed in his Sunday's best, sat in the chair to my right. He ordered his drink then winked at me. I rolled my eyes, because I felt like being annoying.

"You from the area?" he asked, attempting small talk.

I didn't feel like a pointless conversation, but I didn't want to be rude. "Yes."

"Your first time here?"

"No."

He turned to face me, and I knew I was in trouble. He smiled his crooked smile, exposing a slightly chipped tooth, and licked his full lips. Obviously, someone did us all a disservice by telling him they were sexy. They were okay, as far as lips go, but that short thick tongue! *Gross!*

"I've never seen you here, and I know I wouldn't have missed anything as beautiful as you." His eyes smiled.

If I were another woman in another life, I probably would have talked to him. He had a football build with a slight gut, but nothing unappealing, and was average height. He wasn't bad looking. Men could be mutts in a pack, but as long as they were neat, trimmed and well-kept, they became attractive. He was a little more than that.

I smiled my rudest smile and rolled my eyes again looking away. "So, since *you've* never seen me I couldn't have possibly been here before?" My smart mouth got the best of me again. I took a sip of my Shirley. "Hmmph. I've never seen you before either, so I guess you've never been here, as you say."

He reared his head back and laughed. I could tell he was used to women pouring over him, but I wasn't feeling it. My life was already complicated.

"I can tell you are a hand full. Maybe I should take my drink and run while I can." He licked his lips again and pretended to go, but just as quickly as he stood, he sat back down. "But I like a challenge."

Across the room, in our favorite spot, I saw Sterling smiling as he enjoyed my interaction with the stranger. I tilted my head to the side indicating I needed him to rescue me, but he didn't budge.

The stranger slid in closer. He smelled good, his cologne reminding me of something Fen wore. But now he was in my bubble, my space.

"I'm married."

"I didn't ask." He looked around. "Besides, if you were my woman you would not be sitting at a bar alone for someone like me who doesn't give a damn about boundaries to push up on you."

I blushed.

"So are you married, or are you trying to get rid of me, because if you are trying to get rid of me, you aren't trying hard enough for me to believe the latter."

I had to smile. This man was pushy, and his conversation told me he was astute as well. He smiled his crooked smile again and turned to his drink holding it with both hands.

"I'm married."

"Are you?" As he waited for my answer, he was studying my face.

The stranger hit a nerve. I didn't feel married in the least. The shockwave from my emotions and the tears I spilled in church earlier hit me again. My years of pretending I had no emotions came over me all at once. Now, I fought back the show of weakness that desperately wanted to flow.

The stranger saw my dilemma and handed me the damp napkin from under his drink. For fear of losing the little composure I had, I didn't move. He slid it in my hand.

"Excuse me." I stood to leave.

He grabbed my hand. "I'll be here if you come back, but you should know I'm a wolf. So, don't come back if you don't want to be taken advantage of because I'm very interested." He removed his hand and turned back to the bar again no longer looking at me. "I'll cover your drink."

Quickly I made my way to the entrance. I knew Sterling would be in pursuit, so I went down the hall to the galley stores and ducked inside the small dress boutique. I grabbed a dress off the rack and ducked into the dressing room. With the door closed behind me, I sank to the floor and finished what I started at church.

Time passed and there was a soft rap on the door.

"I'll be out in a minute."

I stood, and fixed my clothes while checking my appearance in the mirror. My purse! I realized I left it at the bar. I banged my fist on the wall knowing I had to face the wolf again.

My face didn't look that bad. I rarely wore makeup to church, because by the end of service it was messy.

The door creaked when I opened it announcing my coming. I hung the dress on the send-back rack and exited the small area.

Sterling stood just outside the door. His concerned look made me want to run back into the room, but he grabbed my hand, stopping my retreat and handed me my purse with his other hand.

I couldn't look at him. He tilted my head up to his and rubbed my cheek with his thumb. "Let's walk."

He led me out of the building, safe from the wolf, and down our normal path. We shared the silence and walked.

I looked at him closely and for the first time saw the shadows under his eyes and lines on his face. He was going through something as well. "You okay?" I asked concerned.

"I'm good." He smiled and took me to the nearest bench where we sat.

"What happened?"

I looked away, not willing to share the crazy part of my life. I wanted to keep my sanctuary with him separate. "I'm good," I said mocking him.

He smiled, and we sat in silence holding hands.

Chapter Ten

Fen was in the loft when I returned. The shower was calling me. It was always a good escape when I wanted to avoid him.

The spa massage heads spit as they turned on. With my clothes carelessly hung on the door hook, I entered the hot stream of water. The jetted water hit me, massaging my hidden pain. The stranger at the bar should not have been able to affect me so profoundly, but he hit a nerve. And there was Sterling who worried me.

The bathroom door opened. "What's up for dinner? Would you like to go out and get something and take it easy?"

I had forgotten about dinner, and didn't feel up to going out. "I'll cook so we can stay home."

"Lana, you don't have to cook. I can take you out."

I didn't want to go out. People were not on my agenda. Solitude was what I wanted. "We can eat out," I said, giving in to what Fen wanted. Again.

The door closed. I leaned on the wall and cried. I always gave in. Maybe that was part of my problem. I had no identity of my own, and for years, except at work, I didn't exist except through Fen. Without him as my core, I was forced to reinvent me. Now I gave him pushback as I tried to find myself.

Cold air rushed into the shower, catching me off guard as Fen joined me in the water, interrupting my moment of solitude. He attempted to hold me, and I pulled away not wanting him to touch me. Catching me up with his arms around my waist, he pulled me close burying his face in my neck and whispered, "Let me back in Lana. Stop fighting me. I don't even know who you are anymore."

It had been a while since he showed me any affection. His touch always made me surrender to him, so I melted in his arms forgetting the past two months. I felt the overwhelming need to be held, and it was inappropriate to expect that from Sterling.

Washing me slowly, he gave me an opportunity to recompose myself then he took my hand and led me from the shower and dried me. "I know I'm not the best husband, but I do love you."

Love me? What was love? I'd rather he'd tell me his true feelings, even if it hurt. For me, love was a never-ending stream of hurt, and I didn't know if my heart could take any more love.

"What is love Fen, if you're not here with me? Those are just words."

"I love you, Lana."

"You're not here anymore, and even when you are you're not. I never know where you are going, or if you are even available."

"I'm trying to pay for all of this," Spreading his arms he mimicked embracing the house.

"Are you sure, because I told you that material things have never been important to me? I would live in a shack with you if it meant we were together... *really* together."

"We are *really* together." My words hurt him. "You say you would give all this up and go back to the drug infested neighborhood and bug-ridden apartment where we first lived? *Those* are just words." He was becoming agitated.

Fen was accustomed to having his way with everyone. Sometimes I wondered if that was why he was still with me, because of my lack of surrender.

He watched me, saying nothing. I knew that look. He was about to flip on me. "When are you going to let me out of this prison Lana?"

"When are you going to stop seeing her? And don't lie to me and tell me you aren't seeing her anymore. Talk about what you honestly feel, and stop pretending everything is fine!"

"I'm not seeing her!"

"When was the last time you communicated with her? An hour ago? Two?"

"Yes, I've talked to her, and yes, I have seen her, but I'm no longer with her like that." He was pleading for me to believe him.

"Then why talk to her or see her at all?" I could feel my breathing become irregular. My chest heaved as my heart broke from his truth. With her! He was *with* me.

"It's not that simple."

"Why? All you have to do is say 'Rose, I want to save my marriage. I don't want to cause my wife any more pain, so I can't see you anymore. She's important to me, and I love her. We can no longer communicate on any level.'" Breathing slowly, I tried to regain my composure. "What is so hard about that?"

The television was blaring, updating us on forty-five's new mishaps as his own lies were beginning to catch up with him, cutting the silence that followed my question. Fen spun away, walked into the bedroom, and turned the television off. He returned and took me by my hand, leading me to the bedroom and sitting me on the bed.

"I can't totally break everything off with her just yet Lana. We still have unfinished business together."

"What kind of business?" I had never heard anything about this before.

"Lana. It's something I can't get out of."

"What does that mean, and what does that have to do with you disappearing all weekend and evenings. The fact that you have business with her shouldn't have anything to do with not being able to communicate with me!"

He stood and walked away pacing the floor and walking back to me several times as if he were going to answer my question, but changed his mind.

"What does she have on you?" I yelled.

He didn't answer.

"Do you love her?" I asked the question, my voice so low, I was barely audible.

He stopped and looked at me. "I thought I was ready for this conversation, but I'm not."

"So, you do love her?" I asked pressing on. I needed an answer.

"I give you everything Lana, but I will never be good enough to pay your dues. I can't make up for what I did, and I can't take it back, and every time I look, you've got a new hoop for me to jump through."

Watching me, I knew he wanted a response, but I heard no question in what he said. I wasn't letting him off that easily. Something was missing, and he was not going to tell me.

"Some things I can't tell you and I know it sounds ridiculous for me to ask you this, but I need you to trust me. I promise I will tell you everything one day, but until that time, ride with me."

Riding with Fen was tough. The only way to survive was to become detached, but he didn't want that. He wanted me to give myself to him without needing an explanation.

He pushed me back on the bed, laid on top of me, and whispered over and over. "Ride with me, Lana. Please." He could still make me respond to his touch and his voice, even when I didn't want to. Maybe this was why I avoided him.

Moaning in my ear, "I love you," he told me again. "I can't stand you not talking to me and acting like I'm not here." Resting on his elbows on either side of my head, he held my face in his hands. "I made a mistake I will always pay for in more ways than you'll know, but you were never a mistake."

Apprehensively, he lowered his face to mine and kissed me aggressively. Without warning, he flipped me over and ran his tongue down to the small of my back. "I thought about you all weekend. I missed you."

"You never called!"

"I'm sorry."

"You're always sorry," I pouted. Sorry was always his go-to response, and he was believable when he said it.

"You know I love it when you pout." He laughed. "Did you miss me?"

"No."

Lifting me to my knees, he entered me ever so gently. "Do you miss this?" He rode slowly and gently, reaching his hand around, exploring the areas he knew would take me there. I loved that he could please me. I hated that he knew how to push all my buttons.

As usual, my body betrayed me, yielding to his touch and moving with each stroke. The air sucked out of my lungs, and I gasped as he pushed deeper. I moaned answering his question when I didn't want to.

One. Two. Three. He held it there and pulled back only to allow me to catch my breath. "I know your body because it's mine, Lana. I went to Lana 101 just to please you."

He pleased me, alright. We never had an issue in that area, which was why I never understood why he stepped out. Maybe it was why I was so hurt.

Maybe I suspected that any woman who was with Fen was sure to be pleased. Why would Rose give him up? Fen was good looking, kind hearted, attentive, and a millionaire. His only downfall was he could be selfish. He did not like me to spend time with anyone except him when he was home, and lately, I wanted no part of him.

The waves of pleasure were coming, and I started speaking in tongues, which turned him on.

"Talk dirty to me, baby," he said as he reached his limit and released, holding me tightly.

Now what?

We lay in each other's arms as though the past two months had not happened. But nothing had changed. We still had unresolved issues. I still didn't know where Fen went when he disappeared, or why he sometimes left in the night after a text message.

"I love you, Lana. It will be okay. Let me fix it."

"Fix what?" He always referred to everything so mysteriously. What was *it* and why did *it* need to be fixed? *It* didn't need to be fixed. *We* needed fixing.

He became mysteriously quiet again. No answer.

"This is why I just can't with you, Fen. You tell me to trust you, and then do everything to make me not trust you. Why?"

"I can't talk to you about everything."

"Why?"

"Because it would hurt you!" He was yelling.

"You mean like now?" Frustration was pushing me. "You don't think the things you're doing now, or have done before, hurt me? What could you possibly say that would make a difference?"

He lay back on the bed. I could tell he wanted to talk, but his guilt or anguish kept him from going any further in the conversation.

Even in his sins and mystery, he was so damn lovable. The simplest thing for me was just to walk away, but I didn't. I wanted to, but I couldn't. God held me right there.

Chapter Eleven

My intimate encounter with Fen knocked me off kilter. I didn't know what I felt, what I was doing, or where I wanted to go with him. My trust was shattered, and he was in my head all day. My confusion grew worse when he came in and went right back out, telling me he would be home kind of late. Was I a fool? And, what the hell was *kind of* late.

I prayed a lot and didn't hear much from the Holy Spirit, but I didn't blame Him. I wouldn't talk to me either. It wasn't like I was taking his advice. Sterling was my hindrance. I just wasn't willing to let him go.

Sterling and I continued to see one another. My commitment to church returned, and I bawled every time I went. I needed to see Mother for counseling, but I didn't. I knew what she would tell me and I already knew what to do, but I just couldn't make myself do it. I asked for forgiveness every day.

"You've been quiet lately. I'm usually the quiet one," I said.

Sterling was staring into his drink. He was usually full of life and laughter, telling stories about his co-workers or something he witnessed. When he looked at me, his eyes were sad and distant. He rubbed the side of his glass, playing with the condensation that built from the cold ice.

I took his hands. They were shaking, but then I realized it wasn't just his hands. He was trembling. "Sterling, talk to me." The water built in his eyes, resting on the rim of his soul, threatening to spill.

I stood, still holding one hand, and waved to Ebony, our waitress, with the other to let her know we were leaving. Sterling reached in his pocket, but I stopped him. "I'll take care of it. Let's walk." It was my turn to take care of him.

The air was brisk and our path crowded with the attendees from the concert that had just let out. Sterling was oblivious to the mass of people and the bumps and occasional pushes, but I was becoming annoyed.

He squeezed my hand to calm me when a group almost knocked me over, letting me know he was still present. He was still shaking. Something was wrong.

Peering into his face, I saw that his eyes were blank and his jaw twitched. I didn't say anything. I just wanted to be there for him as he needed in that moment.

We sat on our favorite bench, and I continued to hold his hand and rub his back. Bending his head low, he rested on his knees, and I stroked his head.

"You can talk to me, Sterling. What's wrong?" I was worried. He was scaring me.

He sat up and looked across the flowing river. The current was moving swiftly today. There was a Ferry returning from Old Town, which was just across the water in Virginia. Virginia. I thought about my grandmother, and I didn't know why. He was still shaking.

"Just be here Lana. Just be here," was all he said in a hushed voice. So, I was there for him and continued to rub his head like a mother would a child.

Something happened he was not willing to share with me. I felt like an outsider in his life. When we were together nothing else and no one else mattered. But for the first time I realized other people did exist for him.

I kissed him on the cheek and the tears came. It broke my heart to see him cry. My throat grew tight as I tried to be his rock. He needed me, and I wanted to be his strength as he had been mine over the months.

I couldn't give him up. I wouldn't give him up. I loved this man. So, yes Fen, it's possible to love two people at the same time, as selfish as it may be.

Chapter Twelve

I didn't see Sterling for a couple of weeks, but he kept in contact, sending me short text messages. One message told me how much he appreciated me being there for him on that strange night. He said he needed me, and I came through.

He needed me. Someone *needing* me was new. Fen always said he loved me, and only used those words out of desperation. Needing seemed so much more profound.

I smiled and held my phone close to my chest when I got the message. It made me feel important, loved, necessary, and needed.

"Girl! What are you doing?" It was Mother staring at me with her atern stare and one hand on her hip. "Come in my office." Like a mischievous child, I obediently followed.

I had never been in her office before, but it was quaint and tastefully decorated. There was a fancy white jacquard love-seat with corded fringes on the bottom posted up against the wall. Above the love-seat was a family portrait of the Bishop and their children. I looked around but saw no pictures of Jesus or a cross.

"Have a seat." She waved her hand at the chair in front of her desk, and I knew she was serious.

Turning my attention back to Mother, I sat in the seat, but became distracted by the décor again.

Inside the office credenza were family pictures and a few photos of deceased church members. Books completed the empty spaces, mostly Bibles and study books.

"Who is he?"

Caught totally off guard, my mouth dropped. Who was who? What did she mean? How did she know? "I'm not sure what you mean, Mother."

"You came here broken up a couple of months ago. I know you have been having marital problems for a while, but now you're smiling and grinning. That's new love."

I didn't understand. New love? Did we wear love like a badge where everyone could see? My personal life was just that... personal. I never wanted to give anyone anything to judge me by. "Why do you say that?"

"You just had the opportunity to deny me twice, but instead you chose to ask me a question."

The clock on the wall caught me off guard. No one had clocks hanging anymore, yet she did. My mind wandered again at the distraction. I slid back in the chair and waited her out. I didn't want to lie, but I began to wonder what role Sterling would play in my life. Had he made such a difference that my appearance had changed?

I felt the smile just under the surface wanting to burst through, but Mother would scold me. How would I tell her no, when she said I had to give him up? Because I was sure that's what she would advise me to do.

"I told you before you can come and talk to me when you were ready. Be careful of the things you let into your life, daughter. We are not of this world and we cannot do what everyone else does."

"Yes, ma'am."

"How is your husband?"

"Fen?"

Her eyebrow lifted. "Do you have another?"

I laughed. "Fen's fine."

Mother studied me for a moment before she finally dismissed me. "Well, tell him we would like to see him too. I know he works hard, but he needs to find time for God."

"Yes, ma'am. I'll tell him."

Wanting to escape her watchful eye, I stood and made my way around the desk to hug her goodbye.

"Remember what's done in the dark will come to light, daughter."

Her final words hit me. My life wasn't perfect, but I had not sinned. I knew what I was doing wasn't completely right, but I was not intimate with Sterling. We shared a kiss, just one kiss, and it was on the cheek.

No sooner than I entered the hall, another woman, I didn't know, walked past me, eager to get to Mother. When the door closed behind me, I heard the woman burst into tears. Relieved I had escaped answering any more questions; I went directly to my car. There stood Loquacious. Maybe no one told her mother about the names you gave your children because she fit her given name. She talked endlessly.

The short light complexion woman was waving frantically to get my attention. Did she really think I could miss her standing there? "Sister Fenney!" she yelled as I approached.

The customer service smile I had acquired over the many years of calming guests instantly framed my face. "Hello, Sister Brown."

"I was trying to catch up with you inside, but Mother *scooped* you up so quickly."

I almost burst into laughter at the way she said the word *scooped*. She gave the word character. "What did you need?"

"I was building a committee to prepare for the teen fashion show fundraiser. Sister Joyce suggested I asked you."

At first, I wanted to say no, but I thought it would be a good idea for me to occupy my spare time. I needed to do something to get my mind off my dismal life. In spite of my dislike for church committees I committed.

"Sure, I will be happy to help out. What can I do?"

"I'm not sure yet. We are just getting started, so we will decide roles at our first meeting. It's here at the church at seven this Wednesday."

"I will be here, Loquacious."

On my way home I thought about what Mother said. *What was done in the dark would come to the light.* I guessed what Sterling and I were doing *was* in the dark. Then I thought, if our relationship were justified, and then there would be no problem in Fen knowing Sterling. Instead, Sterling was my secret, and I guessed that was what made the situation wrong. Instead of being on the up and up, we were on the low low.

Abstain from all appearance of evil.

The Holy Spirit was talking to me, but I still wanted to see Sterling. We were not sinning, but I could see how it would appear if Fen ever saw us together. If he saw us holding hands, I was sure he would have questions. Actually, I'm sure there would be more than questions.

I remembered the first time I met Rose, who I sometimes called Thirsty. I knew immediately there was a connection between that woman and Fen and I had plenty of questions.

We were at a contractor's social event. Fen paraded me on his arm the entire evening. We shook hands, and he introduced me to the officials he did business with, and the contracting representatives.

I was so proud to be there with him, and had primped all day. I spent hours with the Dominicans taming my unruly hair and getting my make-up done. I wanted him to be proud of me, too.

I met other contractors and their spouses as well as vendors. Fen hovered, and shared jokes about most of his colleagues. We had been working so hard it was the most fun we had in a while. We danced, laughed, and ate. But like Cinderella, the clock struck midnight and instantly my time as a princess was over.

Suddenly he became aloof. If he had not introduced me, no one would have known we were together. I asked him to sit, and he gave me excuse after excuse why he wanted to stand. If I sat, he stood by my seat. I was used to walking in heels all day, so I stood with him. After shifting several times, he walked away briefly, then returned, seemingly nervous. Then I spotted her.

Across the room, a woman sat staring at us. She was brooding. Her arms crossed her chest, and eyes followed Fen's every move. I could see he had spotted her too, as his eyes veered every so often, darting between the two of us. He was scared. Who was she?

Fen excused himself and went to her. He sat on the couch beside her, and she turned away from him. His head was bent into hers and he appeared to be whispering. They looked too familiar, and she was unnaturally too upset to be just a work associate. Astonished by what was unfolding before my eyes, their apparent intimacy made me feel uneasy, awkward, and finally pissed off.

Over the months leading up to this moment, Fen was always missing in action, coming in late and a few times he was missing on the weekends. Now I understood why and felt like a fool.

He returned to where I stood. Without looking at me he asked, "Are you ready to go?" I glared at him, now understanding his mood change.

Deciding to treat the situation like I did my work affiliates, when they pissed me off, I smiled and pretended to be unshaken by what had just transpired. Fen always believed me to be shy and naive, but tonight I would give him the full show of who I could be.

"It's so early! We can't leave yet." I threw my arms around his waist and tried to kiss him. He shifted and gently pushed away from me.

"Come on and dance with me," I said with as much excitement as I could muster under the circumstances.

I pulled Fen's hand and led him to the dance floor. He danced with little enthusiasm and continued to dart his eyes in her direction. How obvious could he get?

As I glanced in her direction and could see she was staring at me now. When she saw she had my attention she rose from her seat and sauntered across the room. The closer she got the more tensed Fen became.

"Come on." He took my hand and pulled me from the dance floor, but we were cut off before making it to whatever destination he was guiding us to.

He stopped abruptly.

"Hello Russell," she said as she looked me over, trying to decide whether or not I met her approval. She turned her attention to him and smiled. Her eyes roamed over his body, stopping where no other woman should have been looking except me. Directing her attention back to me, she made sure I saw her movements and his reaction.

The perspiration beaded on his forehead as he said nothing, afraid of what would happen next. He was angry. Instinctively I reached for his hand, and he slipped it out of mine. She smiled as though silently indicating he had done well not to hold my hand. Again, she turned her attention to me taunting me.

"My name is Rose Sanford. I work with your husband on a *regular* basis," she said, emphasizing the word regular.

She moved closer to me, and Fen blocked her from getting too close. She was pissing me off. WHO WAS SHE?

"Move Honey. I didn't get a chance to shake Rose's hand properly." I reached my hand out to take hers, but again Fen interfered. Immediately all my suspicions were confirmed and here stood the living proof.

"Bae, what's wrong? Don't be rude."

Stepping around him, I extended my hand, sizing her up at the same time. She was slightly taller than me, and had me by some years. I never knew until then that Fen was into older women. Her hips were wide and her breasts large, but fake. We were about the same complexion, and she wore fake hair. I couldn't determine whether it was a weave or wig. Maybe it was hers, but for that night it was fake. A beauty she was not, but I couldn't say she was unattractive either. Maybe I was biased.

"My name is Milana, but my friends call me Lana. I am Fen's *wife*." Now it was my turn to emphasize my point.

The smile she wore so confidently disappeared. She stood brooding. She was immature, but I could see that from across the room when she was pouting. I was expecting more from her, especially since she approached me.

"Russell, may I speak to you for a minute?" she asked and turned to walk away as though she knew he would follow.

"Oh, not tonight Rose. Tonight is not a work night, but I am sure he will call you on Monday."

Abruptly, she stopped and turned to face me. She looked me over before turning her attention to him for his answer. There was an awkward silence before he spoke.

"I will catch up with you on Monday, Rose."

Hurt flashed across her face for a brief moment before she turned back to me. "Well, enjoy the rest of your evening, and it was nice meeting you, Lana."

"Milana."

"Oh! I apologize. I thought you said they called you Lana."

"*What* I *said* was my *friends* call me Lana," I corrected, showing my annoyance.

And there was that smile again mocking me, letting me know she was the elephant in the room, but I was the only one who was not supposed to be able to see it. Oh, I saw.

"Then I will speak with you on Monday, Russell." She walked back to the other side of the room and returned to the seat she left, watching us again.

"You ready to go?" Fen was irritated and eager to leave, but not as irritated as me.

"No. I am enjoying myself, and there are still other people to meet." I wasn't letting him off that easily. He was going to stay, and endure every uncomfortable moment.

"I've had a long week, and I'm tired, Lana."

"You don't want to go home with me right now *Russell* because rest is not what you would get." I cut my eyes at him and looked across the room at Rose who was still watching. Slowly, I turned to face him again. "The rest of the night *you* can call me Milana."

That was a long night for him. As badly as I wanted to leave and cry, sulk and demand answers, I made him stay, watch and squirm while she took it all in.

She continued watching us for the evening. Finally, his rejection got to her, and she left the room upset. A few minutes later, Fen excused himself.

"I'll be right back."

"I wish you would." I challenged him, daring him to follow her.

He stopped to look at me, but only for a second. He sucked his teeth. "I'll be back Lana," he said and continued his exit.

Infuriated, I was ready to leave. My feelings were hurt, and a war was lost just by his one simple decision to follow her. *Now* it was time to go.

The girl at coat check was very instrumental in helping me escape. The evening started out grand, but like Cinderella, my time was up, and I had to go before I came out of my masque and embarrassed Prince Charming in front of his royal subjects. I was humiliated by a woman I knew nothing about, and his gesture of concern showed me she was important to him.

Where did I stand in all this? It was clear she knew all about me. She knew he was married. Right? She might have heard something different, but the truth was I was his guest of honor

I walked through the corridor following the direction of the coat check girl. Outside of the side entrance sat my chariot, now a pumpkin, with the sign in the window as she had instructed. Before the building door closed, I heard Fen call my name from down the corridor behind me, but I didn't stop.

I stepped into the car closing the door hard behind me, startling the driver. "Where to ma'am?"

"Anywhere. Just drive please."

The side door I had just exited exploded. I could hold the tears no longer. "Just go! Please!"

The man swiftly pulled from the curb when he saw Fen approaching his car, leaving him. As we distanced ourselves I could see him half run then stop his efforts in defeat.

I didn't know the truth or the story that brought me to that point. I didn't need to. All the missing time and late nights came rushing back to remind me how stupid I was.

The windows of her eyes told a story. The lustful way she looked him over, the hurt from his lack of effort to demonstrate her importance in public, and his awkwardness when we were both there. That was all I needed to see.

Visions of them lying together brought me to the edge of hysterics. I knew I had to get out of the car.

"Take me to the GM."

"Yes ma'am," he replied and made the next U-turn.

It was late when I arrived to the resort. I had no clothes with me, so I stripped to my birthday suit and crawled between the cool covers, exhausted from the day's adventures. There were numerous calls and texts from Fen, but I didn't want to hear anything he had to say, so I turned my phone off. Exhaustion outweighed my anger.

It was time to rest.

Chapter Thirteen

Remaining at the resort for three days gave me the opportunity to calm down, but did nothing for my hurt. It was time to go home and face the music. Fen wasn't there when I arrived, but I was sure he would return as soon as he received the text message indicating someone had entered the premises.

I was wrong. He didn't return until the next morning deepening my hurt.

I was dressed for work and having my morning tea when he arrived. We needed to talk, but I no longer wanted that conversation as my anger rekindled from his tardiness in returning home.

Avoidance was my best friend. I never liked to have the difficult conversations. My insecurities usually got in the way, and my mouth followed.

Standing at the top of the stairs, in the entrance of the kitchen, he watched me, not saying a word. The circles under his eyes told the story of his past few days. His clothes were wrinkled, and I could smell the alcohol. He had been drinking.

I felt the room getting smaller and close in on me the longer he stared. I didn't know what he was thinking, but it couldn't be good, and I didn't care. If he went back out the door, I wouldn't have been surprised.

I walked to the sink to wash my cup. I was about to put it in the drain when I felt his arms encircle my waist. Wriggling out of his grasp, I returned to the island to get my purse.

"Can we talk Lana?"

"We did," I answered, feeling the hurt and annoyance all over again.

"When?"

"When I asked you not to go to her, and you did anyway." I continued on my path to the steps.

"You didn't ask me anything! You dared me and gave me an unspoken ultimatum."

He rushed to block me from going down the steps, and I knew I would be late for work. Returning to the island I put my purse on the counter stool and leaned back crossing my arms.

"I... I was worried sick about you. I didn't know if you were safe or if something happened to you."

"Something did happen to me." My jaws were tight, and I clenched my teeth. "I discovered my husband was a liar and cheat."

His left hand stayed on the back of his neck as he paced in front of me. "I never lied to you, Lana."

"Lana, I have a meeting. Lana, I have to check on the project. Lana, I have employee issues," I said reminding him of the lies from over the years.

"Those were not lies. They were true."

"The lie was showing up hours later, leading me to believe you were there the entire time, and you were with someone else."

"You have questions. Ask."

"You have answers. Do tell."

"Then you don't have any questions."

He threw his hands up and walked to the coffee maker. Reaching into the basket, he pulled out the flavor he wanted and popped the pre-made cup into the machine, his arrogance heightening my anger.

I grabbed my purse and continued to the steps. I heard him rush across the kitchen island to the top of the stairs and down behind me.

"Are we done?" He grabbed my arm.

I snatched away from him. "The conversation or the relationship?

"Both." His anger was showing.

"You have the answers, so ask yourself the questions."

My chest lifted and fell. I wanted to slap him, but my Grandma Ruby taught me not to put my hands on a man unless I wanted him to do the same. She said you treated people how you wanted them to treat you. But I guess Fen's rude mother taught him nothing about how to show respect to others. Maybe if I cursed him out and busted a bottle over his head, he would feel at home. That was how his parents solved things.

"You're smart mouth, Lana," he moaned and reached back as though he were going to smack me.

"You owe me answers and an apology, and there isn't a word I should have to say to get either. You should have come in the door with both."

"You should have come home three days ago!" He yelled.

"You have the nerve to talk to me about coming home."

"We keeping score now?"

"Says the man who has much to count!" Now I was yelling. I wouldn't give him my tears. The first stone of my Mexican wall was in place, and he had the choice to tear it down before it got higher or continue to build. He was a builder.

I turned to continue to the door. He stopped me again, this time grabbing around my waist. "Stop Lana. This isn't how I wanted this to go. Don't leave. Can we talk?"

The heat of his breath was on my neck. His heart pounded on my back. I stopped resisting. Arms crossed I stood, waiting for direction.

"Come back upstairs and let's sit down and talk about this."

I stood still thinking about my day's agenda. He must have thought I was going to say no.

"If you don't want to go upstairs we can go in the office," he suggested and gestured for me to enter.

I couldn't think of any reason to say no other than I didn't want to talk. I wanted to be angry. No, I chose to be angry. I felt entitled to my anger. The numbness began when I got into that car three nights before. Nothing seemed to matter anymore.

Indifferent to the situation, I put my purse next to the stairs in case I had to make a speedy exit. I went into his office, which was the only room on the first floor.

He must have been distraught. Everything was in order. It was the one room I refused to clean. I noticed he updated our picture with one from our last trip to the beach. We were laughing. I could remember when the beach photo boy took the picture. There was the multi-color two-piece he bought for me. He kept telling me to stop hiding my body, so I wore it to please him.

My head was tossed back and my mouth wide open in full laughter. Fen was in my ear talking dirty. Thinking of the moment made me jealous he was spending time elsewhere. I wondered if he talked dirty to her. I wondered if they laughed and shared similar moments. My mind raced to things I didn't want to think about.

I sat on the love seat, instantly regretting my decision when he sat next to me. I didn't want to be near him. Knowing he slept with someone else disgusted me.

He tried to grab my hand, but I pulled away, not wanting him to touch me. I didn't need him explaining anything to me, but I wanted to know everything. Afraid I would have to face my inadequacies, I wanted to retreat. No one wanted to hear they weren't enough. Sometimes we're insecure and fragile, and at that moment, I was both. I felt vulnerable as if my flaws were on display.

Looking him in his eyes, I asked the first question, "How long Fen?"

He hung his head and let out a long sigh, something he often did when he didn't want to answer a question. "Does it make a difference Lana?"

When I didn't answer, he looked up and my face said everything I didn't. Hiding my facial expressions was the one thing I sucked at.

"It doesn't matter Lana."

"It does matter, or I wouldn't have asked."

"I am not trying to hurt you. Rehashing all the details will not help. It isn't important."

"Dammit, Fen just answer the question! How long?" Now I was breathing heavily, irritated by his evasiveness.

"I'm not doing this."

I stood to leave. If he wasn't going to answer my questions there was nothing for us to talk about.

"Stop!" He grabbed my hand. "Stop." He repeated in a hushed voice. "Three years."

Where was I? That was half our marriage. I could not have slept through three years. How did I miss three years? I put my trust in him. The pit of my stomach ached. I wanted to leave, but there were so many more questions.

"Why?"

"I don't know. It just happened."

"Nothing just happens. Even pissing comes from drinking, so don't tell me *it* just happened!" I waited for a more satisfactory response.

"You were busy, and she wasn't. She was lonely and unhappy at home, so we began sharing." He paused and grabbed his lips. "We spent a lot of time together, working on projects. You went away for training and when you got back you were so damned busy. One thing led to another." He looked at me, I'm sure, to read my expression. There was none. "All of the above."

"I work Fen!"

"You don't have to work. I don't work this hard, so you have to work. I do what I do to take care of you, so you don't have to."

How many times had we had that argument? Not working wasn't an option for me. I was raised always to be able to take care of myself. Besides, sitting at home would have driven me crazy. If it weren't the time factor, then the excuse would be I was boring, or he had to work to give me what I needed. How about the women who had no voice, because they had no means to support themselves, and no income to live without a man?

I completely understood why the married rich and famous women didn't stay married long. They were financially independent and didn't have to put up with the mess. I heard it rumored that the singer Sasha had a baby contract. If she were going to take all the risk, then he would have to pay if certain circumstances arose.

"If I didn't work, I would have to stay. As it stands, I have choices."

"So now you're leaving?" He was concerned.

"What would you do, Fen, if it were me cheating?"

"I would fix those things that were wrong."

"Bull! You would be on the first thing smoking!"

"I wouldn't throw our relationship away that easily Lana, and I resent you thinking I would." He stood and paced.

"You just did! What did you believe would happen when I found out?"

He was silent. Fen was great at business but lousy with life decisions. He cut his parents off as soon as he left home for school not thinking through spring break or summer, or even that period after graduation when most were unemployed.

"How often?" I pressed on with my next question.

Shocked he stared at me contemplating the question. "Why are you doing this to yourself?" He paused, waiting for an answer. When I didn't give one he continued. "I could stand here and run the entire scenario down to you, blow by blow, and leave nothing to the imagination. I would feel better knowing everything was out in the open, but what would that do for you? You think you want to know everything, but you *do not*."

I knew he was right, but I had to know everything. I wanted to find out if he found Rose more attractive. Did he prefer having sex with her, or with me? What did they share? Where did they go? Did any of our friends know?

Quickly, my mind calculated all that must have transpired over the past three years. So much.

My hand covered my mouth when I remembered a specific day and time. It was the day we lost our child just two and a half years ago. The reason the pregnancy ended was that I had a sexually transmitted disease that he passed on to me. But my doctor assured me women could carry and not know, and I could have gotten it years before. The only problem with that was there was just one person I had ever been with. So, Fen had to have given it to me.

I mourned the pain of our loss for weeks. The first week I was alone, because he had to go on a business trip. Now I wondered was he with her on the trip?

We had a little girl. We called her Lena Sade Gayle Fenney. I didn't want to name her because it made the situation that much more painful. I remembered how much I hated that name, but Fen insisted she had mine and our mother's names. I then thought it better because if we had another child I would never have to name her that!

Her memorial was private, consisting of just the two of us. I delivered her at twenty-one weeks and was able to hold her but couldn't take the stress of knowing she would be dead before midnight. Fear of her taking her last breath in my arms forced me to give her up to die alone.

Breathing in, I could remember her transparent skin that was not fully developed. Even now, I wept for her, knowing she took her last breath alone, in no one's arms, because I was a coward.

"Breathe Lana," Fen was saying. I didn't know when I had stopped.

Turning to face him I smacked him hard across his face. I was sure he saw stars. I wanted him to see stars. The side of his face began to turn red. Because I had never put my hands on him before, he was caught totally off guard. If he hit me back, I was prepared to fight. At that moment I wanted a fight, but I wouldn't get one that day.

Blood trickled down his lip where it hit his tooth. He licked the crimson fluid away and cut his eyes back at me sucking his teeth. Shocked and angry he asked, "What was that for?"

"Your extra-curricular activities took the one thing I can never produce again, and you let me believe it was from your past." My lips quivered as the anger continued to rise within. I no longer wanted to talk. Going to work was out of the question as well.

"You knew I had contracted something from you and you let me believe a lie. Our child died Fen!"

His wrinkled forehead told me he knew just what I was talking about. "There isn't a day I haven't thought about Lena. There isn't a moment I don't wish I could take back what I have done," he said.

"You mean what you are doing?" He said nothing. "I guess the remorse wasn't deep enough to stop sleeping with that whore."

"Don't call her that."

The room turned red, and I thought I saw flames because, at that moment, nothing I thought of was Godly. "What should I call her? Rose the whore, because only a whore would lay with another woman's husband."

Silence. Slowly realization penetrated my sleeping mind. "Oh my God! Oh my God!" I looked around feeling the panic of being trapped, with no way out. "You are in love with her!"

I couldn't breathe as I remembered the question of two loves he asked one night. I started hyperventilating. The short breaths became a pain in the lower part of my belly as the hurt from the losses I suffered in those five short minutes welled up inside of me. The pain from the death of our only child, compounded by the betrayal of the only man I had ever known, punched me in my gut. Dropping to my knees, I released a yell reminiscent of a wounded animal.

Fen didn't move. Releasing one scream after another, I cried for my baby and my collapsing marriage. I screamed for what seemed like hours, before feeling his arms lift me to my feet. "Come on Lana."

"Don't touch me!" I snatched away.

"Why don't we talk another time after you calm down?"

He didn't deny anything I said. I had been confused and in the dark, and then I understood everything. The question about loving two women at the same time made sense. The missing time made sense. The times he came home angry, but not wanting to talk about it made sense.

I turned to go upstairs, grabbing my purse along the way. "No, we will talk about this now while I'm angry, hurt, and pissed off."

The tears I promised not to cry for him came for baby Lena instead. Her death was senseless, and there was nothing he could say to me to make me forgive him for her loss or the other babies that would never follow.

I knew people who went through worse, but that was no consolation to me. I thought of the three words 'I love you' that spilled from his lips so effortlessly. Were they a lie? Did he still love me or did he understand what love was?

The good word promised me I would have these trials, but things would work out for my good. I no longer knew what that meant.

That was the beginning of the destruction of our marriage seven years ago.

Chapter Fourteen

Sterling had been busy, so I had not seen him for two weeks. I thought about what Mother said, but didn't want to avoid meeting him just because Fen didn't know him. He would remain in the dark.

"Why do I have to give our friendship up? He hasn't given up anything. He still does what he wants when he wants."

All things work together for good to them that love God.

"I know, but I already told him I was coming so I will go and explain."

The Holy Spirit was quiet. I used His silence as an okay to proceed, although I knew differently.

Outside the bar, in his Sunday slacks and polo shirt, Sterling stood against the pillar. He had been to church.

When I stopped my car, the Valet approached to take my keys. The eager boy opened my door and helped me out as Sterling watched, smiling.

He loved when I wore my hair natural, so the unruly mane blew in the wind. He came towards me, as I exited my car, and immediately touched it. Playfully, I smacked his hand away.

He was carrying two paper bags in one hand and grabbed my hand with his free hand. He seemed different today.

"I brought our lunch and thought we could eat on the path and watch the boats." Without hesitation or an answer from me, he took charge and pulled me along.

After desperately attempting to keep up with him in my Sunday finest I stopped, and snatched my hand from his. He turned to see what happened, but after taking one look at my feet knew. Not thinking about our walk I wore four inch heels. His laugh was so full I began to laugh as well. There was definitely something different about him.

"Would you like for me to carry you on my back?" Bending down on one knee, he pretended he was an elephant allowing his passenger to board.

"My, my, aren't you in a good mood?"

"And no one will ruin it, not even you." He touched the end of my nose with his finger.

Immediately I wondered had I ever ruined a moment for him. My face must have said everything I was thinking.

He reached for my hand, and pulled me to him. "I didn't mean you. You only bring sunshine to the times we spend together."

He lightly kissed me without warning. I was surprisingly caught off guard, because he had never done anything like that before. We spent much time together, but he had never tried to be intimate with me.

His face showed his embarrassment by my reaction. "I'm sorry. I should not have assumed. I..."

"I'm good Sterling. Stop apologizing for what I've...I mean...." I didn't know what to say. I wanted that kiss for months.

"Let's just walk," he suggested, interrupting the awkwardness one kiss had caused.

I stole a glance at him. Was there something different on his face? He seemed so free and happy.

His kiss was all I could think of, and the butterflies fluttered in my stomach. I wanted him to kiss me again. Maybe Mother saw something in me I was not aware had developed.

"This bench is as good as any."

I sat, and he joined me with his small crisp bags. The butterflies fluttered again, and I smiled like a school girl. There was something I came to talk to him about, but I couldn't quite recall what the message was.

From his back pocket, he removed a large handkerchief and spread it between us. From the bags, he pulled two pre-cut sandwiches, chips and pickles. He reached down and revealed a bottle hidden in each pant leg. I was full of excitement. The moment reminded me of the small things that made me happy.

I reached for my sandwich, and he smacked my hand. "Didn't you just come from church?" He winked. "Heavenly Father thank you for the food we are about to partake in and the fellowship. Thank you for the woman of God before me and give me the strength to protect her honor." He looked at me and winked again. "Amen."

Playfully, I waited for permission to eat.

"Woman, if you don't pick up that sandwich."

I obliged him. I didn't realize how hungry I was. The chicken salad sandwich was everything, but more than that, it was my favorite. He listened to me, while Fen didn't know what my favorite sandwich was, even after thirteen years of marriage. I knew I shouldn't compare them. They were two very different men, after all. But I caught myself doing it from time to time.

I stopped to watch him, now distracted by the beautiful lips that had touched mine not thirty minutes before. He was a handsome man. The edge of his hairline was touched with a hint of gray. The shadow from his beard gave him a rugged look, making him sexier than usual. My heart fluttered.

"I missed you." I couldn't believe I said that aloud. He was a significant part of my minds-cape, and my safe harbor from the crazy world I shared with Fen. When we were together, I was free from the complications of my home life.

He was staring at me. It made me nervous. Maybe I said too much.

"I'm sorry I haven't been around much. I had a lot of things to take care of, but they are out of the way now, so I am at your disposal."

Leaning forward, he kissed me again. This time I met him with the same enthusiasm. His lips were soft. The kiss was so gentle. He ran his hands through my roots and gripped them pulling me in closer.

I wanted more, and I knew he did too. I realized then that meeting him was not a good idea, and I probably should have stuck to my plan to call our meeting off.

I stopped abruptly, out of breath, and stood to my feet. My head was reeling. People were watching and I felt embarrassed by my noticeable loss of control.

Standing in my proper Sunday dress, I looked down and smoothed it over, making sure it was neat and straight. I had become one of the many who attended church but was heading straight to hell, selling my soul for a kiss.

Sterling stood and took my hand in his. "You look great," he whispered in my ear.

I wanted him. I needed to run as fast as I could, but where to? He would still be on my mind. He awakened that part of me that was reserved for my husband only. I wouldn't and hadn't shared myself with any other man except Fen, and rightfully so. If I were honest with myself, I would admit that part of me became open and receptive on the first day Sterling spoke to me.

Oh God! Now what?

"I'm sorry I'm so forward with you right now, but I don't know what to do with all these feeling I have for you, Lana. I don't want to push them down any longer, and I know that's not fair to you, but I want to be honest."

I could tell he was waiting for a response, but I couldn't answer him. The heat was rising within me, and I couldn't tell him I felt the same without losing my honor. No, I had no words.

He was so close I felt the electricity from his body. His hands ran up and down my arms, fanning the flames of my low burning fire.

"I have to go," I managed in a low whisper, but I didn't want to go.

"Don't leave. These past weeks I could do nothing but think about you. I think about you more than I want to."

I believed him. The many text and updates I received let me know he was thinking of me. Fen didn't reach out to me as much as Sterling.

Emotions swirled. If not for my commitment, I would leave Fen today to be with this man, but my marriage vows were for better or worse. This situation had to be a test. I had to believe God would give me a way out because at that moment, I was weak.

Leave now. I know what's best for you.

Now He wanted to speak to me, but I knew He knew best. "Sterling. That's the problem. I missed you too, and I live for these moments with you. You are so dangerous for me, and I *want* to cross that boundary with you, but it would make me no better than...." I had never revealed any issues of my marriage before and didn't want to make him think any less of our relationship. Under any circumstance, he would be dangerous for me, even if my marriage was perfect. "I... I've gotta go. I'm sorry."

"I didn't mean to upset..."

"I will call you tomorrow." I kissed him quickly on the lips to savor my last moments with him and headed back to the hotel to collect my car from valet.

"Lana! Please don't go!" His plea pulled at my heart strings.

The sound of his footsteps closed in on me. His long legs caught me before I could reach the corner.

"Wait!"

He grabbed my arm stopping me. People passing began to take notice that something was wrong. My heart was racing. His touch made my stomach flip as he stroked my arm to calm me, but all that did was make me want him more.

"Stop," he whispered. "What's going on? Talk to me."

"I can't. Not about that part of my life."

"Then don't. Tell me what *you're* feeling. I wasn't trying to upset you, but I thought you felt the same for me."

I turned and saw the passion on his face. How could I deny him the truth after all these months? If we were friends, I could share anything with him. Right?

"I love a man who I can't be with, and I am tied to a man who I can't leave. If we're honest, this has nothing to do with you, and everything to do with you. I made a promise I want to break and it is a promise I have to keep. If I were to break this promise, sorry would mean nothing."

I hated the word promise and for the first time realized how important it was. People made promises without giving a thought to what they were committing to. Promises were like lies because once you made the commitment, you hoped and prayed for something you're not even sure you can honor. I didn't know how much longer I could hold onto my promise.

I stroked his face, his jovial mood now gone.

"Is he keeping his promise?"

His words stung snatching me back to reality, the two worlds now colliding. His eyes tore into me. He wanted my answer.

I pulled away, but this time I didn't run. I walked. He didn't follow. I should have gone home in the first place. He poured salt in a wound and awakened a sleeping desire, all in one afternoon. Most of all I still wanted him.

A vow was made to me ten years ago and a promise seven, but they were broken. On the day I found out I lost my child because of Fen's infidelities, Fen swore to never be with her again. Sterling's words dug deep when he asked if Fen was keeping his promise. The day of our conversation about his affair, Fen made many promises and continued making even more after that day.

The morning I slapped Fen we spent the entire day airing our dirty laundry and discussing our relationship. Through conversation, I realized our dead child was his sacrifice for his lies and deceit. Once we discovered we were having a girl, he imagined who she would look like, and what her interests would be. He began looking for schools and wanted me to quit my job to take care of her. He didn't want anything happening to his baby girl.

The day we lost Lena, I was in the kitchen cooking. Without warning the contractions began. It was like someone reached into my lungs and snatched the air from them. We called the doctor immediately. He told us to meet him at the hospital. There his suspicions were confirmed. I was in labor.

They did many tests, but after the doctor examined me, we received the news. There was nothing they could do. I was going to deliver, and she would not survive.

Talking to Fen that day, after meeting Rose, I realized how devastated he was over the loss, and he secretly blamed himself. He believed he was being punished.

"Why did you become involved with her?" I asked.

"You were so busy and didn't have time for me. Rose and I worked together on several contracts. Most of them, she helped me get. She's really a sweet person. She was lonely, and had time for me."

He angered me all over again. I didn't want to hear Rose was nice. He was defending her but didn't protect me when she was boldly in my face. What was most alarming was finding out she worked with him, and he was always at work.

Why was it she could work and he found her to be appealing, but cheated on me, because I worked? That made absolutely no sense to me, but was clear to him.

"That sounds like a victim statement Fen. How many nights was I home while you were with her? That doesn't sound like I didn't have time for you. You had no time for me!"

"Lana, you were *never* home."

"*You're* never home, but you don't see me sleeping with anyone else! You're always at work, and now you tell me she works with you. How do I compete with that?"

"You don't. I'm in love with you. I don't want to lose you."

"Do you love her?"

He hung his head. After a long pause he asked, "What do you want me to do? Whatever you want, I will do."

"I want you to start by answering my question."

"I have feelings for her. I care about her, but I wouldn't say I'm in love with her."

"You're lying to yourself."

"No. I'm not lying," he said convincingly. "She shouldn't be there."

"What are you going to do?"

"I won't see her anymore."

"Just like that?"

"If seeing her means I will lose you, then yes. I don't want to lose you."

"What did you think it meant? You thought it would be okay to continue to see someone else and stay here?"

I couldn't believe what he was saying. I didn't trust him but I needed to. I didn't know if it was about winning and proving to Rose that she was the side chick or genuinely wanting my marriage after all I learned about them.

God hated divorce. My parents were failures in marriage, but who would want a barren woman? There was probably worse out there and better the devil you know. Right? He truly loved me. These were all the arguments I made with myself in my decision to continue life with Russell Lee Fenney.

For months following, he answered the phone every time I called. He spent his nights at home and romanced me as he did when we first started dating. We made plans for our future together and moved on.

Our new way of life continued to go as planned for about a year, and then something changed. The old behaviors returned. When I questioned him, he told me it was my imagination, but my spirit told me differently.

Years later and nothing had changed. The joke was on me. So many dreams shattered... left in a shallow grave... never to be remembered. Maybe they were buried the day Lena died.

Chapter Fifteen

Sterling lived on Capitol Hill, and was an Associate Commissioner in the Department of Education. He graduated from Tuskegee, had his masters from Howard and his Doctorate from American U. He was smart. We shared deep conversations on education, politics, and child-rearing. I could talk to him for hours and sometimes did.

In the beginning, I felt guilty seeing him, but those feelings faded the more time we spent together. Wasn't this the argument I had with Fen? I told him if he spent time with another woman he was cheating. After spending too much time with one person, you begin to nurture that relationship. A man and woman were supposed to be attracted to one another. It was natural. I should have listened to my own advice.

The many conversations Sterling and I shared were harmless until you added dinner, holding hands and kissing. My biggest mistake was I believed Sterling and I would only be friends. The audacity of me to think I was saved enough to never be intimate with him. I convinced myself *I* wasn't doing anything wrong, because *we* weren't having sex and I wasn't like these other women. I was loyal.

As I stood in my closet, I looked at all the dresses on the floor. I cared too much about what this man thought of me. I chose a dress and a matching pair of shoes and hung the others back on the rack. The mirror flattered, but when I was with him, I wondered what he thought of me. *Time to go.*

I picked up my heels and clutch and headed downstairs. Before leaving, I slipped on my shoes and took one final look. We were celebrating Sterling's promotion by going to a high-end restaurant. I checked the time on my phone. "Oh my! I'm late!"

I was late when I arrived, but I guessed Sterling wasn't there either. He usually met me in the parking lot. A woman met me at the door and greeted me.

"Welcome Mrs. McNeil. Your table is right this way."

I blushed because she thought I was Sterling's wife. I complied and followed her through the restaurant to a private room in the back, behind sliding doors. When she opened the door, I saw Sterling sitting at a candlelit table alone. Immediately, he stood to his feet.

Slowly he looked me up and down as I walked towards him. My face flushed. He never heard the question the girl asked, he only answered. "That's fine. Give us a few minutes alone."

My heart raced. My chest pounded. I couldn't breathe. I felt him so close, so handsome, and so intoxicating. It was his celebration, but I felt like the honoree. Our faces were too close. Those lips were so inviting. Oh, my God! I was wet. I had not gotten wet just being in a man's presence in years.

He was still staring into my soul. "How was your day?" he asked me. He was barely audible, but I could not find my voice.

I wanted him, in that room. I needed to run like Joseph, but my feet wouldn't move. His arms encircled my waist, and I didn't resist. I knew all along that if we reached this moment, I would not refuse him.

He caressed me with an ever so gentle hug followed with a light kiss. I wanted more. I was trembling. Then our waitress came. My way out! I cleared my throat and pushed out of his grasp. I walked to my seat and waited for him to pull out my chair.

"Oh! I'm sorry, but the hostess said you were ready." The young girl was embarrassed.

"Oh no, you are fine. I just arrived," I assured her as I sat in my seat.

Sterling ensured I was pushed under the table and placed my napkin in my lap. He lingered running his fingers down my thigh ignoring her presence.

He smelled so delicious. My heart wouldn't stop racing. Slowly he stood and returned to his seat beside me, eyes still glued.

"You look amazing," he said.

"I'll give you a moment and get your waters," the young girl who still stood at the door ignored said. Neither of us responded so she left.

I blushed again, unable to respond. I hadn't seen Sterling since the day he asked me that hurtful question about Fen keeping his promise, and I thought of nothing but him since. He texted me later and told me he was out of line and apologized. We texted one another back and forth over the past two weeks, but I couldn't get the thought of kissing him again out of my head.

"You still don't take compliments very well."

I thought about it. Fen never told me I looked amazing anymore. Every once in a while, he said I looked "nice", but he never said "amazing"! He could have gotten *all* night sex, including the tricks, with "amazing". That word was the beginning of foreplay.

I attempted to put us back on track. "This is a special occasion. Congratulations on your promotion. I am so proud of you."

Now he blushed, flashing his beautiful white teeth. He was happy.

I heard the door crack and knew the poor hostess was peering in to make sure our evening foreplay was over. She walked across the floor with our water and a bucket of ice displaying a bottle of Champagne. "The hostess informed me you ordered this when you booked the room, and it has been on ice as you instructed."

She placed the bucket in the middle of the table with the two glasses of water and empty flute glasses. "Would you like for me to open the bottle now?" she asked Sterling.

"Yes please."

The girl obliged and poured a glass for each of us. I was the happiest I had been in years.

Sterling raised his glass, and I lifted mine to meet his. "To you for your magnificent accomplishments, and may you experience many more." I toasted.

"Thank You." Again, he lightly kissed me on my waiting lips lingering a little too long, taking me back to the day in the park.

My head was swimming, and I hadn't had any champagne. I could not get over how soft his lips were. My heart thumped so loudly I was sure I wasn't the only one who heard. I knew the signs of a man who wanted a woman. He was dangerous and in danger.

He pulled me off my seat and sat me on his lap. It was so inappropriate, but it felt so right. Running his hand up my neck, he pulled me in closer, kissing me until I had no more breath to give.

"I'm sorry about my behavior," he whispered. "I've missed you so much over the past two weeks. I couldn't wait to see you tonight."

His eyes were boring into me. I was his. I was at peace. He was the cure for every pain I had. I loved this man.

Reluctantly, he helped me up and back to my seat. What now?

Dinner was tasteless. I watched his mouth chew, and every chew was sensual. He was elegant. Had the devil taken notes and learned just what man would turn my head and captivate my senses?

"I am talking far too much, and you have barely touched your food. You don't like it?"

"No, everything is great. I'm just not very hungry. I wanted to make sure you had a great time tonight." I smiled and touched his hand. I was also aware what my touch did to him.

He blushed, which always amazed me. It made him look like a teen boy.

The waitress entered to check on us. "Do you need anything?"

"The check," Sterling said quickly. And she was gone.

We walked, as we always did after we ate. This magical man held me close. We had opened Pandora's Box. I didn't know where I was going with this relationship, but I wasn't willing to give it up. Sterling made me feel like a desired woman again. We talked and shared as one, but we were not.

We had been stealing time for months. I could wait no longer. I wanted him, but I wouldn't make the advance. I was still a married woman. I took an oath before God to be Fen's for life. I didn't know how long I could keep my promise. Surely God would want me to have some piece of happiness.

"What are we doing?" His sudden words caught me off guard.

"What do you mean?" I kept walking and thinking fast. I knew what he meant and didn't have any answers. I'd been thinking of him since our meeting two weeks ago. To be honest, I had thought of him every day since we met. What *was I* doing?

He stopped walking and faced me. He ran his fingers down my bare arm. "We have strayed from our agreement to be honest with one another?"

"I don't have an answer. I don't know."

He took my hand in his, and we began to walk again. He directed me to the entrance of the elegant resort hotel.

Be careful what you wish for. I was afraid. I feared God with all my heart and soul, but this pull Sterling had on me was great. Somewhere along the way I had forsaken God, and taken my own path. My God would forgive me. David killed a man to have his wife, Bathsheba. I wasn't trying to kill anyone.

We went straight to the elevators, and up to the fifteenth floor. I felt a shiver as I realized he planned this, and booked a room. The clanking of the elevator reminded me of a guillotine. Maybe the elevator would malfunction and plummet back the lobby. It would be my way out, but it never happened.

The elevator doors opened, and he led me into the corridor. I stopped. He stopped too, allowing me time to breathe.

"Nothing will happen unless you want it to, Lana. I want to be close to you tonight."

Tonight! I couldn't stay out all night! Breathe. My stomach cramped. I needed Champagne.

He was guiding me again. He stopped at the door marked 15-0830. I smiled. The room number, 0830, was Fen's birthday. It appeared God had a sense of humor.

He waved his key card across the entry pad, and we gained access. I checked my thoughts one last time. I knew if I crossed that threshold, he would have to be the one to say no. I checked my apprehensions at the door and proceeded.

The room was beautiful. Working for one of the largest chains of resorts, I had spent time at some of the fanciest hotels.

I could see Sterling had already been to the room to prepare for our arrival. His suitcase sat beside the dresser, and his clothes from work hung on the closet door, as well as clothes for tomorrow. There was also a woman's outfit on the hanger next to his. I spun so quickly I ran right into his arms.

"I thought it was your size."

"Am I staying?"

"Only if you want." His eyes pierced my very soul, begging.

"I, well, I..."

He burst into laughter. I smiled to myself. He hugged me and was still laughing. "This is why I love you so much."

He became serious as quickly as he laughed. Softly, he kissed me. He was testing the waters. He kissed me again, this time more passionately. I melted into his arms as his kisses became more defined. He wanted me, and I wanted him.

Gently he rubbed my arms, barely with his fingertips. I pushed back and paced the floor, deciding where I would go from here. I waited for God to stop me, although I knew he wouldn't. We're creatures of free will, and it was my will to be seduced by him. I prayed, knowing there would be consequences for my actions, because my mind was made up. I was at the point of no return.

He caught me around the waist and pulled me to the awaiting bed. "We don't have to go any further Lana. Just lay with me tonight. I'm afraid if I push, you may disappear and I don't want that."

Lay with him? Oh, he was smooth. He reminded me of the boys in high school, telling you what you wanted to hear to be safe enough to go to that next base. Only he was not a boy from high school, he was a grown man, and I did want to go to the next base with him, and the base after as well.

We lay in one another's arms, and he whispered in my ear, making me laugh and giggle like that school girl. Time moved so quickly, and I wanted it to stop because in a matter of hours it would be morning.

"Tell me something about your childhood," he asked. "I've told you stories about my childhood."

I laughed thinking of my childhood. There was nothing joyous about it.

"Let's talk about something else. My childhood was boring."

"I figured if I hear about your childhood, I could get my mind off the woman lying in my arms."

"But if you can't, wouldn't that make you a pedophile?"

There was that look again. That look called to me even when I was not with him. He was always on my mind.

He kissed me again as though there was a question I had not answered. His lips moved to my neck. I laughed nervously.

"I'm sorry." I was giggling.

"I make you laugh?"

Sterling was a man who had become accustomed to getting his way with women, I was sure of that. I could hear the impatience in his voice. He was at his edge. He was unraveling me inch by inch. I wanted to run. I wanted to stay. Most of all I wanted him.

We were in another season of our relationship. Spring had come, and I didn't want to be without him, but to cross this line would take us into yet another season. I was tired of making excuses to myself.

"Why do you want to lay with me, Sterling? You could have half dozen women who don't come with complications. Why me?"

He lay back on his pillow and let out a long sigh. He was staring at the ceiling, and I was sure I had destroyed any romantic mood he was feeling.

Rolling back up to his elbow, he looked into my eyes. "I think about you first thing in the morning Lana," he started. "I know you belong to another, but I don't feel that when we are together. You only have eyes for me, and you make me feel like I am the only man in your life.

"When things happen, I want to call you and share them with you, but that wouldn't be fair to you. I've wanted you from the first time I saw you. I knew you were married because women like you are not usually available. I wanted to be wrong, but I was correct, and now I take whatever time you have to give me because I have no right to ask you for more, but I love you."

There it was. Those three words that made this all so complicated. I had feelings for him too, but I could not define them as eloquently as he had done. In consideration of his words, I felt it would be best if I left. I could not risk complicating something that had no definition.

"Sterling. You asked me what we were doing. I need to ask you something. If I give in to what I want right now at this very moment, where do we go from here?"

He said nothing. A few minutes passed. "Just knowing you do want me is enough for me to hold you for the night." But I knew he wasn't satisfied. *I* wasn't satisfied either.

I laid my head on his chest and could hear his heartbeat. It was beating quickly initially, and then I felt it slow, until the beat was relaxed and even. I couldn't sleep. Again, I was shown a way out, but I did not want it. I wanted him.

I turned to face him, and the sincerity in his eyes melted my heart. This time I kissed him. He smiled. I kissed him again and reached for the buttons on his shirt and undid them. One, two three... He didn't move. He just watched.

"Breathe." I kissed him long and slowly, drinking him in. Once fully undressed, I began to do the same, and my hesitation was obvious. I had not been naked with any other man except Fen. He knew every imperfection I had, and Sterling had none I could find.

He saw my uneasiness, and helped me undress the rest of the way, smiling with each piece he removed. Once liberated from my clothes, I felt as naked as Eve in the Garden of Eden, my sins exposed.

My arms became my fig leaf as I attempted to cover my breast. He pulled my hands away and held them. My head dropped. I noticed that even his feet were beautiful. He kissed my forehead and lifted my chin.

Still lying beside me, he traced my frame with his fingertips. Turning me around he held me close, and we spooned. He began to tell me another childhood story he loved to share. By the time he finished I was in utter laughter, totally forgetting my nudity.

I turned to faced him and he kissed my shoulder once again awakening my desires. I slipped into his arms, silencing the warning bells ringing in my head. His kisses were gentle, each caressing my need to feel the desire of this man. He stroked my inner longing.

The softest moan sent me to the next level. His touch and his tongue ran over my body, kissing me here and there and making me forget I was another man's wife.

My promise forgotten, I uttered words that were not distinguishable and worshiped at his alter, taking in the blessings he freely offered. Finding my spots, he lingered making mental notes for later.

Parting my legs, he lay there contemplating something. Secretly, I didn't want him to stop, but I was sure he had figured that out by now. He came to his conclusion and crossed the threshold of no return slowly giving me every opportunity to change my mind. Surely for something that felt this good, I couldn't go to hell.

Each thrust given found my response with equal measure. My legs were around his waist pulling him in closer. My back arched as he made love to me like I'd craved for almost a year.

His thrusts were not out of control, nor meant to hurt. They were smooth and gentle, yet desperate and hard. The passion he displayed told me the story of his love for me and the message was received and understood.

"I love you, Lana. I belong to you until you tell me differently."

His words brought tears to my eyes because I didn't just hear his words, I felt them with each thrust. I was confidently lost in the moment because he was there for me. He waited for me. He loved me.

"Whatever you need from me you have it." His words weaved their web around my mind pulling me into his world. "You have me forever. I'm not going anywhere." I could feel his words in my soul, right to the core.

"I want to share your joy and your pain. I want to know your innermost secrets and fears."

He nibbled my ear, thrusting his tongue inside. I moaned. He paced himself, returning to tend to my pleasures, pampering me as he calmed himself.

"I knew it would be like this," he whispered, and our journey began again and continued until I could take no more and my body surrendered, giving into my desires before I wanted things to end.

"Talk to me. Tell me what you want," he asked as he pulled my legs up, sitting me squarely on his lap.

Now we were eye to eye. I kissed him and held on tighter, not wanting to slip from his grip.

"I got you," he whispered and grabbed each mound of my behind, pulling me in and pushing deeper.

"Sterling!" I moaned.

I could hear his breath pick up.

"Talk to me, Lana."

But I couldn't. I made guttural sounds, uttering nonsense. My body felt complicated as he showed me things I had never before experienced.

Smack. He slapped my butt, arousing me even more. I laughed, half moaning.

"You like that?" He whispered as he placed me back on the bed. He rolled me over and ran his tongue down to the small of my back. Gently he bit my right butt cheek then made his way back to the base of my neck, re-entering me.

"Sometimes your smile alone unravels me," I said barely audible. I wasn't good at this talking thing. I found it to be distracting. "I've wanted you since you first kissed me."

"You disappoint me Lana. Only since the kiss?" He continued to ride through his conversation. "I should have stepped up my game sooner."

He turned me to face him disappearing under the sheets again. My back arched. The familiar feeling began to rise again.

"No! Not yet!" I quickly backed up, but he pulled me back to him.

The desperate, animalistic gibberish that came sounded like a howling wolf. Sterling plunged deep and held me tightly. I hollered uncontrollably. All reservations about being there stripped away. Now, completely unraveled, I was embarrassed by my lack of control, but didn't care. I wanted more.

I lay there, drenched and completely spent. My eyes were closed. I wanted to savor what I was feeling, compartmentalizing and cataloging every feeling so I would not forget the joy I felt.

His hand caressed my face. "Stay with me tonight."

I laughed. "I think I have already done that."

When I opened my eyes, he was propped up on one elbow studying me like an astronomer evaluating the constellation. Our lips met again.

"I've wanted you since we first met. I've only dreamt of being here with you like this. This experience has truly been a celebration I will never forget. Thank you."

Time was running out. It would soon be morning. I had lost all my inhibitions. I wanted more.

Reaching up, I grabbed his neck, pulling his head in closer, and once more I kissed him. I pushed him onto the pillows and sat on his stomach feeling his strong muscles flinch.

His fingers twisted in the roots of my hair, locking me in, pulling me down. He flipped me onto my back, but I wanted to be in control and pushed him off, then back to the pillow. He laughed a deep hearty laugh.

"You're in charge. Do as you please," he told me in that magical husky voice. So, I did. This time it was my turn to overwhelm him with pleasure.

My performance surprised and delighted him as I watched his face contort and him beg me not to stop. He had no clue I had secrets of my own kept hidden in the safety of our platonic relationship. I did not disappoint, and now it was his turn to lose his bearings as he unraveled.

"Lana! Lana!" He whispered over and over.

The sun was coming up. I no longer wondered what Fen did with Rose. I didn't care. "Tell me what you want," I taunted.

He laughed. "If I told you that, you might be scared."

We were both drained, as we laid in each other's arms, enjoying our last few moments together before Cinderella returned to her complicated life. He had that thoughtful look on his face once again, and I was sure we were thinking the same. What now?

Chapter Sixteen

Home felt the same as I left it. I came in later in the morning after our morning ferry ride. When I entered, Fen assumed by my attire and bag that I had come from the store. I was irritated he didn't even know I was out all night. I wanted to scream, "I was out all night!"

He seemed more agitated than usual. His phone beeped several times and he looked at his message. Normally, it would have bothered me, but now I didn't care and hoped he had to go out again tonight. Sterling said he would keep the room another night if I could return.

"Did you want anything to eat?" I asked as if nothing had occurred.

"No. I ate already."

I knew what that meant. They went to the pancake house. I use to cook breakfast and text him, and he would still eat out. It would anger me so much that I learned not to cook at all until he got home.

"I'm going to take a shower and lay down." He went upstairs giving me no kiss or hug.

"Okay. I am going to clean up a little here and take out something for dinner. Any special requests?"

"Whatever is fine." He ascended the remaining steps and disappeared.

That was our existence as husband and wife, formalities and courtesies. We tried many times to put things back together. We took trips to romantic places, living lavishly and shopping to return to the same routine once we came home. It always started out with smiles and kisses and sex, but the continuous text messages were hard to ignore.

We shared many conversations about her. The questions I asked were never answered. Why she was there and why he could not get rid of her? He would cut things off and not answer her texts for an extended period of time. The months would stack up, and I would think we were finally past her, but then there would be an indication things had rekindled.

"Do you think I would ever cheat on you, Lana?" I thought that was the oddest question for a man to ask his wife. I was honest with my answer and replied, "As long as we fall short of His glory, I guess it could be a possibility." He claimed because I already believed he would do it, he did. I told him that was the stupidest thing I had ever heard of and a weak excuse. He bought me a new house. It would be another seven years before I found out it had never stopped.

I showered and washed my hair. It smelled of Sterling's cologne. My garment bag remained in my car. I would drop my dress off at the cleaners at work.

I carefully applied my make-up and chose my clothes. I would stop by and see him on my way home from work.

My heart pounded remembering the night's events. I closed my eyes and pretended to be back in his arms. Maybe I wouldn't go to work today.

Fen was in bed. "You going to work?" his eyebrows lifted.

I looked down examining my clothes. Maybe I was overdressed for work, but I was employed at a Casino. "Why? What's wrong with my outfit?"

"Nothing. I just thought it was a little fancy."

I became annoyed as I waited for the compliment that never came. I guess I was expecting too much.

My body shook as though in a trance. I walked to him giving a quick kiss and rolling my eyes as I turned to walk to the door.

"What was that for?"

"I always kiss you goodbye. What are you talking about?" I stood with my back to him not wanting to see his expression.

He sighed. "Never mind Lana." He rolled over and turned his back to me.

Pivoting, I turned and looked at him. "Why did you ask me about my outfit?" I marched back to the bed, feeling angry.

"No reason Lana," he said in his dismissive voice.

Oh, there was a reason. Why couldn't he just say I looked nice? Hell, I may have come home from work to hear more. Instead, he left me with crazy thoughts and imaginations. No! No, I'm not going to be distracted by you today, mister.

I was angry, and I knew it was not a good idea to make decisions when I was, but I did. Once off the block I hit the button in my car and called the hotel.

Sterling sounded wide awake when he answered. "Hello."

"You still want company?"

"I'll order breakfast."

I could hear his smile through the phone, and the heaviness lifted. Calling out wasn't hard. Today would be a slow day, and I usually met with those workers who were struggling with attendance and other issues. They could wait.

As promised, my breakfast was waiting for me when I arrived to Sterling's room. He was showered and dressed, and his bags packed.

"Were you leaving?"

He smiled and placed a napkin on my lap, not answering. Before taking his seat, he fixed my plate. Once seated he spoke.

"Why are you here this morning, Lana?"

"Because I wanted to see you again."

"No doubt," he said looking my outfit over.

Why couldn't someone just tell me I looked nice today! I couldn't tell him I had never made love to another man other than my husband before last night. I couldn't tell him I was going to hell because of my transgression. Instead, I hung my head feeling stupid for being there.

He took my hand, but I pulled it back. I needed to bask in my thoughts. I wanted to be confused, but my thoughts were clear. I wanted to be there with him.

He sat back and sighed. With his head tilted to the side, and watched me, waiting for an answer. I said nothing.

"Are you going to eat?" he asked redirecting.

I looked at the food on my plate and realized I was no longer hungry. Lifting my fork, I stabbed at the bacon and raised it to my lips.

He stopped me before I ate it and took the fork from my hand returning the bacon to the plate. Standing, he pulled me up from my chair and held me. The slightest tremble went through me as his lips met mine. He was hesitant at first, as though thinking... no, debating. I felt him swell and my heart raced and my breathing picked up. He pulled me in closer. If I didn't know why I was there before, I knew then.

I wrapped my arms around his neck and pulled his head in. I wanted last night. I wanted that feeling of being loved and wanted. But, just when I thought it would happen he stopped, pushing me away.

He saw the confusion on my face and turned away. "Why are you here Lana?"

I didn't know what to say. I knew if I didn't say what he wanted to hear he would pick up his neatly packed bags and be out the door and I didn't want that. I wanted to be with him, but my promise to God was to be with Fen. But was I still with him?

Slowly he picked up his bags.

"Don't go," I said in a barely audible voice.

He winced and shook his head as though in pain. He hesitated before replying. "It's best that I do."

I felt angry and hurt all over again. Was I just a conquest turned into 'been there done that?' Did he use me?

"So that's it?"

"It's best."

"For who!?" I didn't mean to yell, but now both of the men in my life were pissing me off. I didn't understand the game either was playing.

"I don't want to be that person who ends your marriage."

Now he was worried about my marriage. "You weren't concerned about my marriage last night!"

He dropped his bags.

"You haven't worried about my marriage since we first met."

"I was selfish! I liked what I saw, and I wanted you. I thought I could have you, but it was too late when I realized I didn't have you and never could. You had me!"

His voice cracked, revealing his deep emotion. "After a while, I thought I could win you over and take you from him, but it never happened. I always saw that little glimpse of respect you had for him, and I wanted that for myself."

"My marriage was over before we met."

He smiled again. "Your marriage isn't over Lana. Go home."

"Then why did you order breakfast and allow me to come?"

"Don't be confused. I still want you, but I realized something after you called this morning. I desire all of you. After last night I imagined us together. You have so much to give, and we work so well together. You are the woman I've waited for all my life.

"When I got my promotion, you were the first person I wanted to call. When I wake up every morning, you're on my mind, and I want to call you, but I can't. You're not mine, Lana. You belong to another man."

He walked to me and kissed me so lightly, it was sensual. "Last night was the biggest mistake I've ever made. I never stopped to think what would happen next.

"All this morning I was out of my mind wondering if he was touching you, did he kiss you, did you make love to him, then you called, and my mind was at ease. I was excited you chose to return to me.

"When you walked through the door, I was relieved. You came back to me! And there it was again. You're not my woman, and I need you to be or not to be, or I will lose my mind thinking about you. I love you Lana, and I don't want to spend another day away from you, but I have no right to ask for that." He picked his bags up again to leave.

I didn't want him to go, but he was right, I was married. "Please spend the day with me Sterling, so we can talk this out."

He turned so abruptly I almost fell back.

"Talk about what? Are you leaving him, because *that* is the only thing I want to hear right now." He waited for an answer.

"I..."

"Why are you with him? I would never let you out of my sight if you were my woman. You wouldn't have time to think of another man. Do you love him, Lana?"

Now we were into the difficult questions. I needed to be careful here.

I turned away from him, and the tears came. Why wouldn't God harden my heart towards Fen so I could move on? At this point, we were only going through the motions. I loved Sterling. I didn't doubt that. But, was it possible to be in love with two men at the same time? The same question Fen asked me years ago and I told him he was selfish. It was confusing to have to ask myself the same question now. Was I any better than Fen?

I heard the door close and quickly turned. He was gone. I lay on the bed I shared with him just hours before, and cried. I could still smell his cologne on the sheets. I wrapped myself in them pretending he was in my arms. I lost control.

I don't know how long I lay crying, but I could no longer breathe. My head pounded and I fell asleep.

When I opened my eyes, the light assaulted my senses. It was probably from the sea of tears I wept. Although my sight was blurred, my vision was clear. Sterling walked out on me, but I totally understood his feelings. We were in a place where I had to make a decision, and I was not ready for that.

I thought about his words. Why did he feel there was still a chance for my marriage? My marriage was over, but if that was true, why did I continue to stay with Fen? Had I gotten too comfortable?

I went to the bathroom to fix my face and check my appearance. My hair was disheveled, my eyes puffy and make-up smeared. It took ten minutes, but I was able to pull everything together. The next decision was what to do with my time.

I thought about my decisions over the past year and became ashamed. I had not remedied anything. I only complicated the situation, and now I'd involved Sterling and complicated his life as well. I hurt him by allowing myself to become emotionally involved, and I devastated him by sleeping with him.

I wasn't naive to believe it was entirely my fault. He knew what he was getting himself into. I no longer had to ask the question 'where do we go from here?' I had my answer.

I never prettied up the situation between Sterling and I. I never played games with him or lied to him about my marital status. We became the movies I'd seen, except there would be no happy ending. In films, there was always one guy who was a jerk, I guess that was Fen, and there was the knight, Sterling. The difference was in the movies; God was not a part of the equation. No one was worried about living by His commandments, and they made things look so easy. Well, I became keenly aware that they were not.

Fen had no idea what I was doing. Therefore, he didn't know he should be hurt. I understood men needed to feel respected, and that was their love language, so I respected Fen and Sterling. I had gotten involved with Sterling because I loved him and initially he was a welcome distraction from my issues at home. Now I had a mess to deal with.

I went to my purse and took out my phone. Although I felt I shouldn't, I called Sterling anyway. I wanted to make sure he was okay. My call went to his voice mail. I left.

The lobby was busy, but I had seen it worse. I figured I would take a walk to the water and watch the people. I didn't want to go home because Fen was still there. My eyes were puffy, and I didn't want his prying eyes watching me and asking me questions I had no answers for.

The Adirondack chairs were empty, so I sat in the center. Men nodded as they walked by and I smiled politely back, but I felt empty. Now what?

Looking across the park, I spotted Sterling. He was standing at the pier looking across the waters at the Nation's Capital. Every once in a while, he hung his head and fidgeted with his hands. I noticed he was carrying a small box that he opened and closed over and over again. I wanted to go to him, but I gave him his space. He was wrestling with his feelings.

I looked around and watched the vendors sell, and the children play. Everyone was compartmentalized into their own piece of the world, and I felt as though I didn't have a compartment. I didn't belong in Sterling's life, and I didn't feel like I belonged at home. The tears burned the brim of my eyes, so I closed them, safeguarding my secrets.

I opened them again to let the wetness dry. Sterling was gone. Did he go back to the room? I really wanted to apologize to him. I closed my eyes again.

Fen would be so disappointed in me when I told him about Sterling, if I ever decided to tell him. Telling him would free me from the fear of being found out, and maybe we could go from there to determine what to do with our lives, but we couldn't stay where we were, I realized that now, but Sterling was still on my mind. I didn't want to give him up, and I couldn't shake him from consuming my heart completely.

I smelled a very familiar scent and opened my eyes. It was Sterling. He was staring down at me, his face broken. We were silent.

After few minutes of standing, he sat in the Adirondack chair beside me. There was that unbearable silence again. I wanted to apologize, but wondered why? We were both consenting adults, and my life was an open book. He knew what we were doing.

He took a deep breath preparing to say something, but stopped. Slowly he turned to look at me, and I watched him as he gained his courage.

"The first time I saw you were at the contractor's gala seven years ago."

I was shocked at his words. Did he know Fen?

"Yes. I know who your husband is, and I know Rose as well." He grimaced at my reaction.

"You were the Belle of the party. I thought you were the most beautiful woman there. You were happy and laughing, enjoying yourself. I thought to myself, now that's a woman I would like to be with."

"When Rose approached you, I realized something wasn't right. Your demeanor changed, and that beautiful smile became fake and taut.

"When Fenney followed her out of the ballroom, all of my suspicions were answered. I always thought there was a thing between them. You left frantically out of the opposite door; something was so wrong."

He took my trembling hand and squeezed. "I thought nothing else of it until I saw you at the bar one night. You looked far from the smiling happy woman I spotted at the gala. I watched you the entire evening. You looked lost and lonely. I wanted to meet you, so I kept coming.

"I asked the guy at the bar how often you came and were you always alone. He gave me all the information I needed, but once I got your schedule down it took quite a few visits to get up the nerve to speak to you."

I was stuck on he knew Fen. "So, you knew who I was married to?"

He nodded. "And I knew your situation, but wasn't sure if you were still together."

He watched me waiting for a response. All of a sudden it hit me... this was all such a mess.

"The more time I spent with you, the more I grew to love you. I didn't want anything deep." He looked away again. "I realized you were still married so I thought this would be a friendship and maybe with benefits. No romance. Oh, how wrong I was Lana. You didn't realize it, but your laughter was mine, your smile was mine your happiness was mine. At some point, I realized I wanted you to be mine as well.

"I thought because you were not happy in your situation you would be an easy mark, and I wouldn't have to make any commitment to you. You were married. But who I came to love was a woman who honored her marriage and held herself with dignity. That woman was who I fell in love with. She stole my heart.

"After we spent the night together and you left, I felt ashamed. I felt I forced you into something you did not want to do."

"But it wasn't..."

"Shhhh!" He quieted me as though afraid to lose his thoughts. "I knew you wanted me as much as I wanted you, but I also knew you would honor your marriage. I got that room because I wanted you and for once in the past year, I didn't care what happened after. I was selfish." He stood and helped me to my feet. "Let's walk."

We walked to the edge of the water and began our familiar stroll. How many times had we walked this path?

He stopped abruptly and turned to me. "Do you love me, Lana?"

"You know I do." My answer was deliberately short. I was afraid of the other questions he could ask that I wasn't prepared to answer like, 'Will you leave your husband?'

"I owe you an apology. I'm sorry I forced you to compromise the person you are. When you called, I was honored that you would spend the day with me, but I felt ashamed."

His words were sweet and kind. I wanted to be with him even more. I still didn't want to go home. I wanted to leave everything and go with him. I silenced the voice talking in my head. I loved him and didn't know if I could be without him. Sterling helped me to forget what my relationship with Fen lacked.

"I think of you as my woman Lana, and I don't want to share you anymore. I don't want another man touching you, and I don't want to settle for pieces of you either. I want all of you or none of you."

Things had gotten real. He was asking me to choose. I didn't want to be forced to choose. What if I made the wrong decision? I had not stopped loving Fen, and I loved Sterling. Why couldn't things stay the way they were?

At one time I was at this crossroad with Fen and asked him who it was going to be. Of course, he chose me, but had he? Things were complicated when everybody was not on the same page. Thirsty Rose didn't require that he make a choice. She said many times she would be second as long as she was with him. So, she continued to eat from the crumbs I dropped on the floor like a scavenger, or was I eating hers?

"I don't know what to say, Sterling. It fills my heart knowing you consider me as your woman." I was lost for words after that. I didn't know what to do.

"But?"

"It's not that easy."

"Sure, it is. It simply requires that you make a decision."

I knew what it required, but it would be me destroying lives. I was losing my mind and needed someone to rescue me from my life. If I were a man, I wouldn't care about the hearts broken. I would be selfish and do what I wanted.

"Can you give me some time?"

"I've given you almost a year."

"A year ago, neither of us knew where we were going with this."

He rubbed my hand with his thumb. He was thinking. "Do you even think about me or us being together? I think about it every time I tell you goodbye."

Those were the type of questions I did not want to answer. Those were the questions that solicited decisions I was not ready to make. Of course, I thought about these things, but I didn't want to make a decision. "Yes."

He stopped walking and looked at me as though he was trying to read the truth in my answer. I looked away, not able to hold his piercing gaze. I had been ignoring the lump that formed in my throat since he stood over me sitting in my chair.

The tears came so quickly I was unable to hold them back. ***Please don't let him leave me, Lord. He's the only good thing I have going in my life right now.*** I knew God heard me, but would have no part in this fiasco I created.

I shouldn't have been crying. In the end, I would have someone, and one of them would lose. I couldn't speak and explain my tears to him. He was the one who should have been crying. I led him down a road with no destination.

I felt weak. Why was I crying? I was much stronger than this. I ran an organization with over one hundred fifty employees reporting to me. I was holding up a false face with a man who lived in the same house who I no longer believed was capable of telling me the truth. Here I was standing with a man who held me together through his companionship, laughter, and trust, which made me stronger. Tears were for a weaker time when I was living a fairy tale that was sold to me from childhood. I had long ago discovered that fairy tales were written by someone as broken as me who needed a happy ending.

I could feel the enemy laughing at me as I was caught up in my own game. I wanted to scream to make the laughter stop, but it continued to ring in my ears, and I couldn't shut it out. What now? I couldn't figure it out so I would have to wait for direction and return to what I knew worked. Prayer.

Had Sterling changed my life, or was it me who had changed? Did he come to me at a time when I needed him the most? I'm in love, and I'm numb.

He held me until the tears stopped, never asking any questions or saying a word. He understood.

Chapter Seventeen

In the morning Fen stood above me. I could feel the shadow of his body before I opened my eyes.

"Why are you in here asleep? Was I snoring?"

"Yes." I lied. I fell asleep while praying the night before. I couldn't sleep thinking about Sterling.

"I'm sorry. I am going to take my shower."

Again, I was alone with my thoughts. Fen wasn't a bad guy. He didn't smoke or excessively drink. He didn't do drugs, and he was a great provider. Most of the time, he treated me like I was the only one in his life. I just knew differently.

I looked around the closet taking in all the beautiful clothes, but they were just costumes to be worn like a mask. I could put on any one of them and become someone else.

I decided to go for a run. I had not run in weeks, but maybe I would feel better after.

The air was brisk and the Harbor streets began to fill. Workers were arriving filling the air with noisy equipment clanking as they dug to build new homes. I waved at those I knew, calling them by name.

Afterwards I looked through the store windows to see what was new, and then rested near the water to watch the people pass. I felt so very alone, which was strange because I hadn't felt alone in years. He was just a prayer away.

I thought about going to the casino to get out of the house. What sense did it make to live near a casino and never go? But when you worked there, it was the last place you wanted to hang out.

Something bothered me, and I felt an argument coming. I thought maybe I was having withdrawals from Sterling, because I decided not to see him for a few weeks. I had been fasting and praying to work through my transgressions. Sterling was in my life for a reason. I thought maybe it was to teach me how I should be treated. Or, maybe it was to teach me not to judge others, unless I wanted the same.

I discounted my value the day I accepted Fen's affair, and I compromised it when I laid with Sterling. Now how did I go back to just holding Sterling's hand without wanting more? I understood Fen's dilemma. There was a lesson in this for me. I judged Fen's sins and disregarded my own.

They say our lifetime here on earth is a blink of an eye in heaven. Or is it that time isn't linear, it is an illusion? Whichever it was, I didn't want to spend a lot of time making a decision, and the ball was in my court.

I had to be at work in a couple of hours, which was a welcome escape, so I headed back home to shower and change. When I returned, I was shocked to see Fen still there. He was sitting at the kitchen counter with his morning coffee. He grabbed my hand.

"You've been a little distant lately. What's on your mind?"

"Work."

"We both work so hard. Why don't we hang out tonight? I have a free evening."

How dare he think he could *fit* me into his schedule. I didn't want to give him my time, and I surely didn't want to encourage him. I wanted answers.

"What did you have in mind?" I could play nice.

"You like to eat at Brussels, maybe we can go there?" He waited for my answer. "What time do you get off?"

"Seven."

"Okay. I'll drop you off and pick you up."

He ran his hand down my behind and grabbed me. I pulled away. The feeling of betrayal gripped me.

"I have to get ready for work, or I'll be late."

I turned and ran to our room. Once behind closed doors, I rested on the back of the bathroom door. My heart was pounding. The exchange with Fen was awkward. I was afraid I didn't love him anymore. But wasn't that what I wanted?

I undressed quickly and stepped into the warm steamy water. Fen entered the bathroom. I dipped my head back. Although my eyes were closed, I could still feel him watching me.

The shower door opened, ushering in a gust of cold air. My body tensed when he touched me causing me to recoil.

"You don't want me to touch you, Lana?" He asked whispering in my ear.

"It's not that. You caught me off guard." The lie rolled from my lips so effortlessly. Was this what I had become, a liar? I wondered if this was how Fen felt when he returned from her. My Grandma Ruby told me as a child, when I lied to her about writing on the wall, that a person who would lie would cheat and steal.

He pulled my body to his and kissed me in a desperate attempt to get my attention. I couldn't breathe and didn't want to open my eyes for fear of him seeing through me.

"Fen, you're going to make me late!" I pushed his hands away and attempted a fake giggle.

He didn't stop. He pinned me to the wall, and lifted my legs around his waist, thrusting himself inside of me. I wanted to scream. His touch was alien to me, but his lust was genuine. He made love to me like a man desperately holding on and the very thing Sterling feared happened.

I opened my eyes to see him looking, not at me, but into me. He searched my face to understand my altered reactions. Leaning in, he kissed me as if trying to catch me in a lie. I responded with a kiss as though it could be our last.

I felt he knew. I didn't care. I felt his fight as he dove deeper and attempted to excite me by using the tricks that had betrayed me so many times in the past.

My body betrayed me again, responding to his touch. I moaned as the heat rose within me, and without warning, we were there together.

Now panting, I closed my eyes again. I felt the soft washcloth dust over me as he washed me and I let him. I had only been with one man all my life, so this was no different. What changed was the man. I was with Sterling and cheating with Fen.

I needed to get out of his presence. I quickly escaped his hold and went to my closet to prepare for work.

I always took pride in how I looked when I left the house so preparing for work was no different. I pulled my wet hair back into a bun before it bushed up and applied my makeup. He watched me as I oiled my body, making me aware of my nakedness. Then he left.

He was sitting on the bottom step when I came downstairs. I had totally forgotten he was taking me to work.

"I can take myself and meet you later," I said trying to avoid his stares and the idle conversation I was sure to come.

"No. I'll take you." He stood and led me to the door by my elbow. "It doesn't make sense to drive two cars later."

"Where are we going tonight?"

"I thought Brussels, but it will be a surprise." He smiled and opened the door to the garage, and it was settled. He would drive and pick me up.

I couldn't concentrate at work. All I could think about was this evening.

My desk was littered from the day before. I returned calls, one at a time, and it wasn't until Courtney buzzed me to say Fen was downstairs in the lobby that I realized I didn't have my cell phone with me.

Seven o'clock. I straightened my desk and grabbed my purse to leave. Luke entered my office.

"Do you have a minute?" He asked.

I was annoyed. I had been there all day, and he waits until quitting time to speak with me.

"Sure." I put my purse on the end of the desk and sat beside it, letting him know he didn't have long.

"Oh! I'm sorry I caught you leaving. This is new behavior for you. Called out yesterday and actually leaving on time today."

I remained silent. He always annoyed me when he came around, and he was never short on rudeness.

"Well okay," he said, feeling the uncomfortable silence. "We have two employees that need to be written up and possibly replaced, so can you get with Whitney to take care of this issue?"

I stood and walked to the door. "I will get with her first thing in the morning."

I waited for him to stand. "Well, you go ahead. You look like you are in a hurry." He walked out of my office and turned in the opposite direction.

I looked at Courtney, my assistant, and she shrugged her shoulders. "Go home before he comes back and finds something for you to do." I winked and headed for the elevators.

Fen was in the lobby dressed in an Italian tailored suit. His hair was freshly cut and his shoes shined by Harold, the shoeshine man, no doubt. Typically, I would have been moved, but I was at a point of indifference.

He sat in the lounge chair with his leg crossed over his knee. He looked like he was in deep thought when he saw me step off the elevator. We met in the middle of the lobby, and he greeted me with a light kiss. I could see his black Lexus LC500 parked in the resort circle. My door was opened by the valet and Fen thanked him by handing him a bill.

"Good evening Mrs. Fenney."

"Good evening," I replied back to the valet, not remembering his name. Fen joined me, and we were off.

He pulled out of the valet driveway and looped back into the Harbor. I could feel him look out of the corner of his eye towards me, but I did not respond.

We pulled up to the Convention Center and we were met by another valet who opened my door and helped me out. Once situated, Fen joined me on the sidewalk and escorted me through the majestic marble floor lobby covered with its scarlet runway carpet. We rode the glass front elevator in silence to the ground floor. His favorite steakhouse was there. When the elevator opened we turned to the left, but continued around the corner to the familiar sports bar.

The hostess looked at me strangely as she escorted us to our table. I felt awkward. This spot belonged to Sterling and me. No one here knew anything about Fen.

As we passed the bar, Dwight the bartender did a double take and gave me a strange look. I wanted to leave.

Our table was dead center in the room, and Fen sat right beside me wrapping his arm around my chair. I leaned on the opposite armrest and looked away.

"If we were coming to the Sports Bar, why are you dressed like that?"

"I thought I'd look nice for my lady and see where the evening would take us. Besides, I wanted to see what was so great about this spot." He looked around taking in the decor. "This is your spot right?"

What did he know about my spot?

He leaned in to kiss me. I accepted his gesture but things were still awkward. I felt like everyone in the room was watching our interactions.

The waitress came to the table and greeted us carrying a bucket with a champagne bottle. What were we celebrating, I wondered?

"Here you are Mr. Fenney." The waitress put the bucket on the table and produced two wine glasses from her apron pocket.

"What is all of this Fen?" It appeared our outing had been planned.

"Can't a man shower his wife?" He leaned in to kiss me again, but this time when he kissed me, it was hard and passionate.

I was caught off guard and took both hands pushing him off me. "You know I don't get down like that in public!" I had never been a public person, and neither was he, so I didn't understand what had gotten into him.

Leaning in, putting his arm around my shoulder he whispered in my ear, "Who is he, Lana? You don't want me to touch you. You don't have any words for me, and now I can't kiss you."

Selecting my words carefully I took a few moments to gather my cool and put it back in place. "What are you talking about? When have you known me to go for public displays of affection?"

"I know I haven't been there for you, and our relationship is on again and off again. But I have never felt as rejected as I've been lately. Who is he?"

"Oh! You don't like the feeling of rejection?"

"Who is he Lana?"

"So, you brought me to a public place to have a serious conversation."

"Who is he, Lana?"

That question again. Maybe I should play his game. I leaned into him, and my alter ego, I called LaQuita, the smart mouthed brat, showed up. I reached over and toyed with his tie. He was seething and I was enjoying it.

"What if I did have a man? You should be happy, because you would be free to do what the hell you want. Oh yeah, that's what you've *been* doing."

He stared at me. Familiar with that look, I continued while I had his attention. "This is what you wanted right? If Lana has a man it's not just Fen, everyone cheats. That would make Lana a bad girl, and your actions would be justified right? I can beg *your* forgiveness and hope you let me back in. I can go back to doing what I want because you believe me when I say I won't do it anymore, and when *you* find out nothing has changed, you can feel like the fool and sit at home hoping I don't come home one day and tell you I'm leaving, it's over or goodbye."

My own words hurt. I was now a cheater, and I had become as callous as him.

I had gone too far. The hurt on his faced surfaced almost immediately. "I will kill any man who touches you," he grabbed my arm. "Do you understand me, Lana. You are *my* wife." He was in my ear whispering, hissing each word for emphasis.

"And you are my husband, but you don't play by the same rules. Do you?" I twisted my arm trying to get out of his grip, but couldn't.

"It's not the same!"

"But isn't it?"

He didn't answer. He was smirking.

"Are we killing people now?" I tilted my head to the side and smiled. No answer. "Me seeing someone else don't work for you?"

I attempted again to snatch my arm back, but he gripped me even tighter. I didn't want to make a scene, so I smiled sweetly. His smile was sinister.

When I attempted to snatched my arm from his grasp again, he released me. I stood to my feet.

"Where are you going, Lana? We rode here together." He attempted to stand and his imbalance made me realize for the first time that he was drunk.

"There is Uber."

"Are you going to disappear for three days again?"

I didn't answer his question because Dwight, the bartender, was watching. He rolled his eyes and did it again. Then I realized he wasn't just rolling his eyes; he was redirecting my gaze.

A chill like none I had ever felt washed over my body. Sterling sat at a high bar table, and I could tell by the look on his face he had witnessed the entire exchange.

He looked angry as he watched Fen. His arms were tensed and fist balled. I wanted to go to him, but did not want to cause more confusion. He turned and looked at me. Hurt filled his face. Embarrassment flooded my senses and I felt sick. Quickly, I moved through the room to the ladies' room.

The room was empty. I paced back and forth not sure what to do next. My attempt to not expose Sterling to the craziness of my life had just come to an end.

By the time Ebony, mine and Sterling's regular waitress, burst into the room I was hyperventilating. Seeing my dilemma, she quickly wet a handful of paper towels and made me sit. Taking the wet ball she put them to my forehead.

"Breathe Ms. Lana." She was fanning me with her other hand.

"Mmmmm," I moaned over and over, trying to release the wave of pain in my knotted stomach.

"Mr. Sterling is in the hall. He asked me to come in and check on you."

She was wiping my head and rambling, but the ringing in my ears drowned out her voice. I knew the sensation; I was about to pass out. It had happened only once before in my life, but that was all it took to know when it was coming.

"You are going to pass out if you don't slow your breathing down. Breathe slower and put your head between your legs."

I did as she instructed. The last thing I wanted to do was to pass out. As I gained control, my breathing slowly returned to normal. Pushing the wet towels away, I stood to my feet and prepared to face my dilemma. I couldn't hide in the bathroom all night. Eventually I would have to emerge.

"Ebony, is he still outside?"

The pretty chocolate girl with the long legs jetted to the door and peeped out. "Yes."

"Can you tell him I'm okay please and I'll call him later?"

Ebony left the bathroom and returned Almost immediately. "He won't leave."

"Damn!"

I went to the mirror and attempted to refresh my face.

"You look fine Ms. Lana."

"Thank you, Ebony."

I took a deep breath and entered the hallway. Sterling was leaning on the wall across from the door. The bottom of his one foot rested on the wall and his arms crossed his body and rested on his raised leg. He looked stoic.

"Where is your phone, Lana?"

That was a strange question to ask. "I forgot it at home."

He nodded as he digested my words. "You haven't had your phone all day?"

"No. Why are you asking me this?"

"Don't go home with him tonight Lana. He knows."

"What do you mean?"

"I've been getting messages from you all day."

"What do you mean?"

Sterling pulled his phone from his suit pocket, and I saw the messages from me asking him to meet me here at the Sports Bar.

My mouth dropped. I was infuriated that Fen would do something like this. He had a lot of nerve. What confused me, even more, was how he knew about us. Now I understood why Fen was putting on such a show. He knew Sterling would be there.

Sterling put his phone back into his suit pocket. "Don't go home with him Lana."

He reached for my arm and touched the now bruising spot from Fen's hold. I winced. He turned to go back to the bar, but I caught his hand, pulling him back.

"It'll be okay."

"He put his hands on you. It's not okay." He paced back and forth angered.

"Stop. Calm down, Sterling. It will be okay."

"It's not okay! He put his hands on you. Look at your arm." He stopped in front of me and pointed his finger in my face. "I am not letting you go home with him tonight. This is crazy!"

"Sterling I have to go. There is so much I need to discuss with him. You're right. This is crazy, but I need closure."

"Closure? You plan to leave me, Lana?" Fen asked as he came down the corridor. He was holding a drink in his hand stirring the ice with the cocktail umbrella.

I thought I would hyperventilate all over again, but all I felt was rage. How dare he call me out! "Let's go Fen! I am ready to go."

I turned to leave, but Sterling grabbed my arm and shook his head no. I gently pulled from his grip with my other hand.

"Don't touch my wife!" He turned and approached Sterling. "Who are you anyway? Some government official or something?"

I moved between the two to keep any altercation from developing. Fen glared at Sterling, who was no longer leaning on the wall. Sterling's look told me everything. It wasn't hurt, disappointment or sorrow, he was pissed. I had never seen this side of him, and I was fearful of what would come next.

Sterling gently moved me out of harm's way and slowly turned his full attention to Fen.

"Mr. McNeil, are you fucking my wife?"

"So, you like hurting women?" Sterling asked. "Look at her arm." Reaching for my arm Sterling raised it to display the fresh bruise from his grip.

"I asked you a question, Mr. McNeil. Are you fucking my wife?"

"And I asked you a question. Do you like hurting women? I'm right here. Touch me." Sterling stood so close to Fen if either of them breathed too deeply it could be considered a push.

"Not here." I tried to calm the situation.

Neither moved. Sterling was visibly shaken. I knew if I didn't get Fen out of that corridor the two would be rolling on the beautiful marble floor.

I started walking back down the corridor. "Fen, I'm ready to go!" I received no reaction.

When I turned, the two were still facing off, sizing one another up, and daring the other. Sterling stood a few inches over Fen, but I knew Fen's background and the adversity he grew up in. Sterling's size didn't intimidate him.

Quickly, I walked back down the corridor and pulled Fen with me as I walked back. He was too drunk to fight me, or hold his balance, so he unwillingly went.

"Stay the hell away from my wife Mr. McNeil," Fen yelled as I pulled him up the corridor.

I took one last look at Sterling and realized Ebony was still standing there as well. Embarrassed I blushed.

Our waitress was standing by our table, worried we had stiffed her for the bill. Taking Fen's wallet from him, I settled the bill and pulled him through the hotel to valet.

There was no cooling down period. That didn't exist when you lived in the Harbor. When we arrived home, five minutes after leaving the Convention Center, I was still fuming.

I parked in the driveway so Fen wouldn't bang the car door getting out in the garage. I opened the garage door and turned off the engine. Leaving him in the car, I stormed to the inside garage door.

My hunch was correct. Fen stumbled up the driveway. Once he made it through the door, he grabbed my behind. I smacked him hard across his face. He seemed to sober up very quickly. Rubbing his face, we were now standing toe to toe. He smiled as though the slap turned him on.

Moving towards me, he backed me into the wall and grabbed my behind, with both hands this time. I fought to get out of his grip, but he leaned on me locking me in with his weight.

I was angry, and the last thing I wanted was to be intimate with him. Shoving him one last time, he stumbled, and I was able to wriggle out of his grasp.

He lunged at me again and went crashing when I moved. Lust was replaced by anger. Struggling, he stood up and reached under my dress pulling it up around my waist and grabbed between my legs. "Have you been with him, Lana?"

I didn't answer, not knowing what to expect from him if he knew the truth.

He smelled his fingers, before grabbing me again. "Did you sleep with him, Lana?" He yelled. "If I find out he has been in you I will fucking kill him. Do you understand!" He was screaming.

"Have you been unfaithful to me, Fen? You don't have the right to ask me who I might be sleeping with. Now your feelings are hurt! Well, I hurt every time I smelled her perfume on you, or you lied about where you were," I sneered in his face. He had unleashed the rage within me that Sterling had calmed over the months.

"You never gave a thought to my hurt. Not once! Ten years Fen! Ten years!"

I shook out of his hold and smacked him again. His pulse quickened, and I could see the tears form in his eyes. But, I knew he wouldn't cry for me. Those tears were because another man had touched his sweet Lana.

Anger overtook my senses and any fear I should have been feeling. My wounds were reopened and the hurt felt fresh, like the first time I felt it. The feelings I had experienced were back on the surface, and I wanted him to hurt the same way he had hurt me.

I slapped him again. My tears burned as they formed. I raised my hand to strike him yet again, but he grabbed both wrists, and pinned my arms to the wall.

My rage within exploded, and I bucked trying to escape his grip, but he held me tight and close this time, until I stopped fighting him.

I screamed, sending ripples of anguish in the air, and he just held me saying nothing. I slid down the wall to the floor, sobbing. But I still wanted him to hurt.

Escaping his grip, I stood. "If I am sleeping with *Mr. McNeil*, I have ten years of fucking to catch up to you! Will you wait ten years for me Fen until I have my fill?"

He stood up, and I suddenly became afraid I had gone too far. "Oh, I already knew you were sleeping with him. You could barely stand me touching you this morning!" His face twisted in anger.

Touché. He was hurt. I could see it in his eyes, but I didn't feel the victory I believed I would feel once he felt my pain. Shame rushed over me.

I hung my head, my testimony gone, with one reckless night and a year of walks. I thought of God's never ending love for me and what I would do, or how I would feel if he gave up on me.

Fen stood staring at me for what seemed like forever and I understood his words when he said he couldn't handle the look on my face when he had done me wrong. He sucked his teeth, walked to the garage door and left, never looking back.

I walked to the door and watched him climb into his car. After a few minutes, he tore out of the driveway.

My heart fell as I sobbed uncontrollably for my careless words. I still loved him, but like a lullaby, Sterling was always on my mind, singing his words of hope and serenity.

I had become great at forgiveness. I stopped counting the number of times I had forgiven Fen for his infidelities. There were so many I lost count. When I believed my limit had been reached, I forgave him again. Too bad I couldn't forgive myself.

I slid to the cold wood floor crying until I thought I would get sick. My back was against the door, and I recounted the events of the evening. Now my mind was on Sterling.

There was a rap on the door. I thought it was a neighbor. I figured the argument between Fen and I had become too loud. I sat still for a moment, not wanting to speak with anyone. They were persistent.

Slowly, I stood and walked across the hall to the front door and looked through the peephole. Immediately, I opened the door and pulled Sterling into the house.

"What are you doing here? He is so upset, and I don't know what he would do to you if he found you here."

He wasn't listening to me. He hugged and held onto me. "I had to make sure he hadn't hurt you."

"Sterling you have to go!" I was crying again.

"Come with me, Lana."

"You have to go!" I looked through the peephole again.

"He's not coming. He's at the bar drinking. I told Ebony to text me when he leaves."

I rested in his arms and let him console me. "I am so sorry you got caught up in this mess. I never wanted this to happen."

He was silent. The tempo of his heart calmed to a reasonable pace. He released and guided me to the step, and we sat in the dark hall in silence facing the front door.

Finally, echoing in the silence, he said, "I won't leave you here."

I wanted to leave with him but knew there were so many unfinished issues between Fen and me. I had to know I gave my marriage everything I could before calling it quits. We didn't get where we were just because of Fen's infidelities. I didn't address the issues in our marriage and harbored ill feelings. My lack of facing all that was wrong in my marriage put me in this situation with Sterling. If I was going to have a future with him, this relationship had to be done.

I turned and kissed him lightly on the lips. "I love you, Sterling. You took care of me when I was a mess and put me back together."

"But?"

"But before I can move on, I need closure from this. I'll have to deal with Fen. He's not going to hurt me. He has never laid hands on me since I've known him."

"He's already hurt you!"

Looking down at my bruised arm, I saw it had become darker.

"Exactly! He's desperate Lana. I saw the rage on his face."

I nodded in agreement. "Yes, he is. This is alien to him. I was his good girl, and he found out that isn't so any longer." I snickered to myself more out of shame. "I guess you can say I'm his good girl gone bad."

He smiled and held me. "He doesn't deserve you."

Sitting and holding one another, we waited for the signal. His pocket vibrated, illuminating the hall. He didn't have to tell me what the message read. He returned the phone to his pocket and held me again.

"I have to go." He stood, pulling me with him. "I will give you the space you need to get a handle on this, but I need to see you, so I know you are good."

I liked the idea, but I knew that wouldn't work. "What if I text you to let you know I am okay?"

"What? You don't want to see me, Lana?" He backed me to the wall and forced his soft lips on mine. I didn't fight him like I had Fen earlier. "You sure you can't see me once a week?"

He was always able to make me smile. "I'll see what I can do, but you know he will be watching me closely and I don't want to aggravate him right now."

"Then leave."

Just then the lights of a car pulled up to the front door. It was Fen, but he was not driving himself. Thinking fast, I ushered Sterling to the garage door at the opposite end of the hall and opened it. He crossed the garage and ducked under the door disappearing into the night. I pressed the door opener to close the garage back and closed the garage house door.

I met Fen at the front door and opened it. He was bent over fumbling with his keys.

Down to the ground, the keys dropped, and he fell into the hallway floor. I watch him roll over, and he looked up at me. "Why are you still dressed? You should be in bed."

He slithered and slipped, trying to stand. Finally, he dropped to the floor and laughed to himself.

"Where is your car, Fen?" He reeked of alcohol, so I was sure they would not let him drive home from the bar.

"It's at the hotel, Lana." Now he was annoyed. "They wouldn't let me drive home. *They* care about me." I heard the hurt in his tone and didn't care.

"Get up."

"No."

"Get Up Fen!" I was tired.

"I can't Lana. I'm too damn drunk." Again, he laughed.

Stepping over him, I ascended the stairs.

"You're not going to help me?"

Without turning, I answered. "No."

When I reached the third floor, I heard a bang on the wall and then another. I found my pajamas and went to the fourth floor to shower. If he made it there, it would take a while.

After showering and tying up my hair, I sat on the bed in the fourth-floor guest room. I heard a crash and then a few choice words. Apparently, he had made it to our room.

My phone, which I found on our bedroom dresser, and was now upstairs with me, lit up. Sterling was asking if I were okay. I answered and climbed under the covers. I was exhausted.

When I woke Fen was sleeping on the bean bag, in the corner of the room, curled up. I watched the peaceful look on his face, knowing it would soon be gone.

I understood what the previous night meant. It was about God exposing my sins before I dug my hole too deep. I was revealed in all my glory, and it was time for my judgment.

I judged Fen and Rose's relationship, and now God showed me how easy it was to fall from glory. He was showing me how easy it was to judge others for their shortcomings. By those same standards, I would be judged.

How many negative words did I have for Fen concerning his unfaithful relationship? He had every right to bring those words back to my remembrance.

I got caught up in the new world's way of living, and somehow, felt worthy to exist in a relationship with Sterling. I felt I needed that connection to live through the hard conditions of my marriage. I didn't want to go to hell yet I shut out all God's warnings. So he let me fall from my pedestal of purity and arrogance.

I watched the man I once thought could do no wrong sleep, looking as innocent as he did at the beginning of our relationship. Where did we fall apart? When did his gaze roam to someone else?

I felt something I hadn't felt in a long time, compassion for Fen. At that moment, God allowed me to see my flaws through him. He was just as fragile as me. Wasn't I just as flawed? Although my moment of weakness was just that, a moment, Fen's were years, but was there a difference? That could have been me, had God not exposed me. I would have continued to see Sterling for as long as he allowed, and remained in the same sordid circumstances with Fen. This was my wake-up call to do things correctly, decently, and in order. The only problem was, I was in love with Sterling. How did I say goodbye?

It was impossible to say what we would or would not do. When the moment presented itself, it could feel right and you could choose to act on it. Even at that very moment, watching Fen, thoughts of Sterling danced just at the edges of my mind.

Life was not long, and we all deserved to be happy, but not at the expense of someone else's heartache. I never meant to hurt Fen or Sterling, but we never set out to hurt anyone. Maybe that was my lesson to learn in this. In the end, someone always loses. We all try to live right, but the devil gets in the way. Or is it us getting in God's way?

I was exhausted and fell back to sleep. When I woke, this time Fen was watching me. Staring back, I watched him in return. He said nothing and the peaceful innocence I saw on his face as he slept was gone. He was hurt. I knew that look. It was the same one I probably gave when he was exposed.

"Are you sleeping with him, Lana?"

His words were clear yet broken. My insides no longer screamed yes. Shame washed over me slowly as the heat of its evidence crept to my face. My heart pounded and I understood what he must have felt each time I questioned him. I didn't answer.

He looked away as the realization of my silence gave him his unspoken answer. His breathing became heavier, as what I suspected was anger rising inside him. His chest rose and fell faster and faster like he was about to erupt. So, I braced myself.

"Do you love him?" he yelled demanding an answer.

Of course, I love him you idiot. Would I have threatened the unity of our marriage on a fleeting whim?

In that small aha moment, I had my answer about his and Rose's relationship. He still loved her, and that was why he could not give her up.

For the first time I had the courage to ask the question, deep down, I already knew the answer to. "Do you love *her*?"

"This has nothing to do with her! This is about you, Lana!" He yelled, and his voice cracked.

I sat up in bed to match his challenge. "This has everything to do with her!" I yelled back, but for once I was in control of my emotions. "If there were no *her*, there wouldn't have been *him*!"

"Do you love him?" He stood, again demanding an answer.

"What difference does it make? You have already created your own conclusions," I answered calmly and lay back down on the pillow.

I would not deny what I felt for Sterling. Fen would have seen through my lie. And every answer I gave after that, he would not trust.

"Who is this man who makes you compromise who you are? You would have never done this unless you loved him."

I stared at him from my safe zone and said nothing. He paced back and forth like a duck at the neighborhood carnival trying not to be shot, then without warning he let out a wail and the tears streamed as he hit the floor on his knees.

He cried making loud, heart-wrenching sounds. I wanted to go to him and console him but I didn't. I wanted him to feel the emotions I felt for so long. His hurt filled a dark place in my soul I didn't know existed. I felt no remorse for my actions or his tears at that moment.

"Why Lana?"

I continued to stare not answering. I didn't sleep with Sterling because Fen was sleeping with Rose or to get back at him, my motives were purely selfish. I did what I did because I wanted to.

"Can you answer that for me, Lana? Why?"

"I have asked you the same questions for ten years Fen. Why is she in our lives? Do you love her? Who *is* she Fen?" I stood to my feet. "Not once have you answered me, so why should I answer you?"

"I was protecting you! I didn't have an answer to your questions, but I didn't want to hurt you!"

"Bullshit! You didn't want to admit you were not perfect. Instead, you lied to me over and over again. You watched me hurt and repeated the same indiscretions, never giving a thought to the consequences of your actions.

"You are the reason Sterling became a part of my life. You pushed me to him. Hell. You took a ribbon and tied a bow around me and gifted him. Whether you want to believe it or not, you wanted this to happen to make yourself feel better."

"Why would I want another man touching you?"

"Because it frees you from your guilt." I waited to see if he understood what I was saying to him, but he looked lost. "If I commit the same indiscretion, then you don't have to assume sole responsibility for our house falling."

He rose from his knees and stood to his feet. "I don't want you to see him again."

The edges of my lips curled. I could not believe the words he was saying. He wanted me to stop seeing Sterling. "I have wanted you to stop seeing that Thirsty whore for ten years."

"Don't call her that!"

The anger in me rose as he stood in my face defending her again. "Whore! Slut! Cunt! Take your pick. They all describe her."

"And which describes you?"

The hurt resonated in my heart. I was none of those things. How dare he compare me to her. I wasn't sleeping with another woman's husband with hopes he would one day be mine. Or had I become all that I accused her of being?

"Which one Lana?" He was waiting for my answer. "Hmmm?"

"You made me who I have become, so, you pick!"

"Don't give me your victim statement. You aren't a victim in this. You had every opportunity to leave, and you chose to stay, and I didn't *make* you become anything." He sighed and hung his head. "We all make decisions, and sometimes they are not our best."

How dare he tell me I made a choice to stay. Didn't he beg me to stay and not leave? I made that choice out of my love for him, and he took it and twisted it.

"How dare you call my love for you a choice and treat it like I was choosing a dress off the rack!"

I turned my back to him and began making the bed. My head was swimming. Maybe I should leave. Why had I stayed? He definitely did not appreciate my decision.

"Why did you ask me to stay if you had no intentions of stopping?"

"I tried to stop, but you always pushed me back to her."

"Who's giving the victim statement now?"

"I'm giving you the truth. I've talked to you for years, and you refuse to hear me."

I stomped to him like a spoiled brat about to have a tantrum. "That's because it was hard for me to tell a lie from the truth. I believe that after a while, you began believing your lies!"

I turned to walk out of the room, but Fen grabbed my arm pulling me back. "Stop running and face this!"

We were nose to nose. I had forgotten how handsome he was. He was freshly cut and shaven. I wondered when I had honestly looked at him. I couldn't remember. When did I get here? When had I become indifferent to his charms?

"I'm not running," I said barely audible. "I'm tired of discussing the same things and going nowhere afterward."

He reached for my face. I pushed his hand away. He tried again, but this time I let him. I wanted to be angry. I needed to feel something where he was concerned.

"Why do you hide from me, Lana?"

He pulled me into his hold. I wondered if he held her like this. Did he speak softly to her or did they just have sex?

I shut my feelings off from him for so long I didn't know what to feel or even how to cry for him anymore. It was easier than feeling the hurt of betrayal.

He kissed me gently, and I could feel the love he still had, but I didn't feel anything. I wanted to feel something.

"When did you stop loving me, Lana?"

"When you showed me I no longer meant anything to you."

"So, you have stopped loving me?"

The pained look on his face saddened me, but he brought this on himself.

"I don't know what I feel for you anymore." Those damned tears I refused to waste on our relationship came. "You hurt me so many times I turned my feelings off." I could hear the laughter as my voice quivered. The enemy was whispering to me, telling me he was playing me again and would never stop seeing her.

The more he stroked, the more the tears came. My chest tightened, and I wanted to run. I didn't want to feel for him again. Feeling for Fen would only remind me of the hurt I neatly tucked away months ago.

I never fought with anyone the way I did with him. We struggled more in the beginning, but since Sterling, I had not felt like arguing.

"How many times do I need to be hurt before I learn you don't want to be with me?"

"I'm sorry Lana, but that's not true," he whispered.

"You're not sorry."

"I see the hurt on your face when I come home. Sometimes it's easier not to come, so why do you stay with me?"

Why do I stay? I couldn't answer his question. I didn't know the answer. I always believed it was because of our vows, but then there was Sterling voiding that answer.

"Why do you continue to see her?"

"The answer is not that easy."

"Why isn't it?"

This time it was Fen who said nothing. He continued to stroke my face.

"We never stood a chance, did we?" I pulled away from his hold and left the loft bedroom.

When I reached the master bedroom, I found a mess from the night before. The nightstand lamp lay on the floor broken in pieces like a metaphor of our relationship. I picked up the big pieces and went to the laundry room to trash them and get the dustpan and broom.

Fen was downstairs now. He took the broom and dustpan from me. "I'll clean up my mess."

With no shoes, I went to the closet to get my flip flops. "Ouch!" Too late. A piece of glass penetrated my skin.

Fen was there immediately lifting me and taking me into the bathroom. Gingerly he removed the large hunk and made me put my foot in the tub. Testing the water first, he put my bleeding foot into the running stream and washed it.

He was so gentle and loving. Again, I wondered if he was like this with her. The stranger was gone, and he was the man I married years before.

"I'm sorry. I should have cleaned this up last night."

I was trembling and trying not to cry again. My trembling caught his attention, and he looked up to find me fighting back the tears.

"Why do you fight it, Lana? Let it go."

I fought harder. I wanted to tell him he had my heart, my soul, and my body, but it no longer belonged to him. It was mine, and I would never give it to him again. Fragile and broken into pieces like the lamp from the nightstand, now shattered on the floor, it could not withstand another break.

He wrapped my foot in a hand towel and carried me to our bed. He laid me on the bed that was still made up, and joined me there.

Timidly he kissed me again and again, my forehead, cheeks, and neck. "I'm sorry Lana. I'm sorry. I'm sorry," he repeated over and again.

I pushed him away. I didn't want to go back to that place of surrender. I liked strong Lana. All the times in the past I was always walking on eggshells, afraid to let him down or lose him to another, but now, although I didn't feel it at the moment, I was stronger than ever. He made me this new person, causing me to test my limits and face my fear of failing.

I was always terrified to fail at anything. As a child, I had to be perfect. I wanted to show my mother I was worthy of her love. I wanted my father to hold me and love me like a father should his daughter, but they were both selfish, caught up in their own desires while their children were not priorities.

I was never the bad girl who found attention in being mischievous. When I couldn't get attention from my parents, I learned to get it from my teachers by attempting to be perfect and mastering their test. In college, I became lost in the thousands and getting the perfect score was more difficult. Then it became a race to have the highest score amongst my peers.

In life, I was beginning to learn your successes and failures had no scores. Instead they became forks in the road, right and left turns, lessons learned or repeated until you got the message in the experience. Sometimes the roads weren't clear, and you had to be still and listen for clues to know which way to go. This was my place in this game of life. I was at a fork in the road.

Shocked by my reaction, Fen retreated to what he knew. "Do you love him, Lana? You have never pushed me away before."

Again, I didn't answer.

"He's not who you think he is."

I still didn't answer. I refused to have a conversation about Sterling, who had absolutely nothing to do with our mess. He may have become a casualty at this point because I didn't know where I was going with him. No, he had nothing to do with us.

"I'm sorry I brought him into your life. It was my own selfishness that caused this."

I watched him and saw the concern on his face. His arrogance had him believing he caused the relationship between Sterling and me. For once I made a decision. I chose to be with Sterling because I wanted to be with him.

"You can't be with this guy Lana."

"Why?" He was beginning to annoy me.

"He's not right for you."

"But you are?"

"I've investigated this dude Lana. How much do you know about him?"

"All I need to know!" I tried to get up, but he quickly pinned me down. "Let me go!"

"No! Hear me out!"

I fought to get up again, but the harder I tried to break free of his grip, the more I hurt myself, and the tighter he held onto me. "Why? Why am I listening to you? You know nothing about him!"

"Do you love him, Lana?"

There was that question again. If he wanted to know so badly, I would no longer spare his feelings. "Yes, Fen! Yes! Yes!"

He stopped fighting me and fell back on the pillows as though hit by a bullet. His eyes were closed, and he was deep in thought.

Reaching up, he pinched his nose. I knew the hangover was getting the best of him now, but that wasn't all that was getting the best of him.

"Do you want me to get you anything for your headache?" I was still trying to take care of him.

His eyes opened, and he watched me. "You don't know him, Lana. You can't trust him."

"And you believe you have the insight of who he is." I stopped. "I'm not having this conversation with you."

I stood to get him an aspirin. The pain from my foot shot up my leg reminding me of my fresh wound.

"Lay back down. I need to get the rest of the glass off the floor."

He shot up and grabbed the broom to continue what he hadn't finished. I could tell he was mulling over something in his head.

After dumping the last of the glass in the bathroom wastebasket, I heard the medicine cabinet open and the tiny pills shuffling in the bottle. The faucet came on, and the sound of Fen slurping water from the tap caused me to grin.

He returned to the door and watched me before approaching the bed and sitting on the edge. "I love you, Lana. I never stopped, but every time I see the hurt on your face or the sadness in your eyes I hurt. It's a reminder of what I've done and can't undo."

"The sadness didn't just show up. All you had to do was stop. You created this mess."

"We both played our part. I wasn't in this alone."

"What part did I play, Russell?"

"You were never there!!"

"I was always there for you. I have no friends because I'm always there for you. I went to training for two months. Then you lost it. I could wait for you to come home every day twiddling my thumbs, but for two months you couldn't wait for me!"

"I'm not made like you, all put together and not needing anything. I need you always!"

His words were no surprise to me. I knew he was needy when we started dating. It wasn't until later that I realized it was his form of control. He would never tell me what and when I could do things, but he used words to make me feel like I didn't love him enough.

"I wasn't always in love with her. The night you first met her I wasn't. You pushed me away after that night and she became my security blanket when I thought I wasn't enough for you. Over time she became important to me. Lately, we exist and are cordial." He was kneeling at my feet, always so dramatic, and it wasn't impressing me.

"Why exist at all? If what you are saying is true, then why do you spend so much time with her? And you think it's okay? Yes, you buy me things, our house is beautiful, but it's never been a home. It's an empty shell."

The walls seemed to be speaking to me lately, whispering. They were telling me I sold out for the American dream. I was haunted by the thought that there was a man who couldn't give me this but wanted to love me with all his heart and being and give me the world... his world.

"I don't und..."

"Let me finish!" Now annoyed at me for disrupting his speech he took a deep breath and let it out slowly, blowing through his lips. "Why?" It wasn't a question, but more of a comment.

"Lana, there is something I have wanted to tell you for so long, but didn't have the courage to do. The more time past the harder it has become." He took a deep breath. "I have a six-year-old son, who I love very much." There were tears in his eyes and a smile on his face. "He's innocent in all this, and for once I wanted to do one thing right."

I felt the air snatched from my lungs, like the wind was knocked out of me. I gripped my chest, now hurting from his words. The one thing I could never give him. A child!

I limped to the window. I wondered if the neighbors were home, because I could feel the volcano rise in me. "Why didn't you tell me?" I asked in a hushed whisper.

He shrugged his shoulders. "I knew you would walk out on me the very moment you found out. I was already holding onto you by a thread. I love you both and felt I had to choose, but I would never be able to have you both."

The clouds moved in on my mind, swirling and turning. I stood, barren, stripped of my privileges as a woman, trumped by a technicality. The Whore played the game to win. Not only did she give him a child, she gave him a son.

"You should have told me!" I whispered so low, I almost was not sure I said the words.

"Then what?" He looked at me for my answer. "Hmm?"

I wanted to go to the kitchen, get a knife and stab him in his heart like he had just done to me. I wasn't prepared for this. How could I have been? If he told me he loved Rose or that he wanted to be with her, but was stuck with me, and a divorce would be messy, I could've handled those words. Hell, I waited for him to one day say those words for the past seven years. But a child I was not prepared for.

"We decided to shelter him from...."

"*We*?" I turned so quickly he stepped back. "*We* are making decisions now? *We*?" I screamed.

It hurt me that Fen couldn't trust me with the truth, but the decisions he shared with her exasperated me more. He felt he had to lie to me to protect his son. What did he believe I would've done? He was making his life decisions with another woman.

"You should have told me," I said again barely audible. "We could have figured things out together."

"There is more." He stood beside me now, peering out the window as though his story was unfolding in the streets. "When I found out she was pregnant I was going to leave you." He turned and watched me, looking for my reaction. "She gave me ultimatums that would have torn us apart anyway. If I fought there would've been a messy court battle, and I would've lost you."

"Why did you stay?"

"You! I stayed for you. I love you. Nothing has changed over the years. I realized she was more desperate to have me, so I called her bluff."

"You thought so much of me that you considered leaving me instead of telling me?"

"You were giving me nothing. I was expecting you to leave me and I didn't want to be alone. Rose told me you would never forgive me and would eventually leave me anyway. So, I held on."

"You let someone else tell you the things you should have known about me. But I didn't leave did I? I'm still here! I've been here through it all, and you still didn't trust me?" My voice quivered.

I wanted to leave. I couldn't listen to anymore. Was this why God wanted me to stay? I went to my closet.

"Where are you going, to him?"

Stopping I gripped the frame of the closet and then turned and looked at him hard, resentful of his words. How dare he!

"Despite what you believe, I do have a mind of my own. I don't need you or Sterling to make my decisions or to direct me. Sleeping with him was a choice. *MY* CHOICE!"

I flipped through my clothes and decided to go back to old school. I needed to get out of there before I became an episode on *Snapped*.

I snatched my ripped jeans off the shelf. "Until the stunt you pulled last night you were never a part of our conversations! Sterling and I were just two people in need."

Stepping into my ripped jeans, I almost fell, and he caught me. I snatched away from him and reached for a shirt.

"Did he tell you he was married?"

I heard him but refused to react. I slid my shirt over my head and the slides I discarded in the bottom of the closet on my feet.

"Please, Lana! Don't go! Let's finish this conversation."

"Why? You already have!"

"We haven't talked about anything. We are just scratching the surface." He was desperate.

I stopped. "Okay. Let me sum this up for you. You have been seeing another woman, while you were married to me, for TEN years! After contracting a sexually transmitted disease from that whore, I miscarried our only child and was told I would probably never be able to have another. Never! You promised me over and over you would end it with her, and like a fool, I kept forgiving you again and again." I was sobbing. Again! UNRAVELED! My mind was ruptured.

"I waited for things to change. You always became the man I wanted you to be every time I reached the end of my rope, but you played on my love for you and screwed me over again and again. No pun intended.

"I've learned to be good at forgiving. Each time I let you back in, you add more shit to the game and push a little further. I should have left seven years ago, but I took my vows seriously and believed love would always prevail. The only thing love did was leave me sterile, barren, and on the outside of your inner circle. Because you have another family and I'm not a member, Fen."

I was out of breath. I was out of hope. I was out of second chances, and I couldn't even blame him. Because, I made the choice to stay.

"Don't leave," he whispered.

"You've given me a million reasons to go. Can you give me just one good reason why I should stay? Just one?"

He hung his head. "Because I love you with all my heart and you are my ride-or-die chic."

I looked at him wondering why he was still standing. I wanted to punch him in the mouth. "You killed her! She's gone! She's done!"

I looked around at the room that held so many of my tears and walked to the door. I paused, waiting for that tiny sweet voice that never left me to whisper something...anything.

Now heal.

Chapter Eighteen

The sanctuary was dark, but that was alright. I didn't want to talk to anyone. I fell on the altar and prayed and cried. I was still angry. There were always unanswered questions, and this was the only place I knew where to find those answers.

"Why didn't you show me this earlier? I feel like a fool." I didn't understand why God would send me so low. I didn't understand why I needed to hurt like I did. "I thought You loved me!"

"Where are You? I need you!" I sobbed profusely. My heart was broken like I couldn't believe. "I need you Lord. Take my scars and my broken heart and cover me with your love. Blanket me in your protection. Take this hurt, because I can't bare it alone. I know I'm not perfect, and never will be, but don't turn from me. I don't have anyone else!"

"I'm nothing without you and I know I haven't listened to you and don't deserve anything from you, but don't leave me!"

I stayed there on my face for what seemed like hours, but I lost all sense of time. I heard the door open and close several times, but didn't care who saw.

I waited and waited for answers. He was silent.

The door opened again, but this time I felt gentle hands stroking my back, and I knew it couldn't be anyone other than Mother.

She stroked me, trying to calm my spirit, but her touch only made me wail. When she couldn't console me, she pulled me into her arms and held me like I wanted my mother to do so many times.

I thought about the time a neighborhood boy waited for me on the corner every day and grabbed my behind. I had no other way home and had to walk by him. When I complained to my mother, she told me to walk the long way, so he wouldn't see me or kick him in the balls and take charge. I understood what she was trying to teach me, but still wanted her to meet me on that corner and slap the boy for touching me. I wanted her to defend me. I wanted the same from God.

I thought of one of many nights she didn't come home and a man broke into our house to steal our television. At eight, I didn't know what to do. When the police arrived, the neighbor covered for her and told the police that she was watching us while my mother worked. I didn't know if he believed her. He couldn't be concerned about a scared little black girl and her brothers, when their mother didn't even care about them. Again I needed rescuing and no one was there, but God had always been there for me. Why didn't He protect me now?

Mother waited until I gathered myself and asked me to come to her office. I declined.

"I'm okay," I said, not wanting to burden her with my sad story.

"No you are not okay, and I'm not asking. I can't let you leave here and not know if you are safe."

I cried again, but not over my situation. I picked up my purse and prepared to leave, but out of obedience, followed her down the hall to her office.

I didn't marvel over the things I saw the first time in her office. I wasn't dancing and singing through joy. Even Sterling had betrayed me. I didn't know if I still trusted God, but he was all I knew. I couldn't understand his plan for me. I was broken.

Mother's question came softly. I was so preoccupied in my thoughts; I didn't hear her speak.

157

"Daughter?"

"Ma'am?"

"What is going on?"

I was silent. I would only air my dirty laundry to God. "I'll be okay." I was not prepared to talk about all I had discovered. I didn't understand these things myself. Mother was watching me, waiting, and expecting me to say something eventually.

When I didn't give her what she wanted, she conceded. "Okay. But know that is why I am here."

Quickly, I left her office. Once in my car, I realized I had nowhere to go. I had just abandoned my home.

I drove and drove with no direction. Fen called, Sterling texted, but I didn't answer either of them.

The outlet was packed. I had to pick up a few things. I needed clothes, but I didn't want to go back home. I would get my things once I had a plan.

It was off season so making a reservation at the GM was easy. I never knew we had monthly rates. I reserved a suite and put it on Fen's business card. He could pay for my recovery.

The suite was nice. I toured all the rooms when I first started, but didn't realize how beautiful they were. I had the bell boy drop my things in my room. After putting my purchases away, I stretched out for a long nap.

I dreamt of a beautiful little boy who looked just like Fen. His large eyes smiled when he did, and his little nose wrinkled when he frowned.

We were riding our bikes in the park. The small boy fell and skinned his knee. When I ran to his rescue, he would not be consoled. He began to yell at the top of his voice, "You're not my mother! What did you do with my mother? Where is my daddy?"

The perspiration and tears streamed down my face and I was frantically panting when I woke. It was dark outside. I scanned the room, not knowing where I was and then remembered. I had moved into the GM.

I went to the bar and got the bottle of water I knew would be stashed in the fridge. The lights from the window caught my eye and I went to it to look at the now lit bridge.

The lights, from the cars moving back and forth between states, calmed me, slowly bringing me back to reality from one of the most devastating days of my life. I stood there watching until the bottle of water was emptied, then threw it in the trash and returned to bed.

I looked at the phone and saw I missed ten calls. Two were from Sterling who never called me. He also left several text messages. He wanted me to call him. He was worried sick.

I took a deep breath and dialed his number. He answered on the first ring.

"Hello!"

"Hi, Sterling." I sounded groggy, even to myself.

"Are you okay? You promised me you would check in daily to let me know you were fine. I thought something happened."

"No. I'm fine."

"Okay. I just needed to hear your voice. Are you home?"

"No." I didn't want to tell him I moved out. He didn't need to know that.

"Did you want me to meet you somewhere?"

"No."

There was a pause. "Are you sure you're alright?"

"I'm sure." I held my breath to get up the nerve to ask the important question. "Sterling. Why didn't you tell me you were married?"

There was silence on the other end, and I knew what Fen shared was the truth. My eyes stung, realizing I had lost everything. There were no good men.

"Lana, we need to talk."

"I'm good. Goodbye, Sterling."

I ended the call, and he called me right back, but I refused to answer. After the third try, he stopped calling, but then came the text messages.

I was done playing games with men, and I was drained. Within a few minutes, I was sleep again.

Chapter Nineteen

Over the following month, I was in overload. I found an apartment to rent in the Harbor. I furnished it, courtesy of Fen, and picked up what I needed from the house.

Although he tried again and again, I refused to talk with him. I thought a lot about Lena and how old she would be had she lived.

Where had I gone? Somewhere along the way, I lost myself. Where was the girl who made safe, sound decisions? Maybe my fate was overdue. Although alone, I wasn't lonely. God returned to me and gave me comfort.

Sterling, the one who held my soul, was on my mind. A lot! I was so hurt to find him to be a liar as well. I knew it was my fault for not asking more questions. I assumed since he spent time with me there couldn't be anyone else in his life. But looking back, I realized that was stupid. We were only together once a week. He continued to asked me to meet him, and I wouldn't reply. His requests became fewer and further apart.

I made an appointment to see my doctor because I was feeling sluggish. Someone suggested I get a vitamin B shot for energy. My trainer told me I needed to change my diet, so I did. I began losing weight and building muscle.

The fashion show planning was coming together. And, I spoke and trusted in God more than I ever had. It was the first time I lived on my own, and I felt empowered. My money was tight without help from Fen, but I was doing it, with God's help.

The doctor's office was hot. The doctor kept looking at me. I became afraid, wondering if he was hiding something. He ordered a blood test and said he would contact me with the results and not to worry. He was sure it was nothing major. I was scared. Just when I thought my life was getting back on track this happened, whatever this was.

I couldn't eat and was sick to my stomach. I stopped going to the gym and stayed on my face.

The pillows in my walk-in closet, which represented my altar, began to resemble the shape of my body. I was there when the doctor's office called with my test results. When I answered, I was nervous. I held my breath when the nurse gave me the result. Her words were lost in translation. I had to ask her twice to repeat herself. We set my next appointment, and the line went dead.

It was dark before I moved from the spot in the closet. Fear encircled me, while I thought of all the things that could go wrong. But, mostly I thought of what I would have to endure alone.

The shower ran for five minutes before I stepped into the hot stream. I lathered, but couldn't help hesitating when I reached my abdomen. Pregnant? After I was told it couldn't happen!

After applying my lotion, I lay naked on my back, wanting to feel every moment as I ran my hands across what would one day grow. Then it dawned on me. I didn't know whose child I carried.

Chapter Twenty

Work picked up as the holidays passed. Christmas was the busiest time of the year for everyone, and we were no different. Courtney, my assistant, was in and out of my office all day with fires to be extinguished. So when she came to tell me there was an irate woman in the lobby who wanted to see me, I became curious. Why me?

When the elevator opened, I could hear her loud mouth, making demands, before I turned the corner. I picked up my pace to stop the noise before she disrupted everyone.

Her back was turned to me when I approached, and she was complaining about every charge on the bill. I never understood why anyone stayed at the GM and then worried about each line item. The hotel catered to the haves. Unfortunately, it didn't exist for the benefit of the have-nots.

"Hello," I greeted as I approached. "My name is Milana Fenney. What can I help you with?"

The woman slowly turned, and my stomach sank. It was Rose. My eyes darted back and forth, looking for Fen. He wasn't there and I could not understand why she was. Mostly, I didn't understand why she asked for me.

"Hello, Rose."

She smiled a polite smile. "Hello, Lana."

I cringed but didn't correct her, not wanting to make a scene in front of my staff. I looked at the flustered desk manager. "I will take over from here, Stewart."

Once the staff cleared the general area, I turned back to the woman who contributed to my woes. "What seems to be the problem, Rose?"

"All of these hidden charges you don't tell your guests about. You just spring it on them in the end." She was shaking her bill in my face.

"Let me see the charges." I gently took the paper from her to avoid a confrontation and glanced at the charges I knew better than my checkbook.

I walked to the desk and told the desk manager to credit the bill one hundred dollars. Once she completed the credit, I approved the transaction and returned to Rose with the newly printed copy and handed it to her.

"I have taken care of the charges. You can go to the desk, now, and they will take your payment for the remainder of the bill. Is there anything else you need help with?"

She took the bill, glanced at it, then back at me. I knew by her look our conversation was not over.

"You think you're better than me don't you?"

"What?"

"All these years you may have been first, but I was still there. I was there for him when he was stressed and needed someone to share with, because you weren't there. You never did understand his needs."

She looked me up and down; as she had the first night we met. The smirk on her lips told another story. She was obsessed with Fen and she would never stop coming for him, which made her dangerous. But why was she here? She should have been celebrating our break up. That should be a win in her book.

"Do you believe you make him happy?" She held her head high and proud, like a child who already knew the answer to the question.

"I'm not responsible for anyone's happiness. But if his happiness is contingent on me, we are not together. So... if he is not happy, then you are not doing your job."

Her eyebrow lifted. She didn't know.

"Okay. Is there anything else you need?" It was time to say goodbye to the crazy woman. I was trying to be nice. I didn't want to have a showdown with her in my workplace. I wanted to go back to work, but she wouldn't let me.

"I will have him. You don't make him happy. What do you think about that?"

"I think you are just as childish as you were when we first met." I was now annoyed. She pushed buttons that were no longer working. I couldn't understand why Fen wanted this woman. She was older, but immature. I wasn't even sure she could have an adult conversation.

I stepped in closer. "Rose, you will never be any more than he has defined you to be, a side chick, eating the crumbs from my table and because of that, he doesn't have to do anything extra. He knows you will be there waiting for the next crumb I feed you, regardless of his mess. You've been put on sale, and marked down because you allowed someone else to determine your value."

My team was watching from the desk, but I was on a roll and couldn't stop. "You started out as his whore, and you will always be just that. That's all. His security blanket. He didn't even have the decency to let you know we haven't been together for months. Does that validate your value?" I looked around. "This is your chance, your shining moment, and where is he? Instead you're here alone, begging me to *give* him to you. Well Honey, I've done my part. I even gift wrapped him for you."

Her shining moment gone, Rose looked mortified. She came to embarrass me and beat me down, but instead she received more than she came for.

I should have been embarrassed, but I wasn't. Truth gave me courage to stand, no matter my story.

"I am the mother of his child! His only child." She was reaching, trying to prove her value to me, but mostly she basked in her belief that I could bear no children.

"And how did that work out for you? You're still the side chick. Girl... bye." She looked shocked by my words, apparently unaware that I knew they had a son.

When I turned back to the desk, my team was beaming. It was not a side of me I wanted them to see, but I felt no shame in my words. "If she needs anything else call another manager," I told them and headed back to the elevators, still amazed he spent ten years with her.

Their relationship was strange to me. She didn't seem like his type, but I guessed my lack of understanding was why we weren't together. Maybe she was different with him.

Why was she here? Fen would have never agreed to stay where I worked; I was sure of that. Something had changed in paradise. I felt she was stalking me.

Chapter Twenty-One

Another month passed and I began feeling flutters as the baby moved. I still didn't tell anyone. I wanted to pass the point when I had miscarried with Lena. God was either punishing me or blessing me. I didn't know which.

I had to eat small meals or risk the chance of getting sick. My workouts changed to walks. Each time I walked the familiar path, I thought about mine and Sterling's walking together. I missed him and thought of him all the time, but I thought of him mostly on Sundays after church, when I returned home.

It had been over four months since I walked out on Fen. I agreed to see him, but when the doorbell rang, I realized I wasn't ready to discuss what was next.

He was dressed casually and was freshly shaven. I could tell he was as nervous as me, but he wanted to look his best.

Surprising even me, I smiled when I saw him, but concern took over. He looked tired and appeared to have lost a few pounds, but he was more defined. I wondered how he was doing, had he been eating right and getting proper rest.

He looked around taking in my decor and nodded. "Your place looks great, but you were always good at decorating. You spent my money well."

I laughed at his humor. "It was the least you could do since I had to leave my home," I teased back.

"You know you...." He stopped. "You're right. It was the least I could do." He watched me for a moment, contemplating his next move, then hugged and lightly kissed me on the forehead. "Let's talk."

He walked to the couch and sat on the end with his hands clasped together. I joined him, and things became awkward. Where should we begin?

"Would you like something to drink?"

"No. Thank you." He was so nervous. "What do you want, Lana?"

"What? Nothing." I didn't understand his question.

He dipped his head understanding my confusion. "I will have my lawyer draw up the paperwork. I know you're not coming back. Why would you?" His hands were stretched out towards me. "You look happy. You're glowing. I haven't seen this Lana in years and I know I was the cause of that. I want you to be happy."

"How are you Fen?" I said out of concern.

"I'll be good, knowing that you're happy now. So, tell me what you want."

I said nothing.

"The house? Alimony?"

"No! No! I don't want any of that."

I slid in closer to him, and he trembled. I took both of his hands. "I want you to heal. You've gone through a lot too. You tried to hold everything together and had no one to talk to in all this. If I don't know anything else, I know you are a private person."

I saw the tears form in his eyes. One escaped, and I wiped it away gently.

He appeared to be fragile. I chose not to say anything about my encounter with Rose. This wasn't about her, for once. Funny how the last ten years of our marriage had been about her and now that we were no longer together, we were concerned about just us.

"I don't hate you or have any ill wishes. I just want you to take care of you. If not for you, do it for your son."

I held him briefly as he cried in my arms. He had done no healing during our separation. It's difficult to heal when you don't understand where you are going.

"I'm sorry." He stood and took a tissue from the box on the credenza and attempted to compose himself. "I'm not ready for this conversation. Maybe I will come back another time, when I'm.."

"When you're what?" I walked to him and held him. I could feel him trembling in my arms. I felt his loneliness, his vulnerability, his hurt and all the things he tried to avoid by keeping his secrets.

I released him and kissed him briefly and went to get him a glass of wine to help bring some normalcy back to our meeting. I could feel his eyes on me the entire time.

He took the glass from me and returned to his seat. After a few sips he let out a nervous laugh. "I feel like an idiot."

"You're no idiot Fen. A little dumb for letting all this slip through your hands."

We both chuckled.

"Are you happy Lana?"

"I'm getting to know me, my likes and dislikes. Why I do what I do."

"You mean like your smart mouth?"

We laughed again.

"Yes. Even that."

"But are you happy?"

I couldn't truly answer his question. I knew I wasn't unhappy or sad. Nor did I regret my decision to leave, but I could say there was definitely something missing.

"I'm at peace."

He thought about what I said and then business Fen showed up. "Let's get started."

We discussed all the particulars. He would keep the company, although I helped him to build it. He insisted on paying for whatever home I found, but I felt that would be awkward, so we decided on an alimony amount. He said it would help him to feel he kept some part of his commitment to always take care of me. We divided our property. I kept my car and he would pay it off. The furniture would remain with the house, but I was welcome to come and get any keepsakes I wanted. He would remain in the Harbor house.

I poured him another glass of wine. "How is your son?"

He looked pained again. "I'm so sorry I took that away from you," he said apologizing for the loss of Lena and my chances to carry another child. I wanted to tell him I was pregnant and make him feel better, but I wasn't ready.

"I'm still hopeful. There are so many other options, and who knows what God's plans are?"

He was wrestling with his emotions again. I could see it on his face. For the first time since I knew him, he owned his mistakes. I was proud of this new growth in him.

"His name is Solomon." He beamed.

"That's a big name to live up to. It's a beautiful name."

"Thank you." His mind was working. "Are you still seeing Silver or whatever his name is?"

I pushed him laughing. "No! After you told me he was married, I left that alone. I didn't need any more complications."

He fidgeted. "I have a confession, Lana." He paused. "I was so jealous when I found out about this guy. He was everything on paper I wasn't. I didn't lie when I said he was married, but what I didn't' say was that his wife died from cancer. He nursed her for six months before she passed earlier this year. He's one of the good ones."

I should have been angry, but I understood why he did it.

"Say something."

I stood and ran my hands down my sides, a nervous gesture I couldn't seem to break. "I should be furious with you, but I understand why you did it."

My mind was racing. I needed to call him and apologize. Was it too late? Oh, I missed him so much. Would he forgive me?

Fen stood with me. "I have to go and take Solomon to practice." He reached out and hugged me, holding me so tightly I thought he would discover my secret. "If you need anything, anything at all, please call me, even if it's just to talk, Okay?"

"I will." Then I thought of Rose. "Be careful Fen. Please take better care of yourself. And you have to let Rose go, or she will be the death of you." I looked him in his eyes to make sure he understood what I was saying.

He nodded and walked to the door. "I don't hate you. I love you, and I always will. We have a lot of history together. In some regards, I guess we will always be family. We were together for over half our lives."

His face was strained as he tried to hold it together. Quickly he kissed me and left.

Chapter Twenty-Two

It had been months since my last visit to the bar. I stood on the outside and looked through the window. The meat market was in full effect. People were smiling fake smiles and sharing fake conversations. I hoped this was not going to be my new future.

The last time I was here was catastrophic. It was the night Fen exposed mine and Sterling's relationship.

Dwight was at the bar sliding drinks, as he often did to step up his tips and I saw Ebony walking back and forth. Then I saw him. Sterling.

He was sitting at a small table off to the side, but he wasn't alone. A young woman who was very animated in her conversation sat with him, her hands flailing. He seemed amused by her story and every so often his head reared back in laughter.

She was beautiful. Her long arms were graceful like a dancer. When she stood, I could see she was tall and eloquent. She wore long belled dress pants and a halter top that matched. Her heels were low, but she appeared to be about five feet, ten inches and needed no help in that area. She was a little younger than I would have expected, but I was sure he didn't want to be alone.

My heart sank. I was too late. He appeared to have moved on and looked happy. I didn't want to complicate his life after turning it upside down, so, I left, never entering the bar.

I couldn't sleep. What would I do if the baby was his? How would I know? "Hello, Sterling. I need you to take a paternity test and then return to your life." No, I wouldn't do that. I decided not to tell either of them.

Time to move on.

Chapter Twenty-Three

Six months. In two weeks I would be past my threshold. I was getting excited and beginning to show, but hid it well. My love affair with my unborn child had begun the moment I discovered my miracle.

I stopped my house search and decided to suspend it until after the baby was born. The Super Bowl was coming on later, and I decided to go to the bar to watch. Sterling wouldn't be there because he usually went to his brother's house for Super Bowl Sunday.

Again, I stood there, looking through the window, watching the strangers at our familiar spot. It seemed strange to be here alone, and I didn't want everyone to look at me as that woman who was busted by her husband, so I changed my mind and decided to go back home, but just when I decided to leave I smelled a familiar scent. I smiled.

"Are you going in or are you just going to stand here and look in?"

It was him. He was standing behind me, so close.

"I haven't decided," I answered still looking through the window.

"Need help making up your mind?"

I smiled.

"Our table appears to be full of strangers, and there isn't a seat in the house."

"Oh, I'm sure I can find you a seat at my table if it's a seat you're looking for pretty lady."

He was breathing in the crook of my neck. I smiled again.

When I turned to face him, I felt the sun shined on my face so brightly, I couldn't help but blush.

"How are you, Lana?"

"I'm good."

"You miss me?"

I couldn't answer. There was so much to share and talk about, but for right now I just wanted to bask in the moment.

"Okay....your name is still Lana, right?"

I laughed. He reminded me of the first night we met.

"Yes." I was sixteen again. I couldn't talk. I wanted to hug and squeeze him to make sure he was real. I wanted to sit and tell him everything.

"Why don't you come in and watch the game?"

He was in my personal space, and it unnerved me. "I'd like that."

Following behind me, he gently guided me through the restaurant to our regular spot in the middle of the room. I was confused, because the table was already full of people. Then I saw her. The tall eloquent woman was there. I stopped walking, but Sterling nudged me forward.

All eyes were on me.

"Look who I found stalking me from the window."

I felt embarrassed as the beautiful woman looked me over.

"Everybody, this is Lana. Lana, this is my brother Shane."

Shane was as tall as Sterling and fit. He was not as handsome, but was a looker as well. He gave me a big hug and whispered in my ear, "I haven't seen him smile that much in months. I'm glad to meet you finally."

Shane turned to a petite woman sitting next to him. "This is my wife Nancy, and my son Brayden."

I nodded to both.

Sterling turned me to beauty. She was still sizing me up.

"This, Lana, is Clark, my daughter. She came home from school to grace her old man with her presence. And this time she brought a guest." Sterling turned to the young man who now held her hand like she was going to run at any moment. "Jamal."

"Jamil," the young man corrected as he shook my hand.

Clark stood and embraced me, which was unexpected. "Thank you," she said and let me go, returning to her seat.

I scanned the table and saw there was only one seat. Sterling walked me to the chair and sat, leaving me standing. Nervously I looked around, not knowing what to do, but suddenly he snatched me into his lap.

Everyone laughed.

"Daddy, get her a chair from another table."

"Not a chance. I want her as close as possible."

He held me as I sat in his lap until he went to the bathroom. I spoke with one of the waitresses, and an extra chair was brought to the table.

When Sterling returned, he looked disappointed I was no longer going to sit in his lap. I leaned into his ear. "See. I didn't run."

"You want to take a walk?"

Before we walked year-round and it was all I did now. I smiled and nodded.

"We'll be back before the game is over." Sterling helped me to my feet and led me out of the restaurant.

The path was empty this time of year. The river moved slowly due to the ice buildup. White patches had formed on the surface from the harsh winter we were having. I was silent, but content to be in his presence.

"I missed you," he said breaking the silence.

"Why didn't you tell me about your wife?"

"You wouldn't meet me, and it wasn't something I wanted to explain over the phone."

"No. Before."

"I didn't want to cloud our time together with talk about those things that stressed us. I wanted our time together to be about us."

"We were friends.

"Why didn't you share the issues you were having with Fenney?"

It was strange hearing someone refer to him as Fenney. He had always been Fen to me. "You should have made me listen."

"How? You didn't return to the bar, wouldn't return my calls, left your home, and I didn't want to bring it to your job, so I prayed about it and here we are."

"What if I never showed? You were just going to leave it to chance?" I stopped walking.

"It was never in the hands of chance," he said and winked.

"I'm so sorry about your wife, Sterling. You shouldn't have gone through that alone."

"But I didn't. You were there when you didn't know you were."

My mind raced to think when, and I remember that strange night he came to me so upset. I stopped and hugged him. "I am sorry for your loss. I can't imagine."

We made it to our bench and sat. "I needed someone to talk to during one of the most difficult times of my life, and you helped me through by being with me."

"Fen told me you were married to hurt me, and I believed him. I owe you an apology because I knew you, and I allowed him to change my view of you. I knew there had to be an explanation, but I lost trust in people. I trusted his words although he lied to me so many times before. Then he came by my place a couple of weeks ago and apologized for lying. He told me you were a widower and that he lied because he knew he was losing me to you."

Sterling smiled. "He came by my office and told me a similar story, and then I understood why you would not talk to me."

Fen went to see Sterling? What was going on? I smiled thinking of his kind gesture. Before I left, I told Fen he was selfish, and I guess he did some soul searching while we were apart. He was growing up!

Chapter Twenty-Four

We were back on again. I saw Sterling often, but would not invite him to my place. I didn't trust I would be good, and he still didn't know I was pregnant. But now it was time to tell him.

I brought dinner because I ran out of time. I put everything in serving dishes, all evidence was thrown down the trash chute, and the table was set.

Nervous did not begin to describe my feelings. This news would either make or break us.

The doorbell chime made me jump. I grabbed my chest to keep my heart from abandoning ship. Before answering, I took two cleansing breaths to calm down.

When I opened the door there he stood, tall and handsome, carrying a bouquet of lilies. Before I could say a word, he gave me a welcome kiss sending my already frail, nervous emotions through the roof.

"Come in." Taking the flowers, I half ran to the kitchen to get a vase from under the sink. I arranged them neatly. At least they weren't roses. I smiled.

The purple vase made them even more beautiful. I placed them in the center of the table where the food was set. I felt Sterling approach me from behind and quickly maneuvered away leaving him standing confused.

"Let me get your drink, and we can start." I disappeared into the kitchen, reappearing with a drink he created at the bar with Ebony. The ice tea with lemon was waiting for me.

"Your place is beautifully decorated."

I stopped for a moment to take in the beauty of the decor. The purples, teal, silver and golds blended perfectly together. The condo was one of my most creative projects and I almost hated to leave it.

Sterling helped me into my seat. "Why are you so jumpy?"

"Oh! Am I?" I knew I was not convincing. "We'll talk after dinner."

His forehead wrinkled as he watched me fidget under his scrutinizing eyes. "Okay."

Bowing my head, I waited for him to bless the food.

"Father we thank you for the meal that has been prepared and the hands of the cook that prepared it. In Jesus name. Amen."

"Would you like for me to fix your plate for you?" I didn't know what else to say. I was afraid I would blurt the words out with no thought.

Sterling chuckled again. "No. I can do it myself." He watched me and returned the question. "Did you want me to fix yours?"

"No. I'm good."

We fixed our plates in awkward silence. The only noise was the sound of the utensils hitting the plates, unnerving me with each clank. I picked up my phone from the table and turned to one of my play list. The sound of the music softened the atmosphere, making our lack of conversation more durable.

Neither of us had dinner on our minds. Sterling tapped his fingers on the table once we were finished, and we sat in the uncomfortable silence. He tilted his head several times, and once almost broke into laughter when I attempted to talk about anything.

He stood to his feet and came to me taking my hand. My heart was beating so fast. My time was up. He led me to the couch and seated me.

"What's going on, Lana?"

I stood pacing the floor for a few minutes. This could be the last time I saw him until the paternity test if this did not go well.

I stopped, facing him. "It's better if I show you." Slowly, I reached down, grabbed the bottom of my shirt and pulled it up over my head. His eyes became as big as saucers and he stood to his feet.

"But, but I thought you couldn't have children?" He ran his hand over my growing miracle in amazement. "How far along are you?"

"I was told I couldn't have children, and I am twenty-six weeks."

I could see him counting in his mind turning to me slowly once realization sunk in. "Is this our..."

"I don't know," I answered cutting him off. "I don't know." Whispering, I repeated my words again. "I want it to be, but I don't know."

Judge not, and you shall not be judged. Hadn't I judged Rose, calling her a whore? Now here I stood not knowing who my baby's daddy was.

Serious Sterling showed up. His face turned stern. "It's our baby Lana."

"I don't kn..."

"It's our baby, Lana," he repeated. "You've been married to Fen all these years and never had a child."

I turned away from him. The story of Lena's death had never been shared. "We did have a baby, but I lost her. That's when I was told I couldn't have children."

"Whooo!" He paced the floor. Walking back to me, he ran his hand through his freshly shaven head. "When you come back on the scene, you come back strong!"

I stood with my back to him. I was ashamed. Everything I despised about fast women had become my reality.

Pulling me back around, he turned me to face him. "We weren't brought back together for nothing. It'll be fine. Stop worrying and let's see how this plays out."

Reaching down, he ran his hand across my belly again. The baby kicked hard. Sterling smiled.

"Does Fen know?" He asked avoiding my eyes.

"No. Only you. They may suspect at work, but I've made no announcement."

He hugged me and kissed the top of my head, still beaming. "Do you know what it is?"

"It?"

I never wanted to get attached in case the same thing happened as before. The fear still gripped me when I felt anything strange, sending me to the phone to call my doctor each episode. She understood my concerns and accommodated me.

He reared back and laughed genuinely happy over the news. Relieved I stooped to pick up my shirt.

"Don't. I want to spend time with my son."

He returned me to the couch and bent down placing his ear to my belly. He spoke in a soft voice and said, "Hey Carter."

"Carter?"

"You didn't even know what *It* was." He teased.

"But what if it isn't your child Sterling?"

"*He* will be our child Lana." He spoke with confidence.

We spent the remainder of the evening catching up on the events of my pregnancy. Fen was on my mind. He was the only one in the dark now.

"You worried about Fen?"

'A little." I was silent for a moment then added, "I would want to know if it were me."

"He will know soon enough."

I was relieved to share my secret with someone. Sterling rubbed and caressed my stomach all evening, not wanting to leave me.

"Tell me about your wife" I didn't know where the question came from, but there it was rudely in the open.

His eyes washed over me strangely examining me. He appeared to be contemplating something. "What made you ask me about her?"

"I'm sorry. That was rude."

"It's okay."

As his mood shifted, he swallowed hard, placed his arm behind his head and stared at the ceiling. The shine in his eye appeared so quickly. I was not prepared for what came next.

A flood of tears overflowed, but he said nothing, mimicking the strange night in the park. I rubbed his chest to console him, but there was no consoling.

Abruptly he turned to me, burying his head in my neck sobbing like a child would to his mother. I held him not understanding.

"I'm so very sorry."

We were a mess of emotions on that night dealing with a new life and death. Sterling was devastated by my question. I began to wonder where we would go from here. Apparently we both had unfinished business.

Chapter Twenty-Five

The fashion show came and went and I found a new name for Loquacious. Stormy.

Mother called me to her office after church. I was dreading this conversation, but I knew I had some explaining to do.

The small office was already occupied by Mother when I was escorted there by the church secretary. This time I felt like the daughter who was about to be placed on punishment. I was sure I dragged my feet when I entered. She looked up, motioning for me to sit and then turned her attention back to what she was reading.

"Hello, daughter." Closing the book, she opened her desk and tucked the thick black book into a file. The drawer stuck when she attempted to close it, but after a few tries it slid shut.

"Well," she started crossing her arms. "I expected to see you on your own, but I called you in because I needed to talk to you." She paused. "Do you have some news to share?"

Not sure which news she wanted to hear, I decided to tell it all and we could go from there.

"I don't know where to begin."

"Well, let me start. First, I would like to say you did a magnificent job on the fashion show. They can't stop talking about how organized, and tastefully it was done."

"Thank you."

She hesitated again. "When is the baby due?"

There was question one. I was long past feeling shamed by my predicament, so I said boldly, "In nine weeks." I didn't want to volunteer too much information, for fear of having to explain my heathen ways. I was still not comfortable in sharing too much with people.

"Does your husband know you're pregnant?" She clasped her hands and looked me in my face.

I thought the question odd. Why wouldn't he know? He was my husband. "No ma'am."

"There are reasons why we ask that you come to us when things transition in your life. One is we can pray for you. We are your overseers, and responsible for covering all our members. If we don't know what's happening, we can't help you."

She stopped and waited for my input. No longer inhibited by my insecurities, I was prepared to bare all. "I left Fen almost eight months ago, the day I came to the church to be exact. We reached an impasse in our marriage, and I had to go."

"Did you pray daughter?"

"I prayed, prayed and prayed some more. When I realized nothing was going to change and there were things happening in his life that were not going to go away I had to let go."

She watched me then looked down. "Were you faithful in your marriage?"

"No," I said without hesitation. "I became too close to a man and later in our relationship we became intimate. I don't know who's the father and this is why Fen doesn't know."

Mother contemplated her next words. "Fen came to see me about a week ago. He told me about his transgressions. He understands he is the downfall of your marriage and he said you were a great wife. He said no other woman would have put up with his shenanigans.

"We spent some time together, and he accepted Christ. Praise the Lord!" She raised her hands and laughed, but as soon as the smile came, it left. "Are you still walking daughter?"

I smiled. Sade would have accused rather than ask me. No, Sade would have welcomed me to hell. Mother was making sure my soul's destiny was still intact. She understood the rise and fall of salvation and wasn't trying to accuse, but her prayers were specific.

"I fell from grace, but I believe I'm on the right track. He knows I'm pregnant, and accepts the possibilities, but I did not tell Fen, because it would complicate an already complicated situation. I know my days are numbered and I will have to tell him soon."

"Does he know of your infidelities or are you trying to hide?"

"Yes, ma'am, he knows. I own my stuff."

She smiled appearing satisfied I still had a chance to make it through the gates. I knew she was concerned, but I never wanted to see disappointment on her face concerning me.

"You know God has his own timing and maybe the separation helped to open your husband's eyes. Have you given thought to getting back with him and going to counseling?"

"I thought about counseling before we got to this point, but he never wanted to go."

"I believe he is open to anything to fix his marriage, but are you?"

I didn't want to have this conversation and was probably why I didn't discuss my personal life with anyone. I didn't want their input in my decisions.

Mother watched me fidget. "Tell me about this new man and have you prayed about him?"

"Mother I stay on my face. I believe God put us together for a reason; he just has not revealed the reason."

"Do you love him?"

"Very much. He's kind, gentle, nurturing..."

"But is he saved?" She asked interrupting my flow. It was just like her to get to the point. What I loved about her was she never cut her words.

I smiled again, knowing she had my best interest at heart. She wasn't trying to tear me down, she was ensuring my safety. "Yes. He's saved."

"I'm not going to tell you what to do, but God can do anything. If you want your marriage then go after it and He will meet you there. Remember God loves you no matter your decision."

Mother shared a few scriptures with me in hope that I would change my mind concerning Fen. I would have considered counseling if Solomon was not involved, because there was crazy Rose to consider I didn't know what changes could occur from us going to counseling as long as Rose was in the picture. I trusted God, but Fen's secrecy didn't allow me to extend that trust to him. I wanted no part of their family dynamics.

Our conversation ended. I know I didn't leave her with the answers she wanted, nor had I filled her in with any missing pieces. Mostly, I hoped she didn't think I had gone buck wild. Besides sleeping with Sterling that one night, and wanting him every time I saw him, I felt pretty normal for a change.

Alone, but not lonely, I was trying to get to know Lana. The new Lana was just a shell of the old. I was stronger and more confident in my abilities and decisions. I had no one other than God and me to rely on, and it felt good.

Sterling and Fen were both parts of my life, but each had their roles to play, and there was no coddling or stroking that I could do to help them through.

New beginnings were coming.

Chapter Twenty-Six

Sterling still worried me since the night of his breakdown. I didn't feel he had adequately grieved the death of his wife.

Clark asked to meet me for lunch, and I agreed as long as it was in my office, allowing me to work during our busy season. I hoped she could fill in some of the missing pieces.

My intercom loudly announced her arrival. She was ushered into my new office, which was now on the waterfall side of the building.

I fought to stay in my old office, but Wayne wanted me near his, because of the many projects I was involved in. I hated that I no longer had the bridge to watch. The movement of the cars and my view of the Nation's Capital calmed me during stressful situations, so I sometimes worked in the conference room.

Immediately following Clark's entrance, the waiter arrived from the restaurant with the lunch I ordered when she called to announce she was thirty minutes away.

The long-legged beauty strolled into my office wearing a luxurious purple designer suit, cream top, and cream pumps. Her natural hair was twisted into a neat bun, and she sported diamond studded earrings. Immediately she went to the window and looked down to the waterfalls.

"This is a beautiful view!"

"Hello Clark," I greeted. Not sure if Sterling had shared my condition. I did not stand.

"Hello, Ms. Lana,"

Clark came from around the barrier I kept between us and hugged me. Backing away, she looked at my huge stomach. "May I touch him?" she asked, excited.

"Yes, you may."

Gripping both sides, she lightly held what she believed to be her sibling. "Dad told me a couple of days ago, and I was in the area and wanted to stop by."

"Have a seat." I motioned to the chair on the other side of my desk.

She followed my directions to her seat and shook out her pants allowing them to fall back in place before sitting. "You look great. Who would believe you are about to deliver a child!"

We exchanged meaningless conversation while the waiter set up the conference table. When he was done I buzzed Courtney. "Courtney, would you please take care of Juan."

"Yes ma'am," she responded and Juan made a quiet exit.

"Let's eat." We moved our seats to the conference table.

Eating was never a priority for me, but I was making better strides since I wasn't the only one being nourished.

"I ordered an array of things. So, help yourself."

"Bon Appetite," she replied and dug in.

We discussed my role in the organization, my educational background, and my family. I smiled halfway through my conversation with this shrewd woman.

"Clark. Now that you have properly interviewed me, did I get the job?"

We both laughed at my humor. I leaned back in my chair now feeling the fullness of my belly. Not wanting to avoid her objectives to see me I became serious.

"Your dad is in good hands, Clark. We don't know where we are going with this and I'm not even divorced."

"You know my dad wants to marry you."

"I know, and I've never lied about my feeling concerning his desires to do so."

"But?"

"But... I am just discovering things about me I never knew or understood. Why I do or allow certain things, or even why I fell in love with your dad in the first place."

"Because he's handsome, charming and has a heart of gold," she replied smiling.

I laughed. "He's all of that and then some, but in order for two people to make it there has to be more than the beauty of love, or the charm of a person, because when things get dirty and gritty love and adoration is not going to bring you through, and sometimes may not bring you home. There has to be a foundation built on truth and trust."

"He said he didn't tell you mom was sick and dying, but there was a good reason for that." She became defensive.

"I'm not saying I don't have trust in your dad. We are still learning one another. It takes time. Besides, I'm not sure your dad has properly grieved your mother's death." I didn't go into the details of the night he broke down in my home. I would never betray his privacy.

"I just don't want to see him hurt like my mother hurt him. My dad's one of the good guys. He will give you the world and leave nothing for himself. Mom was selfish and spoiled. I'm sure my dad contributed to both, but for once I would like to see him come first in someone's life. You know?"

I nodded, listening to the young woman's words of admiration for her father. It was refreshing to hear kind words spoken about someone's parent. I had none for mine that I could think of in that moment. I wondered what kind of parent I would be. I hoped for kind words to spill from my child's mouth as effortlessly as the ones shared with me by Clark.

"I never really knew how wonderful dad was until mom got really sick and he gave the rest of him to take care of her." She paused before finishing her thoughts. "Even in the end I don't believe she even appreciated all his sacrifices, but I will never forget them." A sad look crossed her face.

"I believe in our last moments there is nothing but time to reflect on what we've done with our lives, the people we've hurt, the things we did, didn't do and so much more. But your father is not the man who expects people to thank him for the things he does, nor does he do them to get gratitude. It's just a part of who he is."

"I guess you're right." She thought about what I said, and just as quickly as she had become serious, her mood shifted to carefree and silly Clark, reminding me of her father. "How do you deal with other women falling all over him?"

Again, I laughed at the energetic beauty. "Most are not so bold to approach him in my face, but those who do he handles directly and swiftly." We laughed together as I told her the story of our first time sharing a meal at the Sports Bar and the woman who tried to get his attention.

My next appointment arrived, ending our lunch and conversation. "I'm not going anywhere Clark. I'm only taking it slow."

"I'm just worried about him. I got a good vibe from you when we first met, and I know you care about him."

"So, are we good?"

"For now."

Knowing she meant it, I laughed at her response.

We hugged and I walked her to the door and called in my appointment.

Bonding.

Chapter Twenty-Seven

It was Fen's turn to learn about my condition. My eyes closed to whisper a silent prayer. Not knowing what to pray, I uttered a quick, "guide me, Lord," and meditated on the moment to come.

When the doorbell rang, I was surprisingly calm. What would come would come.

Now thirty-six weeks, I found it difficult to get up. It had been a little over two months since we had seen each other. I was sure he knew the last time we met, but he said nothing.

Using the door as a barrier, I slowly opened it and invited him in. I didn't want the first thing he saw to be my big belly.

"Hey," I greeted.

"Hey to you too," he answered a little tensed.

He knew.

Slowly I closed the door with my back to him, not wanting to turn. He was watching, waiting for me to face him. When I did hurt radiated in his face as he watched me, waiting for my words that were no longer eager to spill from my lips. When I said nothing, he turned and walked to the couch and flopped down.

Head hung, and hands clasped between his legs, he watched the floor. He was upset, but I knew to expect that.

"When had you planned on telling me?"

"I don't know."

Finally, he looked at me. "When are you due?"

"In about four weeks."

He rolled his face in his hands. "But I thought we couldn't...Why didn't you tell me?" He stood and paced the floor. "We have a child coming, and you are still not willing to give us another chance?"

"You mean give you another chance." I was still calm, but I could feel a storm coming. "Our Summer is over Fen," I explained. "The sun doesn't last forever."

"What the hell does that even mean?"

"It means we had our good times and as hard as it was to leave you, I had to." I paused. He said nothing. "I was dying Fen and you couldn't see that."

"I don't understand. They said you couldn't have children."

"You seem disappointed that I've been blessed with a second chance."

He swatted the air as though warding off a pest. "I'm not saying that. I know how badly you wanted this. We both wanted it."

"But?"

"I thought I would be there when we had a child! Now I'll just be looking on from the outside."

Unexpectedly, he came to me and fell on his knees gripping my belly.

"Lana, think hard about this decision. It's not about just you and me anymore."

I stroked his head, wanting to take some of the blame, but refusing. There was still more to tell him. I couldn't look back, and there was no desire in my heart to do so. I had wasted too many tears and spent too many sleepless nights on foolishness to ever go back to that place in my life. It was time to move on.

When I first left, I thought my world would crumble, but I became stronger. I didn't think I could ever wash his scent from my mind, but I had no desire to be with him anymore. If I had not left that night, I am sure I would still be with him now, and Fen would be on his road to destruction, taking everyone involved along with him.

He gathered his emotions, stood and paced the floor again. I felt his pain, confusion, and anguish, which made it harder to go on.

"I have more to tell you."

He stopped and looked at me. He became impatient when I didn't say anything.

"Then tell me." His face was stern, and he dug in for what he knew was more bad news. "Tell me, Lana!" He yelled.

"We won't know until the baby is born who the father is."

Turning his back to me, he went to the living room window and looked out into the city. He was so silent and distant, time stood still. I wished I had put some music on or turned on the television. The quiet was deafening.

Without warning, he turned to me. The look on his face was one I couldn't define, but chills went through me. He took three steps and for the first time since the ordeal began, I was afraid. I closed my eyes and said a silent prayer. He stopped.

He looked through me like the night he realized Sterling and I had been together. "Call me when you have the baby. I want a test."

He picked up his keys and headed for the door.

"Don't go like this."

He spun around again to face me. "What Lana? What do you want from me? You want me to beg? Hmm? You know what keeps me coming? I know you still love me. I feel it every time I'm around you. Well, Lana, I've already begged, and I'm probably not finished. Your love holds me right here, and I'm not done, but if you want this guy, make sure he's who you really want because when I fold I'm done, and you don't want me to be done."

He was gone.

An hour later my phone lit up. It was Fen.

"Are you okay?" I was concerned about him since he left.

"You still taking care of me?"

"I know this wasn't what you wanted."

"It's what I've always wanted. I just wish it was under other circumstances." He hesitated. "I want the baby to be mine. Now I have to live the consequences. Thank you for being honest with me. Now I understand how you felt about me having Solomon and him not being yours. I feel like I'm getting every hurt back I've given."

I didn't respond. Maybe he was, and he had to experience these things in order to understand what he did. I was drying tears for days. There were times I didn't think I would make it through, but I knew I never wanted to find myself in that place again. But once again I was thinking only of the crimes *he* committed. Wouldn't I be judged the same?

"Lana. I know I don't have the right to ask, but consider giving us another chance?"

I was silent. Tears for his pain came because I had been there. "It's time to move on Fen. I don't trust you with my heart anymore."

It took seven years, but I could finally say goodbye. After saying those words, I felt free and honest with myself.

Chapter Twenty-Eight

I was nearing my last day at work. My assistant, Courtney, planned a surprise baby shower and the church another. It was the first time I realized I didn't have any close friends.

I never had sisters, but two brothers yielded me two sister-in-laws. Only my brother, Keanu, lived close by. I saw him and his wife briefly during holidays and cookouts. But the busy lives that Fen and I led didn't yield much time for them.

Clark asked about my family. I missed them. They didn't know Fen and I were no longer together. It was time to let them know everything, especially since the baby could come at any time.

Sterling picked me up to go to a cookout. I was tired and didn't feel much like going, but he never asked for much, so after a few puppy dog eyes and promises to duck in and out, I conceded.

We arrived to the house, and it was amazing. The lawn was well-manicured, with gardens all over the grounds, and I spotted a beautiful gazebo in the corner of the backyard. I already knew where I would be sitting. Ever since I was a young girl, I dreamt of having a gazebo where I could escape and read my books and live out my fairy tales. I smiled, remembering I once had dreams. Now that I was grown, it could become a place of solitude.

I waddled to the door, feeling ugly and huge. Had his family not met me before, there would have been no way I would have agreed.

Sterling's brother, Shane, and his wife Nancy answered the door both smiling and excited. "Wow!" Shane said looking at my huge stomach. "Is this what my wife is going to look like?"

My eyes went to Nancy, and she smiled. "Sterling didn't tell me."

"Sterling didn't know," Sterling replied mouth gaping. "We need to talk."

The two brothers embraced and slapped one another's back. Sterling was so happy for his brother I wanted this baby to be his.

"Your home is beautiful," I said hugging Nancy.

Nancy and Shane looked at one another. "We'll make sure Sterling gives you a tour before you leave." The two laughed before escorting us towards the back of the house and onto the massive backyard deck. Sterling beamed with pride.

"Surprise!" People yelled from their small groups scattered throughout the yard.

Clark ran up the deck steps and did the best she could to embrace me, maneuvering around my massive stomach. My mouth dropped as I scanned everyone. Most I didn't know, but my eyes stopped when I saw a familiar face. My brother Keanu and his wife Tiffany were smiling from the crowd and next to Keanu was my older brother Ozi.

I turned away from everyone and cried. Everyone believed they were happy tears, but they were tears of shame. They hit me like a wave. We were so lost finding our way through our lives; we neglected the things that were precious to us, our family, who were the people who loved us.

Over the years my dysfunctional marriage had pulled me further and further from them because I was so busy portraying this perfect life that I knew would be transparent to them. Now they were here and there was nowhere to hide. The truth would have to be told.

In so many ways I had become my mother, distant and alienated from my family. She wasn't happy with her life. I felt that through her hurtful words and many disappearances. I felt it the most through the harsh lessons she felt she needed to teach me.

Strong arms engulfed me and I knew it was my big brother Ozi who protected me all my life. He knew what my tears meant. He always knew.

"Why didn't you call me, Star?" No one called me that except him.

I turned and held onto him, making sure he was real. I missed him, and although I was the youngest we had the closest bond.

"Shhhh," he whispered. "I understand why and we will catch up later, but now let's celebrate my new nephew."

Relief filled my spirit and I nodded doing as he said, as I always had. He handed me back to Sterling and went to join Keanu, who didn't have a clue and remained smiling.

Sterling wrapped his arm around my waist and held onto me. As people came to us, he introduced them and told me stories about each.

"Aunt Mable, this is Lana." Aunt Mable squeezed me between two of the biggest boobs I had ever seen in my life. They were so big they hung around her waist like a belt.

"I tease Clark and tell her that one day she will have those same mountains." He whispered. One look at Clark and I knew she knew exactly what Sterling had shared with me.

"No you won't." I mouthed to her and she licked her tongue at her dad.

Then there was Uncle Adolph who liked to pinch butts; anyone's butt. When he hugged me Sterling quickly stepped in.

"Whooa Uncle Adolph, this one's mine!" The seventy something year old looked disappointed, but walked away to find someone else to hug.

There was his cousin Belle, who was absolutely stunning. She was dark chocolate with sharp cheekbones and a pointed nose. Her hair was locked and pinned up on top of her head. Her abs and legs were to die for. She made sure she showed them off in her short shorts and midriff top.

"She's a personal trainer," Sterling whispered when he saw me admiring her physique. "I like you just the way you are, so don't get any ideas."

Belle appeared to have latched onto Ozi, and he seemed to enjoy the attention. Soon she was stripped down to her bikini and beckoning for him to join her in the pool. I laughed knowing Ozi was not going anywhere near the pool.

Everyone danced around the beautiful abstract shaped body of water with its Aztec designs etched in the bottom. They sang, drank, ate the catered barbecue, and laughed.

Ozi approached and took my hand leading me away from Sterling and to the Gazebo I spotted when we first arrived. Sterling whispered something in his ear and he nodded in agreement.

"What are you two up to?"

"Just enjoy the evening Star."

There were three sets of steps to enter the Gazebo's platform, and a swing hanging from the roof near the rear where there were no steps. A ceiling fan hung in the trellis style center with a light. On the back was a railing and behind it trees scattered throughout the yard creating a beautiful backdrop.

"This is beautiful!" It was everything I imagined as a child.

He helped me onto the swing then sat next to me. It was like old times when we were kids. We were always huddled up somewhere talking.

"I'm not going to ask you what happened between you and Fen. You can share that with me if you wish, but this is not the time for that."

I hung my head. I felt the shame a girl must feel when she thought she disappointed her father.

He lifted my chin. "Who is Sterling?"

I laughed nervously out loud. "It would be easier to talk about Fen and me." The look on his face was so intense, I looked away.

He turned my head back to him. "Who is this man that Keanu and I knew nothing about?"

I hugged him, again making sure he was real. He rubbed my arm. And gently pushed me back, waiting for my answer.

"I see you love him, but don't you think you need some time between him and Fen?"

I laughed again. "Oh boy. We do have a lot to talk about." Seeing the concern in his expression, I knew I had to tell him something. "Oz, Fen and I have lived in the same house for the past seven years marching to our own drum. I walked out on him almost a year ago. I believe knowing and spending time with Sterling gave me the strength to do that. He showed me how I deserved to be treated, not just loved, but treated."

"So, he's a rebound?"

"Nooo. I wouldn't call him that. He was my friend first." I grabbed both of Ozi's hands. I needed him to hear what I had to say and not judge our relationship.

"So, you were friends with benefits?"

I snatched my hands away. Sometimes, like our mother, Ozi could think the worst of me.

"No Ozi, I'm not a whore! Sterling and I were friends for almost a year before I gave him the goods!"

"I see your smart mouth hasn't changed."

We both laughed.

"Not much," I assured him.

He wrapped his arm around my shoulder and pulled me in close and we leaned back and swung.

"Twinkle, Twinkle, my little Star. I've missed you." He looked through the top of the gazebo. "One thing I can say about this guy is he loves you. But so did Fen." He looked down at me. "Everything had to be perfect for you. He wanted this to be an occasion you would never forget."

"He is so sweet and loving Oz. The entire time he was helping me with my ordeal, he never asked me anything personal. He made me laugh and kept me company when I was lonely, but not once did he tell me he was nursing his dying wife."

"We talked. He told me a little about his life and how you met. He also told me he was the father no matter what and he would be here for you always."

I smiled. That was my Sterling, and I didn't expect anything less. "So Dad, can I keep him?"

Ozi turned serious. His forehead wrinkled. "He's not a puppy Lana. He's a man with feelings, and he has a lot of them for you. Are you ready to make that commitment to someone again? It didn't last with Fen, and he loved you."

"Fen has had a mistress for the past ten years and a six-year-old child as evidence."

I watched the surprise on his face and surprise slowly turned to anger. "Why didn't you call me?"

"So you could come and beat him up?" I laughed again.

I felt like I was ten years old again. No one messed with Ozi's little sister. This was the reason I never told him about the boy who waited for me daily. His older brother was known to carry and I didn't want anything to happen to Oz, but I would sacrifice my mother. What I didn't know, until I was fourteen, was that Oz packed as well. I was sure my mother told him, because after talking to her the boy never bothered me again. I never really dated because boys were afraid to ask me out. He was Sounder, barking at the front door.

He smiled. "Maybe I would have come and knocked some sense into him."

Standing up, he pulled me to my feet with both hands. "We better get back. Sterling has looked this way twice in the last three minutes."

We slowly walked back to the party, me leaning on his chest and him holding on like I may disappear again. "I've only been around him in the last twenty-four hours, but he seems solid."

The last twenty-four hours?

Sterling met us at the foot of the deck stairs. "We need to borrow her so she can open her gifts."

Reluctantly, Ozi let me go, and I was escorted up the deck steps by Sterling. In the center was a table full of gifts and I no longer felt guilty for not shopping. I hadn't expected all of this from people who didn't know me.

Clark sat me in a chair in the middle of the deck and placed a paper plate, with ribbons on both sides, neatly on my head, securing a bow, using the hanging ribbons, under my chin. Shane was aligning the camera to video the event.

Each gift had a sailor theme, which helped me decide how I would do the baby's room since I hadn't decided. The last present was a beautiful box. I lifted the lid. Inside was a much smaller box

"Here. Let me help you with that one. It may be a little heavy."

Sterling removed the small box and bent on one knee.

Gasps and murmurs spread throughout the yard. I was confused and didn't know what was going on. Sterling opened the purple, silver and gold box and presented the biggest Princess cut diamond I had ever seen. Each side was flanked with three smaller diamonds in a triangle pattern, then two diamonds on the band.

"When we met, it seemed like a story that was already written, and we just had to play out our parts. I watched you for two months before I had the nerve to approach you because you were beautiful and scary. I watched you shoot down one guy after another." Everyone chuckled.

"When I finally got the nerve to approach you, I discovered your bark was worse than your bite.

"I got to know you in one room full of strangers and long walks. I thought I had loved to my limit and I would never love again. Love is tricky, and it's not always good times. When you truly lay your heart on the line exposing all of you, love sometimes hurts, but you showed me it's good to love with that right person. That's when I knew you were mine, but for reasons I'm not going to get into, I didn't know how that would be possible.

"I want to look at your smile every day and enjoy the time we have together. Life changes have shown me not to take anything for granted so it makes no sense for me to search for something I already have right in front of me. I just knew you were my promise from God, and that if I endured, like Job, He would give me everything I lost and even more. I couldn't have ask for a better gift."

He was crying. I wiped his tears, and he dried mine. The fear to openly give all of me again disappeared, and the hidden sun returned, with His beautiful countenance shining down on the two of us as a blessing and a promise. This was one promise that wouldn't be broken because *He* is the promise keeper.

"As soon as possible, will you marry me Milana Elise Fenney?" He asked sliding the ring of my dreams onto my finger.

I looked to my big brother Ozi, who was smiling. Keanu was beside him, still oblivious to all the unspoken words.

I just wanted to breathe and live in the moment, and take things as they came, but my personality never allowed me to do that. I was always second guessing everything, weighing them out, calculating, so, in that moment I thought of all the wonderful times we spent together, the laughs we shared and tears we'd spilled. What was left? What would I find out there? I had everything right there in from of me. And like Sterling said, there was no sense in me searching for something I already had. I didn't want to look back at this moment and regret letting the most beautiful and loving man I had ever met slip out of my life.

In the end all we had was now and all I wanted in the past year was him. I wanted to wake up to that sunshiny smile every day and I couldn't get caught up on what ifs. I had to let my past go, because it represented nothing more than a photo album of memories.

The future wasn't promised. There would be overcast and sunshine, but we would make it through together, I was sure of that. The seasons change, but as long as we wore our raincoat, boots and tank tops I was certain we would be okay, even with the unresolved paternity issue we had ahead of us.

"Will you love me with all of your heart, and take care of me when things get rough? When things aren't beautiful, and I need more of you, will you still love me?" I whispered.

"Yes!"

"I'm not perfect, but you showed me that I deserve to be loved." I hesitated. "Make sure you're sure, because if I say yes Sterling, I'm all in. I don't know how to love halfway."

"You're my everything Lana and my love for you is real, it's now and forever yours. You're worth every pound of my love. Let me love you forever and renew your faith in love. Let me show you what love, real love, should feel like."

I took so long to answer, he gripped my hand.

I hugged him and whispered in his ear. "Yes. I'll be yours forever. You already make me a believer again."

He held on tight as he stood with me in his arms. Turning to face family and friends, he beamed as he yelled, "She said yes!" He put me down gently and kissed me. "She said yes!" He whispered in my ear. He wept and rocked me as we danced to the music only he heard.

Everyone cheered, laughed and hugged one another.

My brother Ozi came and hugged me. "I drilled that Bama like he was in my court. He's a solid dude sis, and if you're happy, then I'm happy for you."

They came to admire my ring and say their congratulations. Once that was done I realized how tired I was, but didn't want to leave my family. Ozi ensured me he was there for a few more days.

"Unless you just want to go home, you can take a nap upstairs and rejoin use when you're done. When my people come, you have to put them out," Sterling teased.

"Why don't you take her on a tour," Nancy suggested.

"I don't want to put you out, Nancy. I can go home."

"Well, why don't you go on a tour and then decide."

Sterling took me through the basement with the theatre room and gym. There was a bar in the main room; he referred to as the party room and an in-law suite complete with its own kitchen, bathroom, bedroom and great room. In the back was another room that wasn't finished. Off to the side of the bar was a shower area, and laundry room with steps that lead to the yard behind the house.

We returned to the main floor and saw the office, kitchen, family room, sunroom, dining and living room, before going to the last level. On the top floor, there were four bedrooms, strategically laid out. In the main hall, there were two bedrooms on one side that Sterling explained were Jack and Jill bedrooms, and they were connected by a single bathroom between them. He didn't take me to the other bedroom right away. Instead, we went down another corridor, in the center of the hall that was flanked with books on both sides and stairs on the opposite end leading down into a sitting area and then back up into another bedroom.

When we entered the room, there was silver furniture, and the decor was highlights of purple silver, gold with hints of turquoise.

"This is beautiful. Remember, I told you I was thinking about carrying these colors into my bedroom."

"I know. When I saw this, I knew you would love it. I said 'Self. Lana would love this room'"

I laughed at him teasing me. The bathroom was just as eloquent.

"I forgot to show you the other room at the end of the hall and if you want you can nap there."

We backtracked to the main hall, where he led me to the last room. He opened the door and allowed me to step in first.

I gasped at the beauty of the room. There were sailboats hanging from the ceiling and the most unique gray crib to break up the red and blues. A distressed, gray stained rocking chair, and a full-size bed, decorated with so many pillows, tastefully accented the room.

"When he's asleep we can lay in here and watch him. If you want you can lay in here and nurse him."

"What?"

"This is my first wedding gift to you. This is our new house if you like it."

I covered my mouth. I was amazed at how well he listened to me, from the gazebo to the bedroom decor.

I went to the beautifully decorated bed and touched the boat-shaped pillow. Sterling joined me.

I turned and kissed him, starting something I wasn't sure I was ready to ignite. We avoided this moment since the night at the hotel.

His kiss lingered gently parting my lips as it became more intimate. The question danced in his eyes as he checked for boundary points.

Slowly, he backed me to the beautifully decorated bed and lowered me, pushing the pillows to the side. Careful not to put any weight on me, he ran his hand up my thigh and under my dress.

"I've wanted to touch you for so long Lana. But, I didn't want to cross any boundaries."

I burned for his touch for weeks now. "Take care of me, Sterling." I wanted him since the first night I found him again at the sports bar, but as always I was trying to be the good girl. Now I needed to feel him, to be with him, to know him.

Moving down, he kissed my belly. My breasts were so large. I felt like they were in the way, but he found use for them. Stimulating my every being, he made love to me for the first time since our first time.

I moaned, "Mmm," realizing how long it had been.

"Shhhh," he hissed covering my mouth with his again.

"What you waiting for?" I asked feeling his reluctance. "It's all yours. You can put your name on it."

We both laughed.

"Whose is it?" he asked.

"Yours. You have my heart, Sterling. Take care of it."

"Yes ma'am," he moaned and ever so gently entered me lifting my legs to pull me in closer.

We got carried away in the serenity of our passion, after such a tortured period of turbulence. The higher we went, the higher I became, filled with a love he renewed in me with every stroke, higher and higher, until I was on the ceiling hanging onto a feeling. I didn't want to come down, but to stay there with him, safe from all the things that could destroy the beauty of the love we found some years ago. Free to accept what he was offering, I took it all and held onto it afraid to let it go.

"Not yet," I moaned feeling he was ready. I moaned as the waves began to rise. "I'm here!" I yelled.

He released the inevitable, making a face that made me laugh between the ripples, as I came down. He laughed with me.

Panting, we tried to catch our breath. I was drenched and in need of a shower, but felt more tired than dirty.

"I don't remember you being this loud." He teased.

"I don't remember you making those faces."

"Touché."

He pulled my dress down to make me more respectable and laid with me. The baby kicked.

"You okay?" he asked concerned.

"Yea." I turned to my side to face him.

I thought of the evening's events and looked at my ring. I wanted to admire it again.

"Do you like it?" He beamed.

"I love it."

I looked around the beautiful room again. "How is it that you have known me for only two years and yet you know me so well?"

"I listened to everything you said, remembering every conversation and savoring every word."

"What would you have done if I said no in front of all those people? I didn't even know until that moment."

"Picked my face up off the ground."

I laughed. "Seriously."

"Seriously. What could I do? I don't get bent out of shape when things don't go my way. It just means the timing is bad, or there's better than you out there for me." He winked.

I punched him in his arms then relaxed in their safety.

I didn't sleep very long. The sun was still up when I woke, but I felt renewed. The memory of his kiss lingered on my lips. I sat on the end of the bed but heard nothing. The house was quiet, and the door chimes were not going off. The small push on my bladder reminded me of the weight I carried.

When I entered the hall, there was no movement. I eased downstairs, and all the baby gifts were arranged in the dining room and the kitchen was totally clean. Ozi was standing in his robe, pouring a cup of coffee from the pot on the counter. I couldn't believe he went swimming.

"Hey," I said. I looked at the stove, and it was seven-thirty.

Ozi came around the counter to greet me. "Did you sleep well?"

"Yes, but everyone left already?"

Ozi looked at the time on the stove and laughed. "Yes. We told them you needed your beauty sleep and they should go home."

"Everyone was having such a good time. I didn't mean for them to leave." I was so disappointed to ruin everyone's fun.

"You're such a prima!"

"I'm not! Why do you say that?"

"Lana. It is seven-thirty in the morning."

He laughed so hard I thought he would wake the dead. His laughter was contagious, and soon we were both laughing.

He came around the counter and bear hugged me, kissing all over my face. I laughed so hard I wet my pants. When it wouldn't stop, I realized it wasn't pee at all. My water broke!

I laughed even harder when I saw the look on his face when his feet got wet. "That's nasty Lana. You gonna pee on me and laugh about it?"

"That's not pee stupid. My water broke." My first contraction came, and I laughed through it.

"Let me go get Sterling," he said and ran up the stairs two steps at a time cursing.

Within minutes a hungover Sterling came stumbling downstairs. He found me standing in the middle of the kitchen laughing and my arms out to the sides and a puddle on the floor.

"Are you okay?" He asked, placing his hand on my stomach.

"Yes, but I don't have a change of clothes."

Sterling looked around. "It is entirely too early for this Carter."

Another contraction came. I thought it seemed like it was too quick. But, I knew God had everything under control.

"Let me get you some of Clark's gym clothes she keeps here."

"You need to hurry." He looked concerned with those words, so I had to add, "I'm dripping all over the place."

He disappeared into the laundry room and got a towel, and started wiping me down. He pulled my dress over my head then wrapped the same towel around me. Lifting me, he carried me up the steps and took me down the hall to his bathroom.

The shower was in the middle of the room and formed a circle encased in glass. He turned on the water that came from the ceiling. My now wet undergarments were removed and there was a towel and washcloth already on the side wall. He grabbed the cloth and soap and ushered me into the shower washing me from head to toe. Once done he dried me and helped me put on Clark's gym clothes tucking them under my belly.

Another contraction came, and I bent over.

"Breathe Lana. Don't hold your breath. Breathe through them, breathe through." He instructed me.

"Mmmm." This was a lot stronger than when I went into labor with Lena. I breathed until it went away.

Sterling led me back downstairs and sat me in the kitchen chair. "If you mess up this chair that's okay because it's yours," he said laughing.

He returned upstairs, and Ozi came down. He laughed at my outfit. "You look really pretty."

I cut my eyes at him and tossed my hair, realizing for the first time that it was all over my head. My mouth dropped open in horror. "Stop laughing Ozi and find me something to put it up or it will be tangled when it dries." I tried to smooth it with my hands and twist it around, but it was already drying from getting wet in the shower. The one thing Sade didn't bless me with was her soft controllable locks.

Another contraction came. Oz held my hand through the pain and Sterling walked in the kitchen laughing at the sight of me doubled over with both hands in the air holding my hair in a ponytail. Sterling found a ribbon on my plate hat Clark created the day before, and tied my hair. Then we were off to the hospital. It was a time of joy, but the drama would soon follow.

Chapter Twenty-Nine

As Sterling predicted, Carter Xavier was born at one-fifteen in the afternoon, weighing in at eight pounds-twelve ounces and twenty-one inches long.

Sterling examined every finger and toe, kissing each one. My emotions were in overload when they placed my little miracle on my chest. Blubbering like a baby, I held onto him not wanting to share him with the many aunts, uncles and cousins who came to welcome him to the family. Everyone was there except Fen.

Once the room cleared, and the family returned to their homes, Sterling called Fen. His presence would have brought far too many whispers and questions.

When he arrived, I saw the disappointment on his face. He greeted Sterling and Ozi before turning his attention to Carter and me. He didn't care that Sterling was present. He pushed my hair back and kissed me. "You okay?"

"Yes."

"Why didn't you call me?"

Disappointment radiated in his words. He had been deprived of Carter's birth. The question hung in the air awaiting my answer.

Clark looked at him with contempt, causing Sterling to usher her out of the room. "We're going to give you two some privacy." Ozi followed.

"I thought it better," I answered once everyone was gone.

"For who?"

He walked to the sink and washed his hands. A sleeping Carter lay in his new bed like a cocoon.

Fen lifted him and held him close looking down. "What's his name?"

"Carter Xavier."

"What's his last name?"

"I haven't decided. Fenney for now."

He nodded his head in agreement. "Was Sterling here the entire time?" He didn't look at me as the interrogation continued, letting me know he already knew the answer. I felt the storm building. His hands trembled. He wanted a fight. His eyes darted up, staring me in the face, waiting for his answer.

"This is a very awkward situation, Fen. Everything happened so fast and I was already with Sterling." I tried to explain in a way that made sense to him.

"But you deprived me of the opportunity to experience my child being born!" He yelled louder than I know he wanted, matching his hurt.

Sterling peeped in the room. "Is everything okay?" He looked at me for confirmation.

"Everything is fine Mr. McNeil!" Fen answered, fully displaying his anger.

Sterling entered the room so quickly I had no time to get up and stop what appeared to become hostile very quickly. I only had time to raise my hand, halting his approach.

Ozi entered behind Sterling. He stood evaluating the situation as he was trained to do as a judge. When he saw there was a stalemate, as the two men faced off for a second time, he touched Sterling's arm. "Let's give them a few minutes and go talk."

Sterling didn't move until I nodded my head. Clark now stood in the doorway, confused, looking to her father for understanding.

"You stay outside the door in case you need to come get me," Sterling instructed Clark.

"Okay," a dumbfounded Clark answered glaring at Fen.

Fen sat in the chair closest to my bed cradling Carter.

"I know you're upset, but for a change, I did what worked for me, and this worked for me."

"I can never get this moment back, Lana! There is no re-do button you can push."

"I know this is not what you wanted Fen, but this was best." I tried to stay calm and positive.

"I know this is my fault, Lana!" he said again raising his voice. "You don't have to throw it in my face. I remind myself every day."

Clark peeped in again, and again I raised my hand.

Annoyed Fen crinkled his face and looked at me. "Who is this chick?"

"There was no easy decision. Do you think this was easy? This should be an exciting time for me, but instead I have knots in my stomach, trying to please everyone, and I can't!"

"I didn't think you would deprive me of my rights as a father. What if he turns out to be mine, then what?"

"And what if it turns out that he's not yours?"

"That would work out perfectly in your new life with your new man. Right?" He was standing again.

This time Clark entered the room, walking to the center, and said, with all the calm she could muster, "I don't know who you are or what's going on, but I think it best you leave."

Fen looked back at me. This conversation would not play out today, and nothing was going to come of it.

"Clark is right. Why don't we have this conversation when you calm down?"

"We can have this conversation later, but you're not depriving me of another minute with my son."

"That has not been determined."

"You don't want him to be mine, do you, because that would mean you're stuck with me? Right?" I was silent. "Well, like isn't perfect Lana. Life is not something wrapped with a bow. It's cruel and unforgiving. It watches and laughs at you with each mistake you make."

"Is that what you think? You think I don't forgive you?" My voice softened so he could hear through his hurt. "Fen, I forgave you the night I walked out the door."

"I gave you everything! Tell me one thing you wanted that I didn't provide for you."

"I wanted *you* Fen, but, you couldn't buy that. Buying me everything you think I wanted was easy. You and your time were priceless, and that was all I ever wanted. I didn't want or need those material things. They were for you to make you feel at ease for your infidelities."

He was quiet, which was normal after I pointed out his shortcomings. He was thinking about my words.

"If he turns out to be mine, will you please give us a chance to start over? I promise Lana, I'll be faithful."

"We've been there before Fen."

I became emotional, forgetting Clark was there to witness my words. "You're the worst. You put me through hell. You knew the pain I was in, and it didn't matter to you. Over and over again I endured because I loved you with all my being. You think because I didn't know for years it doesn't count? But ask yourself Fen, did I ever have all of you?

"You fragmented yourself all over the place and continued to walk down the middle of that road. Walking that thin line, you thought you could keep everyone happy. You didn't even see I was dying a slow death inside," I was sobbing, holding my chest. "I don't know how to love halfway Fen, so I rejected Sterling who never wanted to do anything, but give me his all. He stood in the shadows of your hurt, and he didn't deserve that.

"I know it hurts to hear, but I've moved on. Sterling taught me I can't live my life in the shadows of your hurt, so I let it go, all the hurt, all the pain. I let it go so I could forgive you, and me for feeling I failed you. Now forgive yourself. Let it go Fen. I don't hurt anymore, and I will always love you. But I will never trust you with my heart again."

He turned his back and looked down at Carter and let out a cleansing breath. He was trying to regain control over his emotions. "Are you truly in love with this guy Lana, or is he a rebound."

I smiled remembering the night before and the walks at the harbor. I thought of all our conversations. "You want the truth?"

"I asked."

He was looking for closure. "I love him Fen. He's no rebound. We were friends long before we became lovers. We started with a foundation. You and I started with an idea of love, based on our twisted examples. We didn't know how important our words were. We didn't understand time could never be regained. We thought consequences were someone else's reality, but we are living proof they are real.

"So, yes, I pray with all my heart that Carter is Sterling's child, so he can have a fair beginning, which is more than we had or that Solomon was given. One day you are going to have to tell Solomon the truth."

The room seemed to swallow him up. The swing of his body twisting back and forth, as he thought about my words, let me know he was hearing me. After a few minutes, he asked, "Are you marrying him."

"Yes."

"Then I will have my lawyer send the paperwork by tomorrow."

I stood by my bed waiting for his next move or question. He walked towards me and gave me a long hug followed by a kiss. "I will always love you Lana, and I don't care who you marry, you will always be my girl. I... Give the baby Sterling's last name. It will be yours soon."

He handed Carter to me, turned on his heels and headed to the door, walking by a tearful Clark, but not stopping. He had thrown up the white flag and given up the fight.

Clark remained standing in the center of the room. She was confused by what had just happened. Tears flowing, she never moved from her post as she looked at me with contempt.

"I'm sorry you had to witness that," I said.

"I don't understand. I thought Carter was my dad's son."

"He is," I said in a quiet voice.

"Then why does he believe Carter is his child?"

Not sure how much Sterling had revealed about our relationship, I gave her the only answer I could. "You may want to have that conversation with your dad."

"I'm asking you!" She yelled angrily.

"I think you need to talk with Sterling, Clark," I repeated.

"You are no different than my mother. You used my dad just like she did. You don't deserve him."

"I would never use your dad. I love him."

"You have him running around telling everyone about his child. Is Carter his child?" The veins in her neck stood out as she yelled like a child having a temper tantrum.

Sterling burst into the room. "What's going on?"

Clark spun around to face her dad. "Is Carter your child?"

Sterling turned to me questioning me with his eyes.

"Why are you looking at her? I asked *you* the question and why is no one willing to answer my question?"

Sterling pulled a chair closer to Clark. "Have a seat, Clark."

"No! I hear just fine standing." Crossing her arms, she dug in and stood her ground like the spoiled child she was.

"I'm not asking you, I'm telling you. Have a seat!"

Reluctantly, an angry Clark sat on the chair he provided her. Her arms defensively crossed her chest.

"Ozi, can you have a seat too, because I'm saying this only once and this is for your ears only."

Ozi sat in the oversized chair and reclined. The two looked to Sterling to explain.

"I saw Lana many years before I ever said hello. I met her at one of the lowest points of my life. I was taking care of the only person I believed I would ever love. We bonded immediately coming from a similar kinship. She was going through something at home, and I never asked her, and she never told me. Because she never spoke ill of her husband, I had a different level of respect for her. Not *once* did she speak badly of him, yet during that time he repeatedly broke her heart.

"We became friends and confidants, and the later was inevitable. We fell in love."

He turned and looked at Clark. "We had one night of indiscretion, and I realize the chances of Carter being my child is narrow, but I believe he is, as much as I believe we did not come together by chance. All that has happened was orchestrated."

He walked to me. "This woman was told she would not be able to have a child. EVER! Yet there's a baby boy in her arms. This is bigger than all of us."

He walked to Clark and stooped to her level. "She didn't lie to me. She could have, but she didn't. I told her Carter was mine and I didn't need a blood test to prove it. She is not your mother. Your mother was not an honest person, but I won't speak ill of the dead, or air her dirty laundry, but as long as I live, you will give Lana the same respect you give me. Do you understand?"

"Yes Daddy," she replied as a young child would to their parent.

Sterling hugged her. "I love you Clark, but you don't have to keep protecting me. I see people for who they are."

Standing, he walked to Carter and took him. "The only reason we are getting a blood test is for Fenney. He has requested it." He paused before continuing. "I don't want Carter to grow up in life and believe he is less, because of how he was conceived or whose he is, but for now it is what it is." He kissed the squirming baby and quickly Carter turned his head out of reflex.

"Give him to me. He needs to nurse." I reached my arms out and received our miracle.

Ozi was smiling. I could tell that he liked Sterling. He went to him and slapped him on the back. "Man, we need some cigars to celebrate." He was always light-hearted, the optimist and jokester of the family. But even with all his joking, our struggle was long from being over. Now that our miracle was here, the work was just beginning.

Chapter Thirty

True to Fen's word, a courier arrived at the hospital the next day with paperwork. It was our final paperwork for the divorce. Although I didn't ask for anything, Fen gave me the Harbor house and alimony until I remarried, then it would stop. He still believed money was my motivator for being with him.

Quickly I signed, stuffed everything back in the huge manila envelope, and put it in the bottom of my bag. I didn't expect it, but I cried. I cried so much my nurse became concerned, believing I was experiencing postpartum depression. I let her think what she wanted so everyone would stop asking me questions.

Fen called to see if I received the paperwork and I burst into tears again. He was in my room within thirty minutes.

He held me while I cried. "I thought this was what you wanted."

I didn't say anything. Wanting something and receiving it were two different things. By signing the paperwork, I was unhooking the life support from our dead marriage. I wanted to move on, but signing the paperwork made me a participant in its destruction.

"I'm okay." I sat up. Sterling would be there soon, and I didn't need him seeing me in Fen's arms. "I signed the paperwork. It's in my bag. Or would you prefer I send it to the lawyers?" The tears came again.

Saddened to hear my words, he said nothing. I knew he thought I changed my mind. He would never understand how I felt at that moment.

"No. You mail them when you're ready."

He wasn't going to help me end this. Coming to be that tower of strength for me was beginning to wear on him. The clock was ticking. Soon he would not be able to keep it together. I didn't know what to expect after that.

I wondered where his precious Rose was. He no longer had the stress of existing between two women. I never thought about it until then. The change in our dynamics would also change the reality of their relationship. There was no longer Lana to blame or hide behind, there was just the two of them, and they had to deal with the real world he said he escaped when he was with her. Once I was gone, there would have to be someone else to fill the void of the escape in theory. He would soon learn there was no such thing as escaping life.

Sterling walked in and stopped abruptly. Watching the two size each other up, I knew that eventually they would erupt. They wanted the same thing and there was just one of me.

I thought Sterling would be his kind cordial self, but he was flexing. Walking directly to me, he greeted me with a kiss on the lips. "How are you feeling?"

"I'm fine. Waiting for the doctor to release us."

"It will be good to get the two of you home."

Sterling frowned. He was watching me, and then he looked at Fen strangely. Then I realized what he was examining. My eyes must have still been puffy from the tears I cried all morning.

"Everything alright?"

"Yes. Postpartum depression."

I tried to hide behind a smile, but was unsuccessful and could tell by his expression; he didn't believe me. His eyes washed over my face. I shook my head in answer to the unspoken question. It was futile. He knew me better in almost two short years than Fen in our nearly twenty years together.

His awareness made me tumble fast into the abyss I had just fought my way out of. Sitting on the edge of the bed, he held me.

"Do you want me to ask him to leave?" He whispered in my ear.

The nurse entered the room saving me from once again being put in the middle of the two.

"Good afternoon!" She was more chipper than my last nurse. "I am Nurse Tina, and I will be with you until seven tonight."

She stopped updating the information on the whiteboard. "I saw they offered you meds for postpartum depression, and you declined. If you would like to take them, we can give you formula to feed the baby."

Sterling wiped my eyes. Fen looked on intently.

"No thank you," I answered. "I'll be okay."

"Well if you change your mind, let me know. Postpartum depression is real."

She waited for an answer. When I shook my head, she left the room.

"You okay Lana?" Fen asked, more to irritate Sterling.

I could feel Sterling tense. I squeezed him.

"I'll be okay Fen."

"She's fine. I'm here now, so if you want you can go."

Sterling was irritated by his presence. I was familiar with his tone. It was the same tone he gave Fen the night Fen exposed us.

Fen pulled up a chair and sat. He was not going to make things easy for Sterling. Sterling, in turn, sat in bed with me and placed his arm around my shoulders, marking his territory. They had me twisted like the winds of a tornado out of control and all over the place. Both loved me. Another woman may have felt a sense of pride, but I only felt trapped between the two storms.

The nurse returned to the room. "Your doctor ordered this shot for you. It doesn't affect the baby, and it will calm you."

"Can I take it when everyone leaves, Tina?"

"Sure. Buzz me when you're ready." She left the room again.

Resting on Sterling's chest, I could smell his cologne for the first time since he arrived. I let it distract me from what was unfolding in the room. Closing my eyes, I enjoyed the calm. I needed to be alone with him.

"How do you like the new house?" Fen asked smirking.

Sterling snickered. "Are you still keeping tabs on me Fenney?"

"Just protecting my interest."

Oh, my God!

Sterling tensed. Fen hit a nerve. "How is Rose?"

Touché.

Nothing.

"Stop it you two." I kept my eyes closed. "If you want to have a pissing contest it won't be in here."

Opening my eyes, I sat upright, leaving the comfort of Sterling's body. I got up and walked to the bag on the floor behind the recliner. Reaching deep into its bottom, I pulled out the envelope that contained the divorce paperwork.

"Lana," Fen was beginning to object. "I didn't mean for you to..."

"No. I don't want to play this game with the two of you. I'm not a pawn."

Walking to Fen I offered the paperwork, but he wouldn't take it. The hurt on his face was heart-wrenching, but I stood my ground. "Take it Fen." I knelt beside him. "I'm not going to change my mind. I'm sorry I couldn't be what you needed me to be."

"It wasn't you Lana it was me. Everything was my fault, but I don't think this is what you want."

I sighed. This was our closure, and I thought it unfair to display our dirt in Sterling's presence, but it had to be done.

"I was your ride or die, in it for life, no matter what. But you have a whole other family I didn't even know about. Maybe we could have worked through things had you been honest with me, but now we'll never know."

He looked away. I didn't want him humiliated in front of Sterling and thought of asking him to leave the room, but I didn't want my words twisted later.

"I know you love me, but you didn't love me enough to say no to all the things that hurt me over the years."

"I was trying to protect you, Lana."

"You were protecting yourself, Fen. Your decisions had nothing to do with me, but with every consequence, you thought you would suffer."

I paused.

Nothing.

"If there were women, then I could say you have a problem. But, you were with the same woman for ten years. In my book that's another family. What hurts the most is the way you defended her over and over again."

"It wasn't her fault, Lana."

"And there we have it again."

Surprise flashed across his face as he realized he had done the very thing I just accused him of doing.

"I wasn't trying to defend her. I just feel I was to blame in all this."

"Oh, you are, but she owns some blame as well, which you have not allowed her to carry. It takes two to tango, and she knew you were married."

I stood to my feet. "Now take this and go explore the possibilities with her and your son that you could not fully commit to because I was there. No excuses. Use our failed marriage as a relationship lesson. Learn from it."

"So, everything was my fault? You own some of this Lana. Maybe I'm foolish, and maybe I'm blind, but we can get through this."

"I checked out once I realized there was a child involved. Don't bring him up in a lie."

"And if Carter is mine, you will be doing just that."

"I won't lie to him. He will always know the truth about who he is. And I never said this was your fault. I didn't pass judgment on you. I made a hard decision."

"So, you don't love me anymore? Had you not become involved with Sterling we would not be having this conversation? He put thoughts in your mind and pulled you away. You said Rose knew we were married. Sterling knew you were married too." His breath was heavy. "I've never known you to be a hypocrite!"

I could feel Sterling rustle. I put up my hand.

"Yes, Sterling knew I was married, but we were strictly friends for almost a year, Fen. Being with him, even as a friend, allowed me to see I had devalued me. He showed me that I wanted more than just things. I needed your time, but you were spread so thin that when you came home, you had nothing left for me.

"Whenever I said anything about Rose you were so defensive, and when I found out you continued to see her for another seven years after I first found out about her, it told me a story. You not only cared about this woman, you loved her."

He said nothing. The anger had subsided, but he still did not want to let go.

"After you told me there was a six-year-old boy involved, everything in my being shouted, you would never stop. You're a family. I was the outsider, fighting a losing fight."

I took his hand and put the large golden envelope into it. "It's time to let go." Reaching for his face, I kissed him. "It's okay."

"If you still love me, you can't love him."

"You said yourself; Sterling is a good guy. I love him very much and have for a while, but I would not allow a relationship because I was yours and you were due that respect."

"Did you respect me when you slept with him?"

"That's enough," Sterling said now walking towards us. "She's signed the papers and said she…"

"I'm not talking to you. I was talking to Lana."

Now Fen was standing, and I stood between the two.

"What you're forgetting, Fenney is that all of this happened because of what you were doing and what you were not doing. Now you're begging for a second chance when you didn't keep your promise the first, second, third or fourth time."

I turned to Sterling holding onto him, pushing him back and away from Fen. His heart was pounding so loudly in my ear, and his muscles were flexed.

"When I marry her, she won't have to worry about that."

"Yeah, I know, I know! You're perfect. Everyone knows you stood by while your wife was sleeping around on you. That makes you a soft man." Fen was going for all he knew. "Then you did the noble thing and nursed her until she died. Or did you kill her to be with my wife?"

Sterling was trying to lose my hold. "Stop it!" I yelled. "Fen! You have your paperwork. It's signed. Now leave!"

He remained standing in the middle of the room chest heaving. His fist were balled and hanging to his sides. He wanted a fight.

Nurse Tina walked into the room. "Is everything okay?"

"Yes. Fen leave!"

"You heard her. Leave." Sterling repeated.

"I guess since you have back up I'd better go." Fen mocked as though he was frightened.

I felt Sterling trying to free himself again.

"Stop," I whispered. "This isn't you. Don't allow him to make you someone you're not."

Fen left, and I continued to hold Sterling until his heartbeat slowed.

Nurse Tina quietly backed out of the room leaving us alone.

"I'm fine. Let me go." He shook from my hold.

He wasn't *fine*. He was still angry until he heard his son's cry. His face softened, but not for long. He went to Carter, who was now screaming and lifted him holding him close.

"We need to come to an agreement, in case Carter turns out to be his." He sounded defeated.

"He's yours, and that is what I have been praying for."

"But if he is not..."

"He is yours." I cut my eyes at him. "I have given so much, and it is the only thing I have petitioned God for. He is yours."

He smiled for the first time since he arrived and kissed Carter in surrender. This was my family now, and my signed paperwork made all of this possible. I no longer felt guilty for signing.

Chapter Thirty-One

When we left the hospital, Sterling insisted we stay at his house. He didn't want Fen harassing me. Both took a DNA test, and it was now a waiting game.

When Ozi had to leave, I cried like the day he dropped me off at college. He rocked me and promised he'd visit more and expected the same from me.

Clark visited almost daily to see her baby brother and dad, but I could feel the distance. She was changing Carter's diaper when I asked to have a sit down with her. Reluctantly she agreed.

Sterling told me her favorite desert, so I made her brownies before she arrived and had vanilla ice cream in the freezer. The aroma of the brownies filled the air as I heated them and added one scoop of butter pecan ice cream to sweeten the conversation. When I came into the sunroom with my peace offering, her face lit up. She placed Carter in his Moses basket and joined me on the couch.

I didn't know how to start the conversation, so I turned on my work Lana. "Your dad and I are getting married, and you are an essential part of his life. After our altercation the other day, I felt we needed to talk, so I can answer any of your questions or concerns."

She was thinking, and I could tell she didn't know where to begin. I saw the little girl, and realized although she was a grown woman, she was afraid.

"Okay. Well maybe it would be easier to tell you about me and my life," I suggested.

Looking up, with her innocent eyes, she nodded.

"Well, I met Fen in college. I thought he was the most exciting boy I had ever met. I didn't date much in high school because I thought all boys were dumb and immature, but not Fen. He knew what he wanted, and he went after it, including me.

"He was my first and only until your dad."

"Your only?"

"Yes." That one comment told me more than I wanted to know about Clark. I continued. "I thought he was so smart and ambitious." He is still that ambitious person, always finding ways to grow his business, and now it is an empire.

"I ignored him in class the entire semester. He tried to get my attention, but I always had my head in my books, so I had no time for boys. When I said that to him, he told me he was no boy.

"The next day, and thereafter, he showed up in a suit. The first day I laughed, but he got my attention."

She was listening intently, hanging onto my every word. She picked up her spoon and shoved another spoonful into her mouth eagerly waiting for the rest.

"After college, we got married, and he began building his empire to prove he could take care of me. He wanted me to stay home, so initially, I did. I helped him to develop his brand.

"After it became self-sufficient and stood on its own, I became bored and wanted something for myself, so I got a job.

"We fought for months when I took the position, and I moved up so quickly soon I was in management, and I seemed to never to be home, always training. That's when he began seeing a woman named Rose."

"What did you do?"

237

"Nothing at first. I didn't know anything about her for three years."

"Three years!"

"Three years."

"How did you find out?"

"She approached me at a gala. She wanted to make sure I knew there was something between the two of them."

"Did you handle her?"

"I guess, in a way. I let her know he was with me, but he played the middle of the road."

"You let her disrespect you?"

"No Clark. You don't have to be loud, violent or rude to get your point across to a person." I watched her settle back on the settee and side eye me, not believing what I was trying to teach her.

"Well, your point didn't seem to make much of a difference. Nothing changed."

She watched my reaction to her words, but what could I say? She was right. "No, it didn't. That was eight years ago. They have a six-year-old son."

"How did you and my dad get together?" She wanted to hear no more about my past with Fen.

"I used to go to the sports bar to keep from sitting at home alone and there he was; funnier than ever, always making me laugh. We shared stories, dreams, politics, just life. He knew I was married, and he never asked for anything from me or crossed the line. He was a real gentleman.

"He was my friend and confidant and became everything my husband should have been for me. When I looked up, I was in love *and* married, but I wasn't like my husband. So, I didn't betray my marriage."

Clark thought about what I said, but her youth didn't allow her to understand what I was trying to tell her. "Clark, when I said I do, I meant it for life."

"Well, why did you sleep with my dad when you were married?"

"Weakness. I loved him with every fiber in my body. He was gentle. He was kind, but I think what made me make that decision was his patience. He allowed me to come to him. And, I wanted and needed to be with him.

"When I am with him, I don't feel alone. He's my Prince Charming that every young girl dreams of and I didn't get that the first time around. He makes my heart flutter, and he becomes the air I breathe. A single touch from him sends me to sacred places and warms me in the coldest storm."

She was smiling, caught up in my words.

"Okay! That's enough," I said now blushing. I missed him all over again.

"I've never felt that about anyone," she said mesmerized.

"You're so young, Clark. You're still trying to understand who you are and what you want." I took her hand. "Take your time."

She bowed her head. "I'm sorry I judged you, it's just that my mom mistreated and cheated on my dad over and over again. I never understood why he stayed. But, I guess he loved her."

"When people do you wrong Clark, you can't just turn the love off."

"I can." Clark sucked her teeth and sat back on the couch. I had to stifle a smile.

The voice of the alarm announced Sterling's arrival. Clark jumped up from her seat and went to greet him. I wondered if she and Sterling were like that when she was a child. I curled my feet under me and waited for him to come to me.

My phone beeped. It was a message from Fen.

Fen: I've been thinking about you and wanted to make sure you were okay.

Me: We're good

Fen: I was going to wait until the test came back to see Carter again, but was wondering if I could meet you somewhere to see him?

Me: Sure. Let me know

I put the phone down and leaned back on the pillows.

"What's that face for?" Sterling stood in the door watching me.

He made his way across the room and kissed me hello, then sat and placed his head in my lap. "Today was crazy."

I rubbed his head, having learned what soothed him. "What's going on?"

He stretched and looked up. "I don't want to talk about work. How are you and Carter today?"

"We're good. He eats all the time."

Reaching up, he ran his fingers down the side of my breast. They took some time to get used to. I knew it was only temporary, but I selfishly wished I could keep them.

"Clark said you had a talk today. How did it go?"

"I'm sure there will be many others, but I think it was a good start."

"Good. I don't need my two favorite girls feuding."

He sat up. "I'm going to get out of this suit, and we can go to the gazebo and sit a while. Maybe we can take a walk after dinner."

He left to get changed, leaving me to think of how to tell him Fen wanted to meet with me. Doubt filled my head of them ever getting along, but that had to happen if the baby turned out to be Fen's. As fast as the thought came, I remembered my prayer that Carter would be Sterling's.

"Someone's hungry." Clark entered the room and lifted squirmy Carter. "Dad said you were going to the gazebo. Did you want to nurse him before you left, or would you like for me to feed him for you?"

Clark had the bottle I pumped earlier in her other hand smiling. How could I refuse her? "You can feed him, and I will pump when I come back in."

Sterling entered the room and tried to take Carter from her, but she protested.

"Quit it, daddy. I just got him. Go sit with your woman. You can have him all night!"

Sterling settled for a kiss on his forehead then came to escort me out the back door, and we walked to the gazebo swing. It was breezy, so he put his arm around my shoulder, pulling me in close.

"We said we'd be honest with one another, so I have something to tell you."

"Okay."

"Fen texted me today. He wants to meet somewhere to see the baby."

Sterling was quiet. He shifted slightly and bent his head, touching his forehead to mine. He was thinking.

"Why can't he just come here? It's not like he doesn't know where I live." He smiled after the last comment.

"And if he doesn't want to come here?"

"Then I will have Clark go with you. I don't want you meeting him alone."

"He's not going to do anything Sterling."

He studied me. "The last meeting didn't go very well. Can you say it couldn't have gone differently had I not been there?"

He was right. Although Fen was never aggressive towards me, we were on different grounds. I found he was more aggressive when Sterling was around, like a dog still setting his boundaries.

"Are you sure you're done with him, Lana?"

I didn't know where that question came from. "Where did that come from?"

He shook his head. "Never mind."

I had never known Sterling to be insecure, so this was different. "No. Not never mind. Where did that come from?"

Releasing me, he sat up. Round and round, he twiddled his thumbs. "Rose came to my office today."

I could feel the irritation rise within me. I gave her Fen on a silver platter, and she was messier now than she was when Fen and I were together.

"Then maybe it's time I met with her."

"No. No. No. Let's let this thing pass. No one needs to talk to anyone."

"Well, what did she say that made you ask me such a crazy question? Aren't you the same man who was in the room with Fen and me when I had that conversation with him and gave him his paperwork?"

"You're right. You're right. But there is something going on over there. That's why I don't want you to go alone."

"What did she say Sterling!"

"It's not important Lana. I'm sorry I even let her get in my head."

I stood and walked to the gazebo step and leaned. His words were scaring me. Suppose something was wrong. "I've never known you to be insecure about anything." I turned and looked at him waiting for an answer, but realized he was not going to share any further.

I wondered why Fen hadn't told Rose that we were no longer together. Maybe he wasn't with her any longer, like he said. Maybe their relationship was in *her* head.

"Lana. Promise me."

"What did she say that has you spooked?" I asked a final time.

He embraced me. "Promise me, Lana."

I was silent. When he pulled back I saw the concern on his face. "I promise."

Chapter Thirty-Two

The weather was changing as we entered the Fall season. Clark and I sat near the restaurants gabbing. She was Sterling's peace of mind.

Across the court, I saw Fen coming. He smiled and picked up his pace. When he reached us he looked in the stroller at a sleeping Carter, and then turned to Clark. He seemed annoyed she was there but shrugged his shoulders.

"I owe you an apology Clark for our last meeting. This is a very difficult time for me, but it's still no excuse for my behavior."

Clark looked him over then back to me. I simply smiled.

"Yeah. Okay," she replied rudely and nonchalantly.

Fen smiled and slightly smirked. I was sure he thought she was rude as well.

"I just washed my hands. Is it okay for me to pick him up?"

"Sure."

He reached into the stroller and gently lifted Carter, placing him lightly on his chest. "Come here, little man."

He sat on the other side of me. It appeared he was checking out Carter's features for the first time. Again, he smiled to himself as if he remembered a joke.

Clark watched closely. I thought it was to make sure her brother was okay, but I realized she was checking Fen out.

He was dressed in his work clothes, which usually consisted of chino pants and a white button up shirt. Fen worked out regularly, so he was pretty solid, and his thigh muscles flexed through his pants.

Carter began to squirm. I reached to help, but Fen pushed my hands away.

"This is not my first rodeo, Lana. I got this."

Crossing my arms, I let him figure out what to do with a finicky Carter who continued to squirm and began whining. Changing positions several times, he was unable to console the fussing baby. Clark stood and went to sit on the other side of Fen. Taking Fen's arm, she tilted Carter up, and he immediately stopped crying.

"He doesn't like to lay flat."

Fen looked at the young girl and then back at me. I smiled and looked away.

"I had my lawyer start a trust for him."

"Fen. You don't..."

"I know Lana, but if he isn't, I still want to gift him. There would have been one for Lena, so I thought I would do the same for him."

"Okay." Another thing to debate with Sterling. "Thank you."

He was looking at me so intently. I blushed and looked away. I didn't need defensive Clark interpreting my behavior. I was sure Sterling sent her to protect his best interest as well as watching out for me.

Clark continued to let Fen know what Carter liked and didn't like. He held and fed him until he fell back to sleep, then placed him back in his stroller, covering it because the wind picked up. I should have left then, but I stayed longer and we talked about Solomon and the business, but not Rose.

Off in the distance, I saw a familiar silhouette coming our way. Rose! I looked at Fen.

"What?" He was baffled by my expression.

"Why is she here? Fen I don't want any mess, especially around my son." I stood to prepare to leave.

He looked in the direction I faced. "I didn't tell her I was coming here. I apologize Lana."

I didn't say anything. Clark gathered all of Carter's things and swung his book bag over her shoulder.

"So, now that you have another child you forget about us? You don't even know if he's yours." She was loud and breathless from her walk.

"Not here Rose." Fen blocked her path as he had when I first met her at the gala.

I could see Clark looking Rose over, and then back to me. I bowed my head trying not to smile.

Rose became visibly angry by my reaction. "What are you laughing about?" She looked at me in contempt. "I will be glad when it comes back that this bastard isn't his!" She sneered.

I stepped in close to her, but Fen cut me off. "You and Fen may have your disagreements, and you may be foul towards me, but make sure you keep my child out of your mouth."

Fen stood in front of Rose. "Rose, where is Solomon?"

"He's at after school."

"Then go and pick him up. I will meet you at your place to get him."

"Why am I still waiting? You aren't with her. Am I not important enough to you? I've waited almost twelve years. " She pushed him in the chest. "You make excuses. Is that because of him?" She asked pointing to Carter.

I closed the distance between the two of us and Fen lifted me carrying me to a safe distance.

"Come on, and I'll take you home," Fen said, pulling Rose away from us.

She snatched her elbow from his grasp. "I'm not going anywhere until you tell me what is going on with you two."

"I don't have to explain anything to you Rose. Lana is my wife."

"She said you're not together anymore. So why are you running behind her like a sick puppy? She wasn't there for you. I've been there for you." She paused, waiting for an answer. When Fen didn't answer she reminded him, "She dumped you, and you still don't get it! She's never forgiven you and never will. She doesn't love you like I do, and she damn sure wouldn't have waited for you."

Now that the wait was over, and she didn't win her prize, she was furious. "It appears you two have much to discuss, so I'm going home." I attempted to walk away.

"Where is home, Lana?" Rose taunted. "Are you still fucking Sterling? He's a tall drink of water isn't he?"

"Is she talking about my dad?" Now Clark, upset, snatched Carter's diaper bag from her shoulder, dropping it to the ground. With one scoop she had her hair twisted on top of her head in a sloppy bun. Next were her earrings.

Fen quickly grabbed a more volatile Clark, hoisting her over his shoulder and picking up Carter's diaper bag, he planted her beside me and handed her the bag. The two of us stood; ready to square off if needed. But then I saw something as I watched Rose's scowling face, I saw she was miserable. The one thing she always wanted was Fen to herself, and now that he was available, nothing had changed. She was still the side chick I had predicted she would forever be.

I turned to Fen, who looked worn and tired, and realized he had gained nothing and had lost everything by not taking a stand. He was embarrassed. The holes in his soul were visible. The one thing he had the power to make a decision about, he chose not to.

Where had the strong, smart Fen gone? He built an empire and managed it effortlessly, but his personal life was crumbling around him. It was an uphill battle for him, but even though he was running as fast as he could, he could not outrun himself and his mistakes. Learning what those mistakes were was just the beginning. Rose was now the reality he would try to desperately escape.

"Go home, Rose. This is none of your business," he said, causing her to spin out of control.

She tried to slap him, but Fen caught her hand midair. By-passers had gathered, watching the confrontation. People pulled out phones and began videotaping the scene.

"Let's go." He gripped her forearm, holding it tight enough for it to lighten were he gripped.

"I apologize to both of you and will talk to you later Lana."

Quickly, he led her up the street and away from us, leaving Clark and me staring in amazement as we processed what had just happened.

Chapter Thirty-Three

"You're not meeting him again Lana! This is crazy! You don't have to live like that anymore." The wood floor creaked in one spot, annoying me each time he walked on it. "Anything could have happened to the three of you."

"We're fine, Sterling!"

"This time!"

Admittedly, I agreed with him. The situation angered me. Rose was desperate, making her unstable. I thought it might be a good idea to put a restraining order on her, but felt confident Fen would get her back in line. He would never let anything happen to either of us.

"Maybe you should file a restraining order." Clark sat from her favorite spot on the oversized bean bag holding Carter.

"Let's not move too fast," I responded. I was annoyed that she had come to the same conclusion. "Let Fen handle her."

"Fen! He can't always be with her Lana, then who's going to be there to intercept her?" He looked to me for an answer. "I like Clark's idea. You need to report her to the authorities."

"And tell them what? That she called my child a bastard?"

"That bitch is crazy." Clark said.

Sterling looked at her.

"Oh, I'm sorry Daddy, but she is, and like you said, what if Fen isn't there next time to snatch her up like he did?"

"Fen?" Sterling questioned.

"Mr. Fenney," Clark corrected. "Really, daddy?"

"Stop pacing Sterling, and come sit with me," I said lightly to calm him and patted the couch.

He stopped and looked at me. Shaking his head, he came and sat beside me, sighing. Grabbing the back of my head, he pulled me in and kissed me as he calmed down. "Sorry." He looked at me to make sure he had my total attention. "I don't want you to live like that, so, no more meetings until after the results get back, and if we have to deal with Fenney, we will figure things out then." He winked.

"We won't have to deal with it any longer after that," I reminded him.

"Okay. You're right," he answered remembering my prayer.

He ran his hand down the side of my face and kissed me again.

"Oh my God!" Clark stood from the bean bag and placed Carter in his Moses basket. "Does he have any milk in the fridge?"

Sterling stopped long enough to laugh before he started again. I pushed him back laughing myself.

"There is some there, but I'll nurse him."

Clark lifted the basket from the floor. "You won't be here. Go to the Sports Bar or something, but I'm sick of you sitting around like an old married couple. You have plenty of time for that once you're married. I'll stay and watch Carter."

Leaving Carter for the first time was more difficult than I thought it would be, but it was great to be out with Sterling alone. I went back to my place to get dressed because most of my clothes were still there. Making Sterling remain in the car made me feel like a young girl going on a date.

Because he wore his jeans and a white button-up shirt with his team jacket, I decided to keep it simple too.

I put on my ripped jeans and sloppy sweater with my bootie shoes. Looking in the mirror, I noticed Carter blessed me with a little more hips than I had before. I liked what they did to my figure. Now I understood why both Sterling and Fen watched my behind when I walked.

I giggled and walked out of the large walk-in closet. I needed to decide where I wanted to live but already knew the answer. I had grown to love the house and wouldn't think of hurting Sterling's feelings by not living there.

I locked up and rolled the small suitcase I packed down the hall to the elevator. When I stepped off at the ground floor, I almost ran over the County Police Officer getting on. He smiled and greeted me - all eyes on my plentiful bosom, also courtesy of Carter. I blushed as he held the door allowing me to roll out without worrying about getting caught in the door.

Sterling was leaning on the car, but immediately came to grab the suitcase. I stood watching as he put it in the trunk of his car. A new chapter of my life was beginning. Afterwards, he walked to where I stood and embarrassed me.

"You sure?" He whispered.

"I don't want to spend another day away from you."

The officer was leaving the building still checking me out. He smiled and nodded his head. I smiled back then buried my face in Sterling's neck. Hmmmm. He smelled so good. I would have been happy just going home with him.

The Sports Bar had not changed much, but the people had. Ebony was still there, so we asked to be seated with her. She was ecstatic to see us.

"Hey," she said and hugged us. "My two favorite people. How are you?"

"We're great!" Sterling answered as he pulled my chair out and seated me.

The place was empty, as it usually was midweek. We were sitting at our table in the middle of the room in front of the big screen.

"The usual drinks?" She asked leaning on her small clipboard. I noticed she was eyeing my breast. I looked down and blushed. "I'm sorry," she apologized. "Are they new?" She whispered.

I laughed. Sterling smiled and looked away.

"No, they aren't new. We had a baby, and he gifted me with these temporarily."

The surprise on her face was priceless. Mouth gaped open she surveyed the rest of me. "You look great! I would have never known you had a baby. Boy or girl?'

"A boy. His name is Carter, and he is about seven weeks old now," Sterling volunteered with pride.

I watched him smile so big I thought he would light up the room. No longer did he hide his feelings for me, and he didn't care who knew about us. Not that Ebony mattered. She was there the night Fen blew up in the hall.

Ebony left to get our drinks. When Sterling turned, I was still admiring his new excitement for life. His happiness was fully exposed, and no one was taking it from him.

We ordered food and laughed and joked. It had been a long time since we were able to relax. Our laughter felt like no time had passed at all, as though the past months had all been a dream. I laughed at his funny stories and ate until I was stuffed. Afterwards, we hugged Ebony goodbye and went on our familiar walk.

Feeling secure with his arm around me, we walked the path around the shore of the Potomac and watched the capitol lights off in the distance, the foolishness of the day forgotten. He was still smiling.

"You look happy."

"If someone told me a year ago I would be here with you like this I wouldn't have believed them. I can't wait to move on from here and spend the rest of my days with you. "

The whimsical sound of his voice gave our story a fairytale feel and I knew he meant every word he said. I knew the feeling.

"Hasn't the rest of our life already started?"

He squeezed my shoulders and smiled. "Yes ma'am, but that new beginning will feel better when you become Mrs. McNeil."

We decided to take the ferry into Old Town and walk on that side of the river for a while, but after boarding the boat my breasts were so engorged they began leaking and required attention.

Sterling and I took the ride back to the Harbor dock and disembarked. Once back in the car, I removed the portable pump from its bag.

"Can you wait until you get home? Then you can nurse him, and we can sleep in his room."

We hadn't spent much quiet time together since the night before Carter's birth. The night renewed us, bringing us back to the simple things we wanted.

At home he watched me nurse Carter, smiling, as he enjoyed the beauty God created; the miracle of giving. He was always showing us how simple and satisfying it was to share the most intimate part of oneself.

I placed a sleeping Carter into his crib, full and happy. Sterling was waiting for me. I slept there most nights, but tonight I would share it with Sterling... my lover, my confidant, and my friend.

I let him watch me undress, blushing, still shy in his presence. He stood and came to me and ran his hands lightly over my body, stopping here and there. Oh, the gentle touch of his hand drove me to places I wanted him to take me.

Slowly, I began to undress him, taking in every inch of his beautiful body, no longer afraid or ashamed to feel for him. His stomach flexed as my fingers passed each ripple. I counted them, one by one, storing them to memory like a blind person, ensuring not to be tricked by a counterfeit.

I took a long and slow breath, intoxicated by the scent that often drove me wild. But I didn't linger, as my selfish impatience pushed me further. I took full hold of him, causing his breathing to quicken.

Eagerly he helped by lifting me, wrapping my legs around his waist, and kissing me so slowly, I felt he too was trying to commit all that made me who I was to his memory. Seductive and breathtakingly, our lips still together, he gently laid me down. His tongue slowly moved from my mouth then to my neck, as he made his way to the tips of my breast. Gently he sucked, and I moaned, "Hmmm," as I felt the pull of my milk letting down. He hesitated momentarily before sucking again, tasting, savoring every drop like it was gold. Milk ran down my side.

Satisfied with his discovery, he moved on, but this time he did not let himself be distracted before he reached his destination. I gasped at the vigor with which he nursed as though trying to receive the same reward.

"Hmmmm." I moaned.

His body stiffened to the sound, but never stopped, causing me to push back. He pulled me back and buried his head deeper. Oh, how I waited for this moment all evening. I felt free to be with him. He felt like home, and I had finally found my way there.

Before I reached the place he was guiding me to, he made his way back to my now muttering lips to silence me.

"Shhhh," he whispered and entered, pumping slowly and allowing my body to accept all of him.

Again, I moaned.

He laughed a low growl I could feel all the way to my soul. Pulling me up, he seated me in his lap while he knelt. Moving together I met every thrust;

I moaned. He smacked my butt. I responded with a dirty, sensual laugh. I liked that. The beads of our sweat were our lubricant as we slid effortlessly across one another's body. I held on, not wanting to let go, but I knew I wouldn't last long. Instinctively we danced to our personal drums until we both had our fill.

"Ladies first," he whispered.

I praised God for his gift of lovemaking in the tongue of angels as I released with Sterling following right behind me. Remaining seated in his lap, I held onto him as though I was afraid he may disappear.

Gently he laid me back on the bed, rolling over beside me. Pulling me into his arms, we both fell asleep.

Chapter Thirty-Four

Hours later I was awakened by a gentle nudge from Sterling. Groggy and half asleep, I stretched and smiled.

"Hey, you. Did I sleep through Carter's crying?"

He sighed heavily. "Carter is with Clark." He looked away hiding his face. He was dressed.

I sat up on my elbows. "Where are you going? What time is it?"

Now sitting upright, I looked for a clock and for the first time realize there was none in the room. I couldn't have slept through the night because I would have been gorged with milk.

"Lana!" Sterling sternly said to get my attention.

"What's going on?"

"I need you to get dressed and come with me."

His voice was stern. I felt my heart leap to my throat. I didn't understand what was going on.

"Where is my baby?" The tears came so fast.

I leaped from the bed forgetting I was totally naked. Sterling caught me in his arms.

"Let me go, Sterling! Where is my baby?"

"Lana! Carter is fine. It's Fen!"

I stopped and looked up at the man who held me in his arms. The words were alien coming from his lips, yet he was dressed, and for the first time, I realized my clothes were at the end of the bed.

"Get dressed and let's go."

He hugged me tightly and kissed my head. "I'll be downstairs waiting for you."

Standing in the middle of the room, I felt completely lost. I wanted him to stay there with me. I didn't have enough information to process what he had just told me. What happened? Did Fen do something to Rose? Was he in jail and we had to bail him out?

I dressed and went to our room to wash my face and pull my hair into a ponytail. The black sweat suit made me look like a cat burglar.

Sterling was leaning on the front door when I came downstairs. I looked around for my purse.

"Everything is in the car."

He looked so stoic it reminded me of the night when Fen set us up at the Sports Bar. Fen!

The ride was silent. Because of Sterling's demeanor, I was afraid to ask any questions. He held my hand while he drove, but wouldn't look at me.

We drove for a while and turned down streets only slightly familiar to me. Emergency vehicles passed screaming with lights flashing. When we reached our destination the large neon on top of the building caught my eye. It read Trauma Medical Center.

My head quickly flipped back to Sterling, but he wasn't looking at me. He was concentrating on the signs or pretending to. He parked and came around to my side of the car opening the door to let me out.

"What's going on Sterling?" I didn't need his words. His lack of, gave me so many answers. He extended his hand and knelt beside me. I remained on the front seat afraid to move.

"I'm not sure. We'll know more when we go inside. Okay?"

He was gentle with me. He took my purse and helped me out of the car. Now visibly shaking he held me close.

I stood in the cold lobby alone while Sterling went to the desk. I saw an officer approach him and they shook hands. When I looked closer, I realized it was the same officer who nodded to me earlier at my condo.

He looked over to me and gave me a weak smile. I became instantly chilled and shivered as the tears formed in my eyes. This was not going to be good.

The two split and the officer moved to the entrance of a corridor and Sterling came to me. Still not looking me in my eyes, that were now overflowing with tears, he wrapped his arm around my shoulders and led me to where the officer waited. We three headed down a long corridor.

After a series of turns, we came to a large pretty white woman seated behind a reception desk. She looked up from her computer and smiled.

"Hello, Officer Friendly," she teased.

"Hello, Elaine. We need to go to the back."

The woman looked at him and then to Sterling and me. She became serious and reached under her desk and hit a buzzer, releasing the lock on the door giving us access to another corridor behind her desk.

Where were we going?

We walked down the long corridor with its cold, sterile walls. My breathing became labored with the uncertainty of our destination. Finally, we came to a door. It read "MORGUE. "

I stopped abruptly, snatching myself away from Sterling. I turned away from him prepared to run, but my knees buckled. He caught me before I hit the floor, his strong arms protectively wrapped around me as I flailed like a fish thrown from the sea trying to swim where there was no water.

I screamed as he continuously whispered over and over in my ear, "I got you. I got you."

"What happened?" I asked through my wailing; now understanding why the door was way in the back away from everything. It was preparation for the impossible. "Sterling! What happened? Did she do this? Did Rose do this?"

I couldn't breathe. It was like the night in the bathroom at the Sports Bar. I pulled away from Sterling and looked him in the face. Surely, he had answers. "What happened Sterling? What happened?"

Sterling turned looking to the officer for help.

The officer stepped towards us and knelt where Sterling held onto me. His beautiful green eyes calmed me. They looked so sad.

"Mrs. Fenney there was a car accident on the beltway, and Mr. Fenney's car swerved in front of a tractor-trailer."

"What do you mean swerved?" I knew Fen to be a great driver. He wouldn't just *swerve* in front of a truck.

"The witness said there was an altercation in his car causing Mr. Fenney to lose control. They were both killed instantly."

"Who else was in the car?" Sterling asked taking over.

"There was a woman in the car as well. I can't release her name until her family has been notified. According to the witness, she hit him, before he loss control."

Rose! I told Fen if he didn't leave her, she would be the death of him. Words spoken now formed into truth. I thought of how crazy she was acting when she saw him with Clark and me earlier, but more unraveled than usual because she didn't understand our status.

The humming, of the lights in the hall, annoyed my senses. I thought I would be ill as I moaned and rocked. Sterling stroked me like a baby, patiently waiting for me to calm down. Visions of mine and Fen's life flashed through my thoughts; the good, the bad and the ugly.

I thought of the first time we met and how eager he was to get my attention. I thought of the day he proposed to me at the carnival, while on a Ferris wheel ride high in the air and me screaming because I was afraid of heights and we were stuck. I thought of him holding Cater earlier when we met at the harbor.

I wanted to call Mother and Bishop. They needed to know. "I need to call my Bishop," I said through the tears as I tried standing.

"We can do that in the morning. I'm sure Clark will take care of Carter."

Instinctively my thoughts turned to Solomon, and I wondered where he was. Who had him? Was he safe?

Sterling helped me to my feet and gripped me tightly to ensure I wouldn't fall.

"Was there a child in the car?"

"No just the two of them. There is a child at one of Mr. Fenney's residences."

One of his residences? What did that mean?

"What will happen to him?" Sterling asked.

"His nanny has agreed to stay with him until it is determined what to do with him."

The officer looked at me. He no longer flirted as he had at the condo. Once you saw how a person lived, it made decisions much clearer. I saw the pity in his eyes and I fell back into the abyss again.

"You don't have to identify him tonight, Mrs. Fenney." He was being so kind and gentle.

"Can I do it for her?"

"Are his parents alive or does he have siblings?" the officer asked.

"They're estranged, but they live nearby." Again, Sterling was trying to take the load from me.

"I can call them and have them do it." The officer suggested.

"No. He wouldn't want that." No matter what they came up with I knew the responsibility was mine and no one else's. Legally I was still his wife.

"Lana, let someone else do this. You don't have to."

"I know, but he didn't get along with his parents, so it's the least I can do."

I walked to the door wanting to get it over with. Sterling was right there beside me. He would catch me.

When we returned home, Clark and Carter were still asleep. We went to our room, and I stripped, dropping my clothes to the floor.

The warmth of the bed was inviting. I shivered under the covers. I couldn't believe it. Fen was gone.

My mind raced back to our lives together and the last time he asked me again to give him another chance to prove himself. I thought of us growing from inexperienced teens to even more confused adults. I thought about Solomon all alone.

Sterling joined me, wrapping his arms around my shivering body. "I'm so sorry, Lana," he whispered.

The room was warm, but I continued to shake. The new stubble on his chin scratched my face as I buried my head into his chest and cried. Wrapped in the safety of his strength, I wept for a man I loved for more than half my life, and Sterling calmed me. He had been my calm since the first day I met him.

Chapter Thirty-Five

The next few days were a haze. I had to plan a funeral, but my mind was on the child. He was one of the leading factors that influenced my decision to leave my marriage. I voiced my concerns about Solomon living with Fen's parents; after all, they created the mass of confusion Fen had become. When I talked with them, they were more concerned about Solomon's inheritance. Then came the call from Fen's lawyer to review his will.

Sitting in the outside office was unnerving. I didn't know what to expect, but I didn't care about any of it except the boy. I didn't want him to be frightened during this scary time.

"Mrs. Fenney?" The receptionist called to get my attention.

"Yes."

"Mrs. Poe is waiting for you."

She saw the question on my face. "Mr. Fenney switched to Mrs. Poe almost two years ago. He didn't tell you?"

"I didn't keep up with his legal affairs," I explained.

The older lady escorted me to Mrs. Poe's office and opened the door announcing my presence. "Here she is, Angela."

A slim warm woman stood and came from behind a mahogany desk that was much too big for her stature. She reminded me of Michelle Obama. She sported a short fro and a constant smile, which was calming. Her voice was gentle, and she moved around as though she had a full agenda.

Surprisingly, she hugged me when she saw my nerves were on edge. "Sorry for your loss," she whispered. "Come and sit at the table. I find that big ole desk to be impersonal."

Angela Poe, who appeared to be about twenty years my senior, led me to a table already set up for my visit. I sat in the comfortable seat as directed, and she sat beside me as if we were old friends.

She leaned back and smiled. "So, you are the famous Milana. I have heard so much about you in the past two years." Her warm smile was meant to calm my nerves, but it wasn't working.

"I would like to start by saying, despite his indiscretions; your husband loved you very much. Over the past months, he made many changes to his will as if he knew his time was near." I could see why Fen confided in her. Her demeanor was disarming.

"Did you want anything to drink, before we get started?"

I wondered if she meant something hard, because although I didn't drink this could be an exception. "No thank you."

"Okay, then let's get started. We have a lot to cover."

Seeing the confused look on my face, Mrs. Poe touched my hand. "Your husband was a brilliant businessman, but I don't have to tell you this."

Yes, she did. I didn't know Fen over the last years, so I felt she could shed some light on those things I did not know.

"Well let's start with the property. Your husband has left all his property to you and has set up a trust to take care of the taxes over the next thirty years.

"The homes are fully paid for and consist of the Harbor home where the two of you resided. He states if you decide you don't want it and sell it, he would like to have one-third of the net earnings to go in a trust for Solomon and a third for Carter, but he will leave that decision up to you.

"The condo in the Harbor, where he sometimes resided with Solomon, is yours, but he would like it to be turned over to Solomon when he turns twenty-one or has finished college. If he does not go to school and you deem him not mature enough to handle the responsibility, then you may retain it until you see fit to give it to him.

"The home where his mistress, Rose Stanford, resides is yours as well. He states you may do as you wish, but remember it is Solomon's home as well. It was his will that it also be Solomon's when you are ready to sign it over to him. He apologizes for mixing you up in the handling of Solomon's affairs, but he has no one else to trust it to.

"Those are the main homes. Then there are the two apartment buildings in the district, the vacation home in Martha's Vineyard and the office building in Oxon Hill where his office is Located. They have all been left to you with instructions."

My mind was spinning. I had no idea Fen had acquired these properties. I stood up and started to pace.

Angela stood and went to her desk and pushed a button. Her assistant appeared through the door with a tray of drinks and two glasses of ice. She placed the ginger ale and water in the center of the table and left as quickly as she entered with no words, just a sympathetic smile.

Angela pressed a tissue in my hand to dry the tears I didn't know I had shed. I attempted to speak, but couldn't. When had he done all of this?

"Take your time, but there is much more to go over."

I spun to face her. She nodded and waved to the chair where I could no longer remain.

I sat down.

"Mr. Fenney left you his entire business. He said you would know how to run it because you once worked for him."

I laughed at her last words. They were ironic because those words were the reason why I became stubborn and got my own job outside of his business. He always used to say I worked for him. Oh. How I missed him.

"He said you would laugh at that."

She smiled and continued through all the other jargon. Then she became serious.

"None of these things were important to him. He said they were the things he worked so hard for, so one day the two of you no longer had to work. He left a letter for you to read before I read the rest to you."

Angela handed me a thick, sealed letter sized envelope and stood. "When you are done you may push the buzzer on my desk," she pointed to the button on her phone console. It was similar to what I used to call Courtney. She left me alone in the office.

I held the envelope in my hand and was afraid to open it. It was just a letter, but I learned over the years of fighting and disagreements that words held power.

Slowly I opened the envelope. Taking a deep breath, I unfolded its thickness and began reading:

Hello Love,

If you are reading this, I'm gone. I want to let you know I never intentionally meant to hurt you. But I did, and for that I'm sorry.

Lana, you deserve so much more than I gave. At the end of our relationship, I began to understand all the time I stole from us, and that I should have come to you with the truth about Solomon. I didn't, because of our loss of Lena and I couldn't bear to see the look in your eyes, knowing I was the cause of that pain.

You are so loving and I now know you would have helped me and loved him regardless of how he got here. But I realized too much, too late.

Rose. I blamed you for Rose being there, but she was never your fault. She was my insecurities. I never thought I deserved you or that you would always be there for me, especially after the truth of her presence came out. Why would you stay? Look at you.

You are honest, kind, nurturing, loving, smart and beautiful. I totally get why what's his name fell for you. (Smile). I fell for you the very first time I saw you. I didn't even need the class. I only took it because you were in it. When I saw the look on your face the day I came to class in a suit, I dedicated my life to making you happy and taking care of you. But, I guess, the devil got in the way, because I failed.

Rose is messed up and unstable. I didn't learn this until too late. I learned to keep her quiet and away from our doorstep, but at a price. It meant being away from you.

I got a small condo for Solomon and I to escape to, and I guess she thought I was taking him home to you, so she stalked our house after I left with Solomon to see if I showed up. This is how I learned about you and Sterling.

It took forever for you to kiss him for the first time, but she was determined to come with proof that you were cheating on me. When I saw the pictures of you going into his hotel room, I thought I would die then and there. That was my wakeup call, and I got it. I felt what you probably experienced every time I returned home after being out all night or away.

I hurt so badly for what I put you through and thought I would kill her that night for exposing your imperfections. She always wanted to take your place, but it was you that always had my heart. Always.

Rose has no family, and I don't want Solomon to be raised by her. She sometimes scares him, but I am his balance. If I'm dead, he will no longer have the voice of reason to tell him what is right and wrong. Damn, I should have brought him home to you. What I am about to ask you is a lot.

I want you to raise my son, Lana. I want you to raise Solomon.

I put the letter down and paced the office. The tears flowed as I understood the captivity he lived in. He never escaped the hell his parents created; instead he created a new hell for himself. He was never home because he was with Solomon. He was protecting him. He was everything I knew him to be, but he was lost.

The water was warm in the glass now, but I drank it anyway. I couldn't sit and continue, so I stood and read the rest.

Lana. He is such a good boy, and he's smart like his daddy. (Smile). I want him to have a better chance than I had. I know you will love him and protect him no matter who his mother is. Others think you're quiet and meek, but that couldn't be farther from the truth. You are a fighter, but most of all, you're God-fearing.

My lawyer has everything you need to win custody. I have been keeping documents over time, just in case things came to this.

Oh, Milana. Who's going to kiss you now? Oh yeah, Sterling is still there. (Smile). I hate everything about the guy because he is like you. He's a good guy, and I know he will be there for Solomon as well. Damn, I hate that guy.

Solomon knows who you are. He has a picture of you. I told him you were his guardian angel and your identity is secret, so he should not talk to anyone about you. He is brilliant. He asked, 'You mean Mommy?'

Everything I own is yours because you gave me the drive to want to accomplish everything I have achieved. It was always for us. Although Rose's home has been left to you, I would like to keep it for Solomon one day. The taxes have been set up to be paid out of a designated account yearly. Once you get custody of Solomon, you may let her remain there or not. Once you get to know him, you will know what to do.

Mostly, be happy. That's all I ever wanted for you. I just didn't know how to get back to that happy place. Enjoy life and don't work so hard. I have left you enough money that you don't have to work. Enjoy the money and the kids.

Since you are reading this letter, we don't know who Carter's father is. Don't read the results when you get them. He is Sterling's. I had a vasectomy after Solomon. I didn't want to have any more children if they were not with you.

I'm sorry for misleading you, but I was so bitter that I was losing you. Carter could have been our child. The doctors were wrong all along. Lana, I am so glad you are able to be a mother.

Again, I stopped reading and held his letter to my chest. Carter was Sterling's child. I smiled, knowing how overjoyed he would be when he found out the news.

Fight for him, Lana. Fight for Solomon, because no one fought for us as children.

You did give me a final gift. The beauty of your love brought me to Christ, and I was able to accept Him as my Lord and Savior. So, I guess you're stuck with me! See you in heaven. (Smile).

I will always love you. You were my guardian angel through your prayers.

Love,
Fen

My heart was so full! I thought it would burst! He was saved when he died. I praised God where I stood in the office, my hands lifted. I felt he was free and no longer tortured by his choices in life. He could rest in peace.

I took a few minutes after praising God to reflect before I hit the buzzer. Surprisingly, I was still full of joy from knowing he would be with God. I was finally at peace. I heard the door open but didn't turn immediately.

"Are you ready for me?" Angela asked softly.

I was holding the letter to my chest. I nodded.

"I can give you a few more minutes."

"No. I need to get home to share some good news for a change."

I smelled the familiar cologne I had grown accustomed to over the past two years. He was already there.

His arms encircled my waist. "I already know. He left me a letter too."

I swirled around and saw he had been crying as well. He released me and stepped to the side.

There stood the most beautiful little boy, who could have been no one other than Solomon. He looked so much like Fen. My eyes teared up again.

"Hello, Solomon." I smiled, knowing he was safe.

"How did you know my name?" He asked in a shy voice.

"I know a lot about you," I told him and stretched out my hand.

Surprisingly he ran into my arms and held me so tightly I thought he would never release me. His little body was shaking.

"I cried for you, but you didn't come. My daddy said you would come."

Sterling looked at me puzzled.

"I've been a little sad, but I had to push all that away so I could come for you and you wouldn't be afraid anymore."

He wiped his tears. "I wasn't afraid. I was just sad."

How could I say no to taking care of this little angel? I was instantly in love with him. Looking up at Sterling, I was now confused.

"How did you get here?" I asked Solomon.

"Mr. Sterling picked me up from school. He said he was my new daddy."

I was immediately choked up. I held Solomon so tightly he squirmed in my arms. I lifted him and walked towards the door.

"Sterling, would you grab my purse please?"

"Yes ma'am," he answered and picked up my purse from the chair.

"Mrs. Poe. Please let me know when the paperwork for Solomon is complete, and thank you."

"Yes, ma'am." She mocked Sterling. I could hear her smile through her words.

The office people smiled and nodded. A series of 'good lucks' and 'Godspeed' were whispered as we passed.

Once in the elevator I put Solomon down and embraced a grinning Sterling.

Chapter Thirty-Six

The weeks to come were busy. Work was pressuring me to return. After Fen's services, and with all of his accounts transferred to me, I had to review his contracts and papers. Mrs. Poe set up another appointment and helped me to go over everything.

The day I quit I walked into the office dressed in my suit, just as I had on my first day. I was up late completing a new project and was tired. My life had just become entirely too complicated with two new children, a businesses, and a wedding to plan for.

"Luke is looking for you," Courtney informed me.

"For what?" I was not in the mood for his folly. I was irritable.

"I don't know." She shrugged her shoulders.

Sighing, I went to my office and closed the door. After hanging my jacket, I went to my desk and sat down hard.

Why was I still there? Sterling asked me that very question before I left for work. I couldn't answer him.

The nanny we found was good, but there was something missing. Plus, she smiled too much at Sterling. Clark noticed it too.

I had fifteen minutes before the meeting. I wanted to take that time to clear my head.

The knock on my door startled me. Maybe it was because I was half dozing.

"I hope I didn't interrupt your nap."

It was Luke. He was always so rude. He entered uninvited. "Wayne told me to come and get you because he's ready to start the meeting."

Without commenting, I stood and grabbed my jacket and clipboard full of notes. I walked out of the office leaving him standing in the middle of the floor.

When I entered the conference room, everyone was already there. I took the only empty seat in the center of the ten foot long mahogany table. Wayne acknowledged me with a nod.

I couldn't focus as the meeting went on. I wondered how Solomon was doing. I knew he was missing Fen this morning. My milk had me almost gorged, and I needed to check on a contract.

"Well, I would have that information, but Lana has not completed her part of the project." Luke was throwing me under the bus. Again!

"Which project is that Luke?" I asked irritated that he had said my name.

"The numbers for turnover," he answered smiling.

We had been battling since my promotion. He felt his friend and partner should have gotten it over me. Every chance he could he attempted to roll on me.

"Do you mean the spreadsheet I emailed you last Friday?"

Silence.

"Well, I didn't get your email."

"I'm sorry, but I got my read receipt." I waited for his follow-up.

"Why didn't you tell me you forwarded it?"

I was dumbfounded. Did he really expect me to babysit his email? "I completed my project, Luke," was all I said.

Wayne sat in silence watching Luke. Luke seemed uneasy as the silence grew louder even to my ears. Finally, Wayne spoke.

"Did you want her to read it for you too?"

Luke shuffled in his seat, not answering the question that was obviously rhetorical. I was silent, trying not to get caught in the crossfire.

Wayne stood up. The meeting was over.

"Luke, meet me in my office," Wayne ordered, before leaving the conference room.

The room began to empty, but I stayed.

What was I doing? I wanted to have lunch with Solomon, to make sure he was okay. I wanted to hold my baby and savor every minute of his growth. Instead, I sat in my pretty suit, playing reindeer games with a man who was obviously incompetent and who resented the position I had risen to.

"Boss?" Courtney peaked into the room. "You okay?"

"Come in Courtney, and sit with me." She came and sat in the chair across the table from me. I was silent.

"Do you need me to call Mr. Sterling?"

I looked up at the young girl who had flourished in the past two years. Her thick red hair was beautiful and hung past the middle of her back. She had gained a few pounds since she became my assistant. Maybe it was from all the ice cream and waffles I made her eat with me when I was pregnant with Carter.

"You look happy, Courtney. Are you happy?"

She looked puzzled and began entwining her hands, as she did when she was nervous. It was a habit that helped me over the years to know when I was being too hard on her.

"I'm just asking because I want to know." Her slow smile indicated she didn't believe me. I had seen it before. "How old are your children now? And what are they doing?"

She smiled. I saw her love for them immediately shine on her face.

"Haley is eleven now and playing basketball. Ayden is nine. He hates sports but loves to read everything he can on insects, animals and the sea. He hasn't decided what he wants to do just yet. I told him he had plenty of time to explore his options. Then there is Reagan. She is four and autistic which is rare for a girl. She does beautifully detailed artwork."

When she was done, I saw her beaming with pride. I smiled and reached across the wide table and took her hand.

"I'm sorry I never asked about them. I will do better," I promised.

"You've done a lot for us, Mrs. Fenney. You allowed us to stay together and have a roof over our heads. You taught me to be more assertive and to take control of my life. You don't owe us anything. We owe you!"

Her words touched my heart. I knew if I decided to resign, I would have to take her with me. They would ruin her, and she would no longer smile the big smile she displayed for me now.

"I have some tough decisions to make over the next week or so, and I may leave the company. If I do, I want you to come with me. Your salary would remain the same, but your hours would be shorter and your atime more flexible to take care of your children. You would be able to work from home after we get you set up, and no more weekends and late nights."

Her beautiful hazel eyes teared up. "I've been praying to have more time with them," she revealed.

"This has to be quiet until I decide what, when, and how. Okay?"

"Oh, yes, of course!"

I stood, so she stood too. "Oh! I forgot what I came to tell you. Mr. McNeil said he is leaving work to get Solomon. He is having a rough day at school, and the nurse called."

Immediately I headed to my office. I had to go! "Okay. I have to leave, but you have all my numbers, so call me if you need to."

I swiftly trotted to my office to put my things away and call Sterling back. No sooner had I entered, Wayne entered behind me.

"May I have a word with you Milana?" He asked politely.

I stopped moving and looked up from my file cabinet. "Can it wait, Wayne? I have a small emergency," I stopped and corrected myself. "No, I have a huge emergency that I have to attend to. I may or may not be back for the day."

"Okay," he sang and stuck his hands in his pocket. "Then it can wait."

I returned to gathering my things, and it wasn't until I took my purse out of the drawer that I realized he was still standing in the door.

"I'm sorry, Wayne. Was there anything else?"

He kicked at imaginary rocks before looking up. "We're losing you, aren't we?" He asked.

I felt like a little girl about to disappoint her father. "I think so," I answered. "I'm sorry."

"Don't be. I always knew you were too smart to remain here and once you discovered that, you would be gone." He turned to leave. "Come see me when you return. Let's talk."

It was almost an hour since Sterling called the office. He was taking Solomon to his favorite burger place.

The two didn't see me when I entered. Solomon's head was thrown back as he ate an enormously long French fry. Without warning, he burst into laughter.

I stopped to watch the two. Sterling was telling him a story no doubt. Secretly I stole a few more looks before taking my phone from my purse and texting Sterling.

He looked at his phone and texted me back.

Okay. See you at home. I love you.

After a few more looks I turned and went home.

I heard Solomon first. He ran across the backyard at full speed, colliding with me.

"Why are you so excited?"

As he took deep breaths, he tried to catch up to his thoughts. "I was sad today, so Mr. Sterling took me to the hamburger place and I laughed so hard I threw up."

I smiled as he continued to tell me about the waitress who threw up trying to clean it up, so Sterling had to clean it up.

Trying not to laugh I asked, "Where is Sterling?"

Without warning, he turned and ran back to the house, to get Sterling. Within minutes he burst through the back door with him in tow.

Again, he was out of breath.

"Sit and catch your breath, Solomon, before you throw up again," Sterling said pushing him down until he was seated.

The grin on his face was wide and contagious. "Did he tell you about our little adventure?"

"Yes."

No longer able to contain myself, I laughed until my stomach ached. Solomon turned, sporting a huge proud grin. Oh, how he made me miss Fen, but he reminded me so much of him I felt he never left.

Sterling sat beside me and looked in my lap at the pictures of cakes and floral arrangements spread across my legs.

"We decide yet?"

I thought about it all afternoon and decided I really didn't want an elaborate wedding. I wanted a small get together of family and a few friends.

"I was thinking in four weeks, sending out invitations this week, and having a sit-down dinner at the GM."

He beamed. "I was hoping you would say something like that."

"Then it's settled." I thought a little more and added, "And my last day of work will be next Friday."

Without warning, he lifted me from the swing and spun me around. "That's my girl!"

"What did she do?" Solomon yelled from the step excitedly.

"She made a good decision!" smiled Sterling.

Chapter Thirty-Seven

The meeting with Wayne was the first time he and I sat down and shared thoughts about life and the organization.

"So, what are you going to do now?" He was leaning back in his seat with his arms crossing his chest.

"Well, I inherited a company that is pretty self-sufficient, but I need to be hands-on and aware, and I can't do that without stealing time from here." I sipped the sweet tea he brought to the conference room.

"I never got to tell you personally, but I am sorry for your loss. I know you were no longer together, but you did share a life with him."

"Thank you, Wayne. I can appreciate that."

"So, I hear you are getting remarried."

I really didn't know where this conversation was heading, but I didn't feel he was being malicious. "Yes."

"Well, I would like to make sure the room you reserve is covered by the resort as our farewell gift."

"Thank you. Does that include the food?"

"Okay, you're pushing it, but I can definitely give you some kind of discount if I am invited."

"Of course, you are invited," I assured him.

"Then it's settled." We both laughed.

That day became my last day at work. Wayne decided that since Luke thought he knew who should have my job then he would give it to his life partner.

The weeks leading up to the wedding were so busy, I had forgotten about the paternity test. It came one morning when I returned from my run.

I sat at the kitchen counter eating my small breakfast waiting for Sterling to come down, flipping the envelope back and forth between my fingers wanting to trash it, but unable to. Fen told me to trash it, but I still had a desire to read the results for myself, but was afraid. Supposed he was wrong?

"Good morning." Clark entered the kitchen carrying Carter on her hip. She had become the new nanny once she decided to return to school for her doctorate. We made her the offer to stay home, save her money and be Carter and Solomon's nanny. She preferred to be called Au Pair. She was so bougie.

"What's that?" She asked sitting at the counter with me.

Reaching, I took a spoiled sleeping Carter from her arms. "He's asleep, Clark. You are going to make him rotten."

"I know. Then he will be my baby. That's my plan to keep all this sexy."

Unfortunately, I believed her.

"What's that?" She asked again.

"It's the paternity test results."

I could hear Sterling coming down the steps. Quickly she picked up the envelope and placed it in her robe pocket. "We already have the results. Leave it alone."

Sterling, dressed in his navy suit and pink shirt I left on his valet, entered the kitchen, reminding me how he caught my eye over two years ago. He was nearing forty-five, but looked younger than some that were fifteen years his junior.

"Good Morning Daddy!" Clark said, overemphasizing each word and looking at me. She reached in the basket and took a paper cup to fix her father a cup of coffee.

"Good morning Clark and yes I read your paper this morning. Very well written." He kissed my cheek and then Carter's and took the cup from her.

A pouting Clark waited for her greeting. Sterling recognized the look and smothered her face with kisses. It always warmed my heart to see the two of them interact, letting me know I was doing the right thing.

"Why didn't you wake me to go running this morning? How many times have I said not to run alone?" He was leaning on the counter drinking his coffee.

"I know, but it helps me to clear my head."

"I got something for that," he smiled.

Clark shivered. "On that note, I am going to take my shower before I find Solomon in my bed."

Clark disappeared, leaving Sterling and I. Pulling the envelope from her pocket she took one final look before putting it back.

Turning my attention back to Sterling, I closed the folder on the counter. He filled his cup again and sat next to me.

"Are you ready for this weekend?"

I smiled. I couldn't believe we were almost there. We were to be married in five days.

"I can't wait for you to make me an honest woman."

"You are beaming."

He sat on the stool beside me and wrapped his knees around my sides pulling me close. I could feel his breath as he ran the shadow of his whiskers across the base of my neck.

"Stop teasing me. No more until Saturday," I reminded him.

"I'm just reminding you of Saturday." He was grinning.

"Go to work, because I have work of my own to do."

"You sure?" he teased, running his fingers down my arms.

I couldn't wait until Saturday. Being Mrs. McNeil was all I wanted right now. Finally, I was home with the boys and keeping an eye on this empire I had helped to build unknowingly. Being able to help Courtney and others like her was also a plus.

Sterling and I met with the Pastor and Bishop not long after Fen's death, and they were pleased with my choice. Bishop gave Sterling a long speech about the importance of him honoring me. Other than that, he liked Sterling and said he would officiate the wedding.

My dress was altered and delivered two days before the ceremony. Sterling and Solomon were at final fitting for their tuxes when Clark ran into our room.

"Look what I found!" To say she was bursting with excitement was an understatement. The bag read Tim and Tammy. Inside it was the tiniest tux I had ever seen. Clark squealed.

"This is so adorable, Clark!"

"I told you he was my baby," she said smiling down on Carter lying asleep in the Moses basket he had long outgrown.

"Don't you pick that child up! Let him sleep," I teased.

"What time do we leave tomorrow for rehearsal? I need to finish my paper before then."

"Rehearsal is at five and dinner right after. Will you be able to finish?"

"Plenty of time."

"Tiffany is going to stay here and watch Carter while we get our nails done today. You ready?"

"Yes, ma'am."

Chapter Thirty-Eight

The day of the wedding was perfect. Clark, Courtney, Tiffany, and Nancy were there in the suite helping me to prepare.

My dress was elegant but simple. I picked a pale milk plum dress with a detachable lace train. My hair was pinned up and wrapped with pearls entwined. Sterling was so tall. I decided to wear a four-inch heel. I hoped I didn't regret the decision.

"You look so beautiful," Clark whispered.

She was dressed in burgundy with hint of tan, and gold accessories. Courtney, although she was my assistant, was as close to a friend as I would get. She was wearing matching colors to Clark, but a differrent dress. I could remember Clark telling me, "The help is not wearing what I am wearing." Bougie.

It was time. Everyone left me alone. Nancy was coming back to get me when everything was ready, and Tiffany had Carter.

Sitting in silence was welcoming. It gave me a chance to say a final prayer and prepare for the walk. I thought of the day I married Fen and how different it was. Broke and young, our preparation was much simpler and the reception was in the basement of the church. Our food consisted of potluck and made with love by family members and college friends, long forgotten. Fen's death validated that we all had an appointed time to die and mine and Sterling's meeting was not an accident. He was always to be my husband.

Then came the small rap at the door.

When I opened the door, I was shocked to find my brother Ozi. He was supposed to meet me downstairs.

"What's wrong?"

"I decided to come and walk you from here. Is that okay?" He took my hand. "You ready?"

I had been ready since Sterling asked me. Taking one look over my shoulder to make sure I wasn't forgetting anything, I confidently walked through the door and closed it to return as Mrs. McNeil.

As we walked through the hotel, I thought of the many times I had seen other brides making the same walk. People stopped and took pictures, becoming a part of my history. Soon those photos would be posted somewhere or shared with others. The employees wished me well and waved. Some took the walk with us to the grand room. Others came from different parts of the hotel to see Mrs. Fenney for the last time. I looked up and saw Luke standing at the balcony. He smiled and lightly waved. I waved back.

Once we reached the ballroom, I saw Nancy standing outside, ready to signal my arrival. She beamed as she snapped pictures to share later, getting in the way of Shaw, the hotel photographer.

Ozi turned to me. "If I could, I would tell you that this time will be perfect, but then that would be a lie. What I will say Sis, is that I trust Sterling to do the best he can to protect you from all that he can. He will be there through every experience, as I was when we were children.

"I'm happy to give you to him, and then maybe I will know when things happen in your life." He winked.

"You're going to make me cry, Ozi."

"That was my intention. So, when you walk towards him, he will see those tears and believe they are there for him. I'm the hype man."

"Okay. Now you just ruined the moment."

We laughed.

"Ready?" Nancy asked.

Ozi wiped the tear from the corner of my eyes trying not to mess up my make-up. "Yes."

The doors opened, and everyone stood. My eyes went side to side as I smiled at those I knew and those I had yet to meet. Once I reached halfway down the aisle, my eyes were focused on Sterling, who stood so handsomely at my destination.

His smile did not disappoint. The sunshine he had been basking me in for over the two years, shined as bright as ever. Solomon stood close and just when he was about to run to me I saw Sterling reach down and touch his shoulder, instantly calming him. I puckered my lips, and air kissed him, making him smile.

Bishop and Mother beamed like proud parents as I arrived to the altar. The two were donned in their official robes, looking noble.

"Who gives this woman?" Bishop asked.

"I do," Ozi answered and turned to sit with his wife.

I thought it would be Sterling who would be nervous, but it was me who shook like a leaf. I felt him take my hand.

Our guests were asked to be seated as the ceremony began. Then we came to the part where we each shared our personally written words that Clark insisted we do.

Sterling turned to me and cleared his voice.

"Milana when I met you, you were my happiness during a sad time. Just when I thought my life was about to be empty and lonely, you appeared. Just as God breathed life into me at birth, you breathed for me when I felt I no longer wanted to.

"You are the example of a righteous woman for my daughter, although grown, and your love for God has returned me to Him: to trust Him again.

"I could not have imagined a woman as beautiful as you," his voice cracked, *"In my lifetime I have seen so much and thought things would only get worse, but you walked in. That entire night, I was mesmerized by you.*

"Although you were going through something no one would have ever known. You were kind and thoughtful, and your smile captivated me.

"Your innocence baffled me. You still had so much hope for man; I had given up the idea that there was hope for me. But no." He shook his head. The crowd laughed. *"You held onto a dignity, despite your circumstances that gained my respect for you, which I still have today. It's a respect that tells me you will be there for me in sickness and health, and in good times as well as bad. You didn't set the bar; you moved it to a whole new level. You were all I needed."*

"When you invited me into Lana's world, I recognized that I was given an invitation only a few would possess in a lifetime. I experienced a love that many only dream of, and have no hope for; a love many are still searching for in their own relationships: A love I've searched for all my life. I found it in God, and God was in you."

"Outer beauty isn't an issue for someone as beautiful as you, but that inner beauty is rare, and that's the beauty I wanted and needed. The rest is a bonus."

"When you share with me, you touch my heart. But when you look at me, I know that you see the real me, the me I show to very few, and it's then when you touch my soul.

"I thought I experienced love before, but I learned you are my first love. You are the air I breathe Milana, and I am honored you said yes."

He took his thumbs and holding my head wiped my tear-stained face with them. Lightly, he kissed my forehead, and I heard the sounds of hearts breaking. He was mine.

I reached in the sleeve of my dress and realized I left my speech on the dressing table in the suite. As quickly as I panicked Clark was there to calm me like her father had so many times.

"Just tell him what you told me," she whispered in my ear.

In his face, I saw all I wanted to say and felt. His one tear fell, and I wiped it away.

"In the beginning, God created the heaven and the earth. And the earth was without form and void: and the darkness was upon the face of the deep. And the spirit of God moved upon the face of the waters. And God said let there be light: and there was light. And God saw the light that it was good. And God divided the light from the darkness. I was the Earth without form and void, and you were that light in the midst of my darkness allowing me to see those things I couldn't. You were good.

"And God said, let there be lights in the firmament of the heaven to divide the day from the night. And let them be for signs and for seasons, and for days and years. The light God has given you has shined for me through the seasons of my life, sustaining me, allowing me to rebuild my strength to withstand my next battle.

"And God made two great lights; the greater light to rule over the day and the lesser light to rule the night: He made the stars also. You, Sterling, are my sun and my moon and my stars.

"In those six days God created so much, and He saw it was all good. And when I look at you, I know He created you too, and all that is good within you.

"Sterling, you are the most loving and kind man I have ever known. You accepted all my faults and mess but only saw me, in the midst of that mess, loving me anyway.

"So, we stand here on our sixth day of creation, and I say 'It Is Good.' I give you my heart and all that goes with it. I Love You so much, Sterling."

His head hung. He was crying. Standing on my tiptoes, I wrapped my arms around his neck, cradling his head and held him. "I love you so much," I whispered in his ear.

Mother and Bishop allowed him time to gather himself before moving through the rest of the ceremony. Tears dried by my dress, he beamed through the candle lighting and our first communion together.

"You may kiss your bride," Bishop announced.

I thought he would attack me, but instead, he gazed at me for a moment, savoring the moment, then as quietly as he came into my life, he leaned in and kissed me so gently. Every time I thought it was over, he started again, and again. Foreplay.

Everyone cheered, reminding us we were not alone. I turned to Clark to gather my bouquet only to find her in Courtney's arms crying. Courtney waved me on signaling she had Clark and tore my bouquet from her hands to give to me.

"I introduce to you for the first time, Mr. and Mrs. Sterling Clark McNeil."

Everyone rose to their feet as we waved and nodded, passing through the center aisle. Solomon held tightly to Sterling's other hand, and did not let go. He smiled and waved to everyone as well.

We had to redo Clark's makeup, but she was even more beautiful than before. Shaw took thousands of pictures, some serious and many silly. Sterling introduced me to his colleagues, but mostly he kissed my neck and talked trash about what he would do to me later.

Solomon clung to Clark most of the evening, but Nancy took him and his brother to their room and waited for the hotel nanny service to show up with the nanny I personally handpicked. Clark was free to dance and enjoy her evening.

Jamil or Jamal, whatever his name was, was now replaced by Tony, who was happy to see Solomon go to bed. Sterling seemed to like him more than the others and hoped he stuck around for a while.

Wayne asked me for a dance, and told me how beautiful I was. He made an offer for me to come see him about coming back or consulting, but I turned him down, knowing it would stretch me too thin.

As a wedding gift, Sterling, Ozi, Keanu, Shane and Tony did a dance that I was sure would be the talk of the decade. I didn't know Sterling had such skills and I could feel more hearts breaking.

A few women from his office danced with him. Clark butted in on one of the dances. She said she didn't like the woman and every time she came to Sterling's office the woman was grinning in his face. "There won't be any Rose repeats here. Besides I don't like her."

Sterling and I made our rounds and thanked everyone for coming, took pictures and encouraged them to stay and have a great time. It was time for us to retreat to our suite.

The night was young.

Chapter Thirty-Nine

I was nervous. Although we had been in this place before, it was the first time as Mrs. McNeil. It was with honor and not blemish. I was free to make love to him, and felt the anticipation at the thought of doing so.

Alone and standing in the middle of the Bridal Suite, Sterling circled me rubbing the scratchy stubble of his freshly shaven beard across my neck sending chills through my waiting body. Softly he kissed my neck, making me wait as he slowly unbuttoned my dress.

The satin buttons running down the center of my back annoyed me as he undid them one at a time. He played with me, deliberately making me wait until he unbuttoned the final one. I regretted getting such a complicated gown.

Reaching from behind, he slowly ran his fingers down my arms while pushing my sleeves off. Again he kissed my back and didn't stop until he reached the top of my matching satin panties and pulled them down and his teeth lightly brushed my behind. I shivered in the middle of a room I had just complained was too warm.

Stopping at the base of my behind, he removed my panties the remainder of the way with his thumbs, as he kissed me between my legs.

"Hmmmm." I moaned.

The only thing remaining of my clothing was my bra, which he undid with one pop. It fell to the floor in the pile now building. With the exception of my jewelry and shoes, I stood completely nude, but no longer naked.

He circled twice, looking me over and smiled. I reached for him to remove his clothes, but my hand was smacked away. He shook his finger as though I were a child touching what I was not allowed to touch. I smiled. I was no stranger to his foreplay, but I was impatient at that moment.

He stopped in front of me and removed the bow tie that hung around his neck, discarding it on the heap of clothes. His shirt was next, followed by his shoes.

He lifted me in the air, allowing my gown to completely fall to the floor. Reaching under my thighs he raised me in the air and placed my legs on each of his shoulders burying his face in my freshly waxed purse; something Clark insisted I did. I was grateful I listened.

"Ummm," I moaned, trying to be quiet.

Slowly he lowered me to the bed while I was still on his shoulders, savoring his meal.

The heel of my shoes caught the cover snagging it. Reaching down I attempted to remove them, but Sterling smacked my bottom indicating that was a "no, no." I smiled again.

He resumed. My back arched and my mouth opened. The language of the angels returned as I thanked God for his precious gift of lovemaking. When Sterling heard my secret language, he stopped abruptly and flipped me over, removing my shoes and then smacking my behind again. It stung but was so sensual. I smiled once more, and laughed under my breath.

I felt him in my hair removing the pins one by one. My hair shifted, toppling over and down my shoulders and back. Without warning, he snatched me back, placing my legs around each side of him. The heat and softness of his lips kissed each cheek, exciting me all over again. He was unpredictable.

A soft cry escaped me, and I sucked in my breath, feeling the gentle bite, branding me as his. His hands ran up my sides until my breast lay one in each. He played with their peeks, making my purse tingled.

Thrusting deep, he entered, causing me to arch again. I squeezed my legs around his waist, feeling his muscles flex back. Instinctively I squeezed. This time he moaned. Smack! I squeezed again. This time he smacked me twice. Again, I smiled.

Realizing his position, Sterling pulled me to a sitting position in his lap, tucking my legs under and on each side of him. He tilted my head back and gently nibbled my ear lobe and then thrusted his tongue inside.

Reaching both hands around to my purse he teased. I squeezed again, and the boat was in motion as he began thrusting deeper, taking my breath with each push.

"You already put your name on it. Now what?" I asked.

He laughed a low guttural laugh. "Since you won't let me run this show you're on time out and will wait."

He lifted me and pushed me face first to the covers. Before I could recover, he flipped me over to my back and watched my face to read my feelings, no doubt. He could see I was excited. He smiled before ducking his head back between my legs, resting them on his shoulders. This time he turned up the heat as he fingered me from the front and behind. This was new, and the sensation sent me soaring, endangering our adventure before it really got started. Sterling, recognizing my love language, stopped abruptly and flipped me again, pulling me back to his lap.

"Are you going to let me run this now?"

I remained quiet, afraid he would stop. He re-entered, thrusting deeper, hitting my secret place the first time, and holding me there until I calmed. The boat rocked again. The corners of my reality blurred as the darkness closed in. I quivered, and the waves came. I was arching my back to receive everything he offered. The language of the angels overtook my senses. I couldn't stop them. They were coming.

As I squeezed, gripping his manhood, I held on tightly. I climaxed to a level we had never experienced. When the waves stopped, my body started over again.

"Sterling!"

"Say my name again," he teased.

"Sterling, Sterling, Sterling!" I was yelling now as the third and fourth wave came.

He continued to rock the boat, so he could meet my conclusion. I squeezed again, and he moaned. I could feel another wave coming, as though the previous four were one.

I thought I would pass out; our drenched bodies were sliding back and forth. His turn.

He hollered sounding like a wounded animal in the wild. I smiled.

His body jerked as he gave two final pumps then pulled me back into his chest, where I rested. We were both panting, out of breath from an accomplished adventure.

I reached behind me, and ran my hand down the side of his face. He was smiling. Taking my hand, he put my fingers in his mouth licking them one at a time.

Foreplay.

Chapter Forty

The next morning, I woke to kisses on my face. I smiled, remembering the night before.

"Common. I made us a nice bath to share."

"No!" I said playfully. "Again!"

He laughed. "Later."

"If I get in that bath all my milk will run out."

"And I won't let a single drop go wasted."

I felt complete in that moment. I turned off my mind, which was always in overload, trying not to understand how we got here. I just wanted to enjoy all of it. We were happy; all of us, and that was all that mattered. We were a family.

Epilogue

Clark sat watching Solomon entertain his little brother, Carter, from the gazebo swing. It was a little chilly and the winds swirled in the air.

"Solomon! Come here and put on your sweater."

Solomon stopped and ran to her. "Why are you crying, Clark?" He traced her tear with his tiny finger.

Clark sniffed back the tears and kissed him on the cheek and then hugged the concerned boy. "I'm not crying, angel. It's windy, and some dirt got in my eye."

"You want me to blow it?" He wrinkled his nose looking into her eyes. "I don't see anything."

"I think it's gone now." She hugged him again. "Thank you."

Solomon returned to Carter, running around him causing him to spin in his stationery walker. Carter squealed, laughing every time he caught up with his brother.

Opening the paper, she read it once again. She remembered the night her mother died. The day before, she spent the evening with her so her dad could go out, no doubt to meet Lana.

Her mother was never really kind to her. It was her father who showed her love and comforted her when she needed it, but the closer her mother came to death, the nastier she became. That night she was extra. Nurse Booker warned them, but Clark was not ready for the cruelty her mother would dish out.

"Your father was the most popular man on campus. He was so proud of his stature. He could have any woman he wanted and he wanted me." Her mother smiled at the memory.

Clark was warmed by the moment, smiling and thinking of her daddy walking around proud and chest out. She giggled because he was nothing like that now. The dad she knew was conservative and reserved. He was funny around those who knew him and protective of those he loved.

"Oh, the other women rolled their eyes and talked behind my back, but I didn't care. I had what they couldn't have.

"When I found out he was sleeping with other women I was so hurt. I thought my world would crumble."

Clark was shocked by her mother's words and thought it was the drugs talking. Her father was the most perfect man she'd ever known. Her mother was the cheater, not her dad. She wanted to snatch every cord from her mother's machine and allow her to die a painful death. Hadn't she done enough to make his life miserable?

"We had a big blow up argument, and he told me I was no more than a piece of ass. He said I had to know this was not forever; it was college. He broke up with me."

Clark quietly listened to her mother deface her father. Secretly, she wished she would die and leave them alone to be happy. She hated her mother, but couldn't get away from her. She saw her every time she looked in the mirror, always wishing she looked like her beautiful father.

"And as usual there was dutiful, boring Sterling to pick up the pieces and put everything back together. He was your father's roommate, and consoled me through the breakup. I missed my cycle and slept with Sterling so you would have a daddy.

"After Sterling and I were married, Cliff told me he broke up with me because he knew Sterling had a thing for me. They were boys he said and it wasn't like he was going to marry me. He told me you got a good one."

Clark couldn't believe the words she was hearing. Her dad was not her father? She didn't understand why he wouldn't have told her over all these years.

Her mother continued with her story. "I never forgave Sterling for me losing the love of my life. It was his fault Cliff and I were not together." She looked at her daughter. "Never trust a man. Have who you want when you want. They aren't faithful and if they are, they'll bore you to Sterlingville."

"Why didn't he tell me? You're lying. He would have told me!"

Her mother popped her lips. "He was too dumb to figure it out. Your father isn't the brightest. He was blessed with looks but had to be lacking somewhere. Don't worry. He thinks you're his."

Clark looked at the paper again before tearing it into tiny pieces. She would keep this secret to her grave. "Why did I open it," she whispered.

"What?" Solomon asked.

"Nothing baby. I was talking to myself."

"Rose used to talk to herself," he said sadly. He stopped referring to Rose as his mother once Lana and her dad were married. They were daddy and mommy now.

Clark thought of the day her mother died. Her mother was nasty to her dad, calling him names. She heard her call her dad a coward. "Can't you do anything right?" Clark heard her say. "I never asked you to do anything for me!" Clark's eyes teared up thinking about it.

"You wait until I'm about to die to become a man. Well tell the bitch I will be gone soon and she can have you to herself! Does Clark know her daddy isn't as perfect as she believes? Won't she be heartbroken!"

Clark walked into the room, attempting to protect her father. "I know, and I'm glad he finally has someone to share his life with, who can appreciate his kindness! So, shut your mouth and die. Leave us in peace!"

"Clark!" her dad yelled standing to his feet.

"Why don't you tell your dad about our conversation last night while he was out with his bitch, Clark!" her mother taunted.

Clark lunged at the machine that dispensed her mother's medication. Her father caught her before she could get to it, lifting her in his arms and returning her to her room. Clark shook loose, ready to return to her mother's bedside and finish the job, but her dad grabbed and bear hugged her as she cried in his arms.

"Why doesn't she just die and leave us alone? I hate her. She's been mean to us all our lives," said Clark holding onto her secret.

"Die!" she yelled.

"You stay here. Do you hear me, Clark?"

She never disobeyed her father. He was all she had in the world. "Yes, Daddy."

She cried as she lay on her bed, and listened to her mother's ranting. Why had she left school for the semester? She should have stayed and returned once her mother died, then she wouldn't feel like she did. Her mother had taken from her the one thing that was sacred and special to her, her Prince.

Then it was quiet.

Clark tiptoed to her parent's room and cracked the door. Her father sat in his chair with his head hung. Her mother was finally asleep.

"Daddy, get some rest," she encouraged. She knew that watching over her mother was exhausting for him. Then she noticed her mother's machine was turned off. Looking closer at her father, she saw the syringe in his hand. She ran to her mother and took her pulse.

"She's gone. She won't be taunting you anymore." Her father spoke now in a low whisper.

Clark went to her father and hugged him. He was shaking. "Daddy. What did you do?"

Clark looked around for the syringe she had just seen in his hand. She picked it up from the floor and shoved it into her pocket. "Daddy, I have to call Nurse Booker and let her know Mom died. You stay here."

Clark called the assigned nurse. Sherena Booker was there within thirty minutes. Sterling remained sitting in the chair where Clark told him to stay.

Clark cried her fake tears for Nurse Booker but had mixed feelings about her mother dying. She loved her because she was her mother, but over the years learned to hate the person she was. Her concern was for her father, who was distraught over a woman who disrespected and mistreated him for years, because of a guy who didn't want her in the first place.

Nurse Booker took care of the arrangements to have her mother's body picked up. She offered to have the doctors prescribe a sedative for her dad. He rejected the medication.

After the house was cleared out, Clark urged her father to get out. She suggested they stay somewhere else for the night. He agreed, so she booked a room for the two of them.

Once they were in their hotel, her dad paced the room not able to calm himself. No matter what she said or did, he wouldn't settle down. So, she was surprised when he told her he was going out. When he returned, he lay in the other queen size bed beside hers and slept.

The winds were picking up and the newly fallen leaves swirled in the air. "Come on, Solomon. It's time to go in. Carter has to take a nap."

Clark took her brothers in the house and fed them. Her dad and Lana had gone to a dinner party. She was happy her father had found happiness. For once, she felt like a part of a whole family. But, she lived in fear that her secret may tear them apart.

Carter was in his bed, down for what she knew would be a short nap. She gave Solomon the option of watching a movie or reading in his room. He wasn't much for television, so he chose to play on his tablet in his bedroom.

Once they were settled, Clark retreated to her room to take a shower. She had a date tonight after her parents returned, and needed to prepare.

In the shower, she ran her hands over her growing belly. She would soon have to tell her family that she was expecting, but she wanted to wait as long as she could. She and Tony had not decided what to do, but they were running out of time.

Tony was a good guy like her father. He loved her immensely and was excited about the baby. He wanted to marry sooner rather than later, but she had reservations.

She looked in the mirror and staring back was the woman who haunted her with her words of freedom... her mother. In her mother's last days, she freed herself by telling Clark the truth surrounding her paternity, thereby imprisoning her daughter with a truth she could never share.

Fen was fine. When she first met him, she hated him. He was the man who threatened to destroy her father's happiness, but she felt an unnatural attraction towards him.

She had not planned on sleeping with him, but when she went to his townhouse to threaten him, she met a charming and smooth, strong and sensual, mysterious and transparent, smart and witty Fen. She understood why Lana stayed with him as long as she had. He was everything she believed she wanted in her young inexperienced life.

He invited her in, but was initially irritated by her visit. Irritation was replaced by curiosity, and she was soon caught up in his web of attraction.

They were interrupted by several calls that pertained to his business. He was direct and unbending. All of it turned her on. Her father and Fen were nothing alike.

"Did Lana send you to talk to me?" He asked. The hope in his eyes made her feel sad for him.

"No. I came to tell you to back off of her. She's with my dad now."

He laughed at her, which both angered and excited her. "What's so funny?"

He didn't answer her; he just smiled and leaned back watching her. His swagger was disarming, catching her off guard.

He stood, walked to the small bar, and poured a drink. "Would you like one?"

"Yes. Thank you."

Up went his eyebrow.

"What?"

"Are you even old enough to drink?" He teased. "Let me see your ID."

She laughed but reached for it anyway. He put his hand up stopping her from going any further and poured her a drink. When he returned she could see he was worn down and tired looking. His hands shook. Maybe he was nervousness.

He took a sip and leaned back on the couch and closed his eyes, unusually comfortable in her presence. Suddenly he sat up.

"Lana is happy? Truly happy?" he asked.

"Yeah, she is."

"And she's not just taken by your father's kindness and charms?"

"No. She's happy."

"How do you know? You hardly know her."

He had her confused for a minute, but she remembered how Lana glowed when she spoke of her father. Fen was shrewd. "No. She is in love with him."

His face looked pained, as he shook his drink. He threw his head back taking in its contents with one gulp, then stretching his mouth into a dry smile, as though the drink was sour. The ice cubes clanked against the glass now empty of its liquid. He stood to get another. When he returned to the couch, he sat hard.

"I can't go quietly into the night and let her go that easily. If that means challenging your father, then so be it."

She admired his words.

He sat forward in his seat swinging his drink between his legs. "So, you came to threaten me, Miss McNeil?" He smiled.

"Yes."

They drank, and he poured out his heart telling her how much he loved Lana, and if he had the chance, he would do things differently. Clark saw his torment, his stress, and his heart. He became a real person to her and not the jerk she thought him to be. She was no longer there to protect her father. Power exuded from his body. His words touched her.

Seducing Fen wasn't difficult, he was drunk and lonely. She fucked him over and over until he had no more to give.

He was skillful and passionate. He did things a young girl didn't know existed, and then fell asleep in a drunken stupor.

She left before he woke. She called him the next day and before she could say anything, he apologized. He told her it could never happen again and that he took full responsibility.

There was much she could learn from Lana. She wondered how one woman ended up with two wonderful men.

"I won't say anything if you don't. It would destroy both Lana and my dad, but you need to let them be and back off," she threatened.

"Are you still threatening me, Miss McNeil?"

She smiled, and he hung up.

When she saw him again at the harbor, she became excited and secretly hoped Carter was his so she could see him again. She hoped Lana did not see her desire for him. She didn't want to cause any conflict over something that could never be.

When he died, their secret went with him. She felt the pain of his death and held Lana when she wept after her dad left for work, understanding her loss. He was a good man. He was just misplaced.

The boys were in the nursery with Lana. She needed to finish preparing to meet Tony. She kissed both boys good night, and returned to her room.

She took her time as she applied her makeup. She wanted to look immaculate. Tonight she would tell Tony she would marry him. Tonight she would build on the curse her mother began; tonight she would become her mother.

Soon Fen's legacy would live on in Solomon, Carter and her baby Tres.

The End

A Note from the Author

Ephesians 6:12 (KJV)

> *For we wrestle not against flesh and blood, but against principalities, against powers, against the rulers of the darkness of this world, against spiritual wickedness in high places.*

This was one of the most profound verses I have ever read in the bible. It has become my go to verse when trying to understand people. This verse constantly reminds me that I can look at the person in front of me or the master they serve.

I know you are probably saying, people chose to do what they want to do, and I would agree. We are free will beings. But if you take the time to evaluate all that goes into a decision, you will find there is an intense thought process. That process is confounded with what influences us.

Lana had a deep love for God, but like many she was afraid to put her total trust in him. Proverbs 3:5 says Trust in the Lord with all thy heart and lean not unto thy own understanding 3:6 In all thy ways acknowledge Him and He will direct thy path. As fallible creatures we believe what we can see rather than what God has promised us. 2 Corinthians 5:7 for we walk by faith, not by sight, living in a manner consistent with God's promises. He is the real Promise Keeper, and Lana believed she was.

With each disappointment from Fen, Lana began to take matters into her own hands, believing their relationship was hopeless. She became impatient with God and not willing to wait on that perfect resolution that only He can provide in His infinite timing. She allowed the enemy to feed her childhood insecurities of never being enough. She strived for perfection that was only accomplished by one, Jesus Christ. She prayed, but would not get out of God's way to allow Him to work, thereby feeding Fen's insecurities unknowingly.

Sterling became a distraction. He fed her desires, by being what she felt she needed and felt she deserved, but her time with him made her focus on her husband's shortcomings, causing more resentment towards him for his infidelities. We can always find fault in anyone, if you look hard enough, forgetting the faults we have.

After sharing with other women I saw that woman take infidelity personally, but infidelity is a sin against God. It speaks to a man's character and insecurities, whether in his relationship or in himself. Fen talks briefly about his insecurities in the end. He never believed he deserved to be with Lana or that she would stay with him. He felt he wasn't enough for her, and didn't live up to her standards, even dressing in a suit every day, while in college, to prove he was enough. In reality those standards where in his head, hence his insecurities.

He was more than enough for Rose, who lived with her own demons, and he stroked her insecurities while feeding them at the same time by staying with Lana.

It still amazes me how as adults we forever remain seven years old, never seemingly able to grow beyond our parent's imperfections. It took me many years to realize that I was enough for God and if I was enough for Him, then I was enough for any situation he put me in, because He prepared me for that moment.

Author Diva Dorreen is a Southern Maryland resident. She is married with six children and ten grandchildren.

As a child she learned to escape through reading and began imagining her own stories, but never penned her first book until 2008. A co-worker, who read the book, asked what ever happened to the book and encouraged her to publish it. That book became *Love is Patient Love is Kind* in 2015. She hasn't stopped writing since, and said she will write until she is unable to.

Books by the Author

The Heart Series
Love is Patient Love is Kind: Book 1 (2015)
Faith Hope and Love: Book 2 (2016)
Agape Love: Book 3 (2019)

UnRaveled (2018)